Blood Sky

By

Judith Ennamorato

This book is a work of fiction. Places, events, and situations in this story are purely fictional. Any resemblance to actual persons, living or dead, is coincidental.

ISBN: 1-4107-1731-3 (E-book)
ISBN: 1-4107-1732-1 (Paperback)

Library of Congress Control Number: 2003090759

This book is printed on acid free paper.

Printed in the United States of America
Bloomington, IN

1st Books - rev. 4/14/03

<u>**Dedication**</u>

This book is dedicated to the memory of my brother Thomas John MacAdam.

BLOOD SKY

Prologue

In the year 1570, the Iroquois, among the most politically sophisticated people of their time, established the Confederacy of the Five Nations of Iroquois. Those who later drew up the U.S. Constitution based some of the most vital clauses on the principles set in this confederacy. The five united tribes called themselves *"Ongwanosionno"* or "We are of the Extended Lodge." The general term *Iroquois* was given to them by the French; a combination of the native words *"hiro"* meaning "I have said it," a phrase they used to end their speeches, and *"koue"* a cry of sorrow when drawn out and an exclamation of joy when briefly uttered. Hence, we have the "Iroquois League of Nations."

The remaining five tribes consisted of: Mohawk: People of the flint, or Man-eaters, a name given them by the Algonkian; Onandaga: On top of the hill; Cayuga: The place where the locusts are taken out; Seneca; It is a projecting stone, and Oneida: Standing stone. The Tuscarora or Kemp Gatherers were to unite in 1772 making complete the present day "League of First Nations."

The League occupied the territory extending from Lake Champlain to the Genesee River, and from the Adirondaks southward to the territory of the Conestoga. In 1649-50 they proceeded to defeat and disperse the Huron and Tionintati nations who later joined to become what is now known as the Wyandott, as well as the Neutrals in 1651, the Erie in 1656 and the Susquehanna in 1675.

Champlain, on one of his early expeditions to Stadacona, called *Kebec* by the Natives or 'Where the River Narrows', presently Quebec, joined a party of Algonquin and Huron natives against the Iroquois Confederacy. This caused the Iroquois to become bitter enemies with the French and, while remaining firm allies with the English, opposed every move they made until the end of the French regime in Canada in 1763.

After the arrival of the Dutch from whom they procured firearms, the confederated Iroquois immediately made their power known by extending their conquests over all of the neighbouring tribes. Eventually their dominion was acknowledged from the Ottawa River to the Tennessee, and from the Kennebec to the Illinois River and Lake Michigan.

Such was the influence of the Confederacy, and so striking their advancement in their savage state, that Francis Parkman, the dean of United States historians, stated in his work on the Jesuits in North America:

"Among all the barbarous nations of the continent, the Iroquois stand paramount. Elements, which among other tribes are crude, confused and embryonic, are among them, systemized and concreted into established polity. The Iroquois is the Indian of Indians. A thorough savage, yet a finished and highly developed savage. He is perhaps the best example of the highest elevation which a man can reach without emerging from the primitive condition of the hunter."

The Iroquois were rightly feared warriors, but they also had a remarkable gift for democratic government. This quality was much admired by such people as Benjamin Franklin to name just one. Of the character of the Iroquois, one of the Jesuit missionaries in 1636 said, "You will find in them, virtues which might put to blush the majority of Christians. There is no need of hospitals because there is no beggar among them, and indeed none so poor as long as any of them are rich. Their kindness, humanity and courtesy not merely make them liberal in giving, but almost lead them to live as though everything they possess were held in common, none can want food while there is corn anywhere in the camp."

The Jesuits learned, however, that there was another side to the Iroquois personality – a barbarism too grotesque for the good missionaries to understand yet too important to go unrecorded.

BLOOD SKY LEGEND AS SEEN BY TARACHIAWAGON

Long ago, even before the time of counting, when knives were forbidden for fear of drawing the blood of brothers, *Wawnatta*, a Mohawk warrior came home from battle, bloodied, pale and depressed. He announced to his elders the contents of a dream or vision he had experienced the previous night. He had seen the cultural hero of the Mohawk, *Tarachiawagon* – He Who Holds up the Sky.

"If you wish me to continue my protection over you," *Tarachiawagon* told the warrior dreamer, "hear my words and hear them clearly. Rejoice now in your freedom and rejoice in the purity of your hearts, for the season shall soon fall upon you when these natural blessings will be lost to you forever! Your freedom and innocence shall be torn from you as surely as the cougar rips the flesh from its unsuspecting prey. The cougar will appear in the form of an *O'seronni,* a man with white skin covered in hair. Beware, for he bears the split tongue of the serpent and he will force his vile system of belief upon you. He will place law above love in the land and strict institution over the free growth of the *Ongwanonhsioni."*

"There will be much sorrow among your brethern, for brother shall raise up the hatchet against brother and much blood will flow. The heavens will weep in their grievance and shed upon you great tears of blood. (1) This is a sign to the *Onqwanonhsioni* that their loss of freedom is at hand. No more will the tender melody of the tiny sparrow be as one with the growl of the wolf, for the balance, the real balance of nature, will be upset forever. The natural laws of the Creator will be crushed under the demonic forces of the unnatural man-made laws of the split-tongued white cougar. *Hiro* – I have spoken."

> *(1) Red rainfalls, though not common, have been recorded numerous times throughout history, as have black rains that give the appearance of ink. Science is largely mystified by such phenomena.*

CHAPTER ONE

September 19, 1665, 4:30 p.m.

Separated by 800 miles of verdant wilderness, the infants came forth into the world at precisely the same instant. Their initial cry was simultaneous, their first breath drawn in unison-a unison that bordered on the uncanny.

The blonde infant, red-faced and angry, continued the screaming; upgrading the tempo until the pitch was almost unbearable. Her wizened visage was so contorted it was difficult to decipher where her natural features would settle once she tired of her initial tantrum. The moment Marjolaine retrieved the babe from the confines of Jeanette's womb she'd experienced a sense of apprehension. In an attempt to thwart the disquieting emotion, she focused on thrusting her forefinger down the newborn's esophagus, emulating as best she could, the deft movements of her mentor in the art of midwifery; a Grandmere Muriel, midwife to all and sundry in the small French settlement of Fort Ville Marie. The learned midwife had stressed the importance of unblocking a newborn's esophagus to ensure total elimination of any mucus that might obstruct the breathing process. Congratulating herself for not having choked the infant with her callused finger, Marjolaine initiated the cleansing of the little one.

For some strange design she was adverse to the touch of the infant's flesh, pure and delicate in appearance, yet prompting chills to surge sporadically up and down the domestic's spine. She bound the screeching infant in a small woolen blanket, designed and woven to perfection by the same hands that had gently eased her into the light of day. Hoping her mother's scent would calm the brat she placed her at Jeanette's breast, but the act angered the infant further as her tiny head struggled madly to free itself from the confines of her sleeping mother's bosom. Cupping her hands over her ears in a futile attempt to block out the unearthly squeals, Marjolaine leaned against the elaborate cherry-wood wardrobe, hand-hewn by Jeanette's husband, Jacque, as a wedding gift.

Staring vacantly across the large room that served as kitchen and bedroom, she focused her gaze on the great flagstone-hearthed fireplace. Her eyes scanned the numerous hooks attached to the immense stone structure boasting the necessary cooking utensils: stock, stew and dripping pans: a gridiron, firedogs and a lone shovel. A set of flatirons sat on the ledge beside a tin lamp and some homemade candlesticks. A steel cauldron rested on the hearth beside the raging fire. The bulky rocking chair situated in front of the open fire was occupied by the frame of Father Arter who'd assumed his position for the better part of two hours having been hastily summoned at Jeanette's urgent request, her highly religious bent intent on the earliest possible baptism for her firstborn. She was only too aware that new mothers were forbidden to enter the church for forty days following delivery, as they were considered unclean. As well, Jeanette was concerned about the weather forty days hence, as their local parish, like most in Ville Marie, was not heated due to risk of fire, and her newborn might be struck with pneumonia. She was perplexed as to why so many women and girls of the parish insisted on appearing at mass with, as Father Arter would say, "displays of Satan," even on the frostiest days of the year. They'd show up with nude arms, shoulders and throats, their heads bared. As young ladies will, these girls were merely mimicking the latest fashions from France; however, a number of them had been excluded from the sacraments as a result of their apparel. Evidently the Bishop had issued a pastoral letter condemning the wearing of indecent gowns, revealing scandalous views of nude shoulders and bosoms.

Indeed, it had been the Bishop himself who ordered the priests to refuse absolution to females who wore these fashions either in their own homes or in public; however, the French government got wind of this and retaliated by ordering the New France clergy to stop harassing the women in this manner.

The old priest rocked the chair slowly, rhythmically, the beat of the rockers on the crude wood floor emulating the pounding of Marjolaine's heart. A selfish, insecure and petty soul, he was staring hypnotically into the fire, his small black eyes glazed, the corners of his mouth slightly tilted, granting him an almost satanic countenance. His overall facial tone resembled that of a person about to enter into a hedonistic experience.

Marjolaine feared the priest, and had never trusted him. Intuitively aware of his sinister nature she avoided contact with him at all cost, her weekly confessions whispered instead to Father Opaire in the dark, musty confines of the confessional. It had been Father Opaire she'd wished to see today, but as luck would have it his assistant, Father Arter, had arrived at the Langevin's door. Without so much as a word to Marjolaine he'd swept brusquely past her toward the oak rocking chair, the hem of his black cossack trailing behind him like the Prince of Darkness himself.

Mindful of the priest's mission, Marjolaine drew a deep breath and began to walk toward him. Overtaken by a sudden dizzy spell she reached out to grasp the rough surface of the large maple table placed upon a once colourful braid rug, her gaze involuntarily drawn to the old man's bony hands. He was grasping what appeared to be a vial of holy water, his spider-like fingers clenched so tightly around it as to render his knuckles white. His shadow, magnified against the log wall in the flickering firelight, elongated an already hawkish nose, evil in its appearance. He was uttering in a barely audible voice, incantations that Marjolaine assumed to be Latin, the tone of the words reminiscent of her weekly vigils at mass. She was aware of his laboured breathing and lascivious expression. Droplets of spittle escaped from the corners of his mouth. A small black fly buzzed listlessly above him before taking refuge on his nose, its hairy back legs rubbing furiously together, as if triumphant in locating the perfect oasis.

Too timid to disturb the priest's deep musings, the apprehensive girl prayed that the ear-shattering squalls of the newborn would induce him to vacate his trance and get on with the business of baptism. As if reading her thoughts he shifted his gaze from the fire to stare directly into her anxious gray eyes. A perverse grimace crossed his lips. Like a jack-in-the-box he popped up from the rocker and headed for the quilt-covered bed upon which the heads of Jeanette and the wailing baby were visible, whereupon he conducted the swiftest baptismal ceremony since the birth throes of Christianity. Through Marjolaine's disbelieving eyes, he seemed to render the sacred ritual somehow indecent. Eyes burning with fervor and with a melodramatic flair he sprinkled a few drops of holy water onto the infant's head. The moment the hallowed fluid came in contact with the babe's translucent skin she took on the appearance of one in spiritual torment; her shrieks became course and lewd, almost blasphemous in timbre. Roughly shoving the vial into his pocket, the priest spun around to once again face the terrified domestic, the delirious gaze in his sunken eyes smacking of some corrupt victory. Then, just as suddenly as he'd arrived, he was gone, the reverberating slam of the large oak door momentarily stifling the howls of the newly baptized babe and shocking the dumbfounded domestic back to her senses.

Through it all, for reasons known only to God, Jeanette remained blessedly asleep. Fearful that the infant's fuss would awaken her mistress, Marjolaine picked her up and began to fervently rock her, breaking into a chorus of *Au Claire de la Lune* in an attempt to drown out the infantile screams with her own delicate voice, a competition she readily lost. She accepted this defeat with aplomb since she had never been able to sing with any merit because of her bird-like voice, a characteristic that, when coupled with her lack of ability to take a stand on any subject, contributed to her nickname, *Souris* or Mousey. Contrary to what most people thought, she was knowledgeable in most areas; however, by nature she was shy and unassuming, hesitant to express her personal opinions lest she be publicly proven wrong, an embarrassment to her of the worst kind. She loathed being the center of attention and her shyness was a deeply personal burden. This unfortunate lack of confidence in her innate powers of comprehension proved to be the sole flaw in an otherwise beautiful nature.

Jeanette, deprived of strength and still partially oblivious, was momentarily aware of an almost maniacal shrieking and what appeared to be Marjolaine's child-like singing. Unable to force her heavy lids open, she drifted back into a deep, restless and dream-filled sleep.

Her dream took her to the sight of a campfire; the blood red tongues of flame spiraling upward in the distance toward a funereal black sky. Beside the fire sat Father Arter in a rocking chair, his clawed hand beckoning to her as she cowered in the distance, her howling infant clutched tightly to her breast.

"Bring the child to me!" he ordered, his voice raspy and echoing hollowly in her ears. Powerless to halt her steps, she walked trance-like toward him. His cavernous eyes glowed like scarlet coals. Her heart thumped unmercifully; the hair on the back of her neck bristled from fear. As she approached him she glanced down at his skeletal hands that appeared to be growing larger by the second, throwing his

body out of proportion. He held a miniature firebrand fashioned from iron and bearing a small symbol at the tip, a symbol so miniscule she was unable to decipher it, despite the lucidity of the dream. Plunging the brand into the raging fire, he deftly spun it around, heating it as he mumbled to himself, occasionally breaking into uncontrolled, manic laughter. Satisfied at last that the instrument was white-hot, he reached out and roughly grabbed the infant's left leg. Frozen with fear, Jeanette could only stare in terror as he withdrew the incandescent brand from the fire before swiftly gouging the tip of the scalding instrument under her tiny thigh. The hissing sound and the pungent odor of burning flesh searing her nostrils instantly sickened her. The baby, momentarily shocked into silence by the unexpected and painful violation to her body, emanated a tiny animal-like whelp before losing consciousness. Aware of a burning sensation around her ankles, Jeanette glanced downward to find the hem of her nightgown aflame. Unable to move, she stood helplessly as the biting flames engulfed her, the crazed laughter of the old priest resounding in her brain.

The last thing she saw before awakening was the hideous sight of Father Arter's head being ripped from his shoulders by some unseen force, his vile laughter continuing as the disembodied head tumbled into the raging fire.

CHAPTER TWO

September 19, 1665, 4:30 p.m.

Dancing Leaf was pleased. *Shonkwaya'tihson,* the Creator, had delivered her of a female. The birth of a *yeksa'a* or female child was a joyous event for the Mohawk tribe, a tribe that revered the female life force. Matriarchal in government, the *Onqwanonhsioni,* or "Real People" were very much aware of the benefits derived from a female birth; the main advantage being that the child can, in turn, give birth to more offspring, thus ensuring the strength of her prospective Clan, in this case, the Clan of the Wolf.

From where she lay, Dancing Leaf was able to glance through the entrance of the birth hut and drink in the rich scarlet hue of the sky. She wondered at the strange blood-red rains that had fallen from the sky earlier in the day. The rains had commenced at the same time her labour began and she had taken this to be a bad omen. The old people had sat huddled together in their longhouses, solemnly whispering amongst themselves, their faces bearing expressions of sad acceptance. In the back of her mind she vaguely recalled the legend of *Wawnatta's* vision, recounted to her many moons before by Old Grandmother as they worked side by side in the vast cornfield that lay inside the palisade village of her people.

She realized now how foolish she had been to believe that the red rains foretold impending danger, for her girl-child had signaled her arrival into the world with a lusty, healthful cry and her body appeared to be perfectly formed.

Dancing Leaf's desire for a daughter had been fired by the ill-fated outcome of her last pregnancy, a pregnancy that had resulted in the birth of twins, male and female. Although double births were a rarity among the *Onqwanonhsioni,* custom dictated that twins, regardless of their apparent strength and hardiness, be slain immediately, for it was known they possess at birth, uncanny, occult powers given them by the devil spirit *O-nes-sohn-ro-noh.*

The twins, according to convention, had been dutifully smothered prior to their fourth inward breath. The old midwife, Crippled Sparrow, had carried out the distasteful task. Consumed with guilt from that day forward, Crippled Sparrow believed that she alone was responsible for *O-nes-sohn-ro-noh* sending the twins to Dancing Leaf. The source of her guilt lay in the realization that she had neglected to perform the age-old ritual common to all midwives of the tribe, a rite that was to be carried out just previous to aiding in the delivery of newborns.

Midwives were obliged to eat the flesh of boiled bitch puppies immediately prior to drinking the broth they were boiled in. It had not been a conscious act of neglect on Crippled Sparrow's part, but rather a matter of forgetfulness, her memory fading after eighty-two summers. As she performed the double infanticide she appeared to be outwardly composed, an air of purpose surrounding her as she skillfully snuffed the life out of the ill-fated infants, but deep inside she harboured feelings of guilt and self-hate. She had tried to console herself in the knowledge that the *Onqwanonhsioni* did not practice infanticide in times of famine as did some other tribes, but only when infants were born with a pronounced physical handicap or, as in the case of twins, a spiritual malady.

In direct contrast to her emotions following the extinction of her newborn twins, Dancing Leaf was elated to find that this delivery had produced but a single child. The delivery itself had been extremely trying despite the constant administrations of crushed snake rattle Crippled Sparrow had given her to hasten delivery and ease the pain. The infant herself had seemingly disregarded the excruciating throes she'd been subjected to. It had been a footling birth, one foot presenting itself where the head should have appeared. Upon seeing this, the old midwife's memory took her back to another time when she, as a young girl, had been witness to another such birth. The experience had been terrifying; resulting in the loss of both mother and child; her mother and the child that was to have been her brother.

"Aaaii, what is happening to me? My mind retreats like a stalked deer!" She directed her thoughts once more to the task at hand. Gently tugging on the tiny bronze foot, she prayed to *Shonkwaya'tihson* that its hidden counterpart would follow. Unbeknownst to the old woman, the other leg had become entangled in the life cord and was not to appear so easily. Again she yanked on the exposed limb, and in doing so, the diminutive hip socket of the concealed leg tore loose from its natural hold. Beads of sweat poured from her wrinkled brow.

7

Reaching as far as she could into the birth canal, she released the imprisoned leg from its grasp. Dancing Leaf's agonizing screams unnerved the old woman. As the girl's guardian, she had taught her that these unseemly cries were unnecessary.

"To cry out in pain is to shame your people. The only thing worse is tears." She had repeated these words time and time again to her young ward, adding, "Women prove their courage in childbirth just as a man proves his in battle." She would chastise the young mother later for this weakness.

Upon her emergence from Dancing Leaf, the infant had cried out lustily; then, just as suddenly became silent. Dancing Leaf, in her terror, fearing the breathing had halted altogether, attempted to snatch the infant from the grip of the midwife who had just severed the umbilical cord with her teeth. As she reached out to retrieve the papoose, her legs, weak and feeble from the long hours spent crouching in the birthing position, gave way, causing her to fall sideways, her long black hair narrowly missing the fire that burned on the ground beside her. Ignoring the incident, Crippled Sparrow proceeded to pour a few drops of wolf oil down the infant's throat to cleanse out her system and feed the guardian spirit that lives in her soul. Placing the newborn face down on a large wolf skin that lay opposite the woven cornhusk birthing pad, she slowly knelt down, pushing to the back of her mind the searing pain that shot like burning arrows through her arthritic knees. Placing her papery hands on the babe's puny back, she gently rubbed the little face into the rich gray fur of the dead animal. This ceremony was so antiquated that its initial purpose had all but been obliterated from the memory of the *Onqwanonhsioni,* but it continued to be carried out in deference to the Great Spirit who had originally wished it so.

The pleasurable sensation of the thick luxurious fur was the infant's first conscious sensory experience, an experience that would remain imbedded in her soul, never to be completely forgotten. Her second conscious sensory experience was to hold neither the pleasure nor the memory.

Wrapping the child in an otter pelt, the old woman clutched the bundle tightly to her withered bosom and left the birth hut, walking as swiftly as her aching legs allowed, to the river, her moccasin clad feet treading the familiar needle strewn path in the twilight. The fresh air invigorated her. This was her favourite season, *Seskhoko:w,* her people called it, "the time of much freshness". She inhaled deeply as she walked, allowing the wind spirit to replenish her senses by way of a soft, perfumed breeze that swirled gently around her, toying with the fringe of her doeskin skirt before making its way up into her nostrils, whirling inward, purifying and regenerating her disposition. Thus refreshed, she chided herself for her irritation at the sound of Dancing Leaf's screams. She would not mention the incident to the other *yakonkwe* or women in camp lest they tease or deride the girl.

Reaching the shore she walked upstream, thankful for her privacy. Had the infant been born just two days before, the river would have been filled with villagers, for that had been the time of the Great Medicine Ceremony. Following many prayers of thanks to *Shonkwaya'tihson,* the whole village had submerged themselves amongst the profusion of red and gold leaves scattered haphazardly upon the water's surface, bathing and splashing, performing an age-old ritual guaranteed to ward off sickness during the long winter months ahead.

Rounding a tree-canopied curve on the shore, she caught a brief glimpse of something moving beside her. Glancing into the stand of trees she saw them, two of the little people, half-hidden among the lush foliage. Less than two feet high, their wizened faces were staring in the direction of the otter-wrapped bundle she grasped. She was dumbfounded. Although she knew the little people lived deep in the forest she'd never seen them, as they generally appeared only to the most spiritual to whom they bore messages or warnings. What had they to say to her, a mere midwife. Then, just as suddenly as they'd appeared, she watched them flee back into their forest home. It never occurred to her that they might have emerged in celebration of Blood Sky's birth.

Reaching the sacred location at the shore, she removed the otter pelt from the papoose, and bracing herself carefully over the waters edge, swiftly plunged the tiny body into the frigid water. Although she'd executed this final birth ceremony hundreds of times in the past, she never felt comfortable carrying out the testing of a newborn's tolerance, especially during a cold season. She was only too aware that more often than not the infant contacted pneumonia and succumbed shortly after. This in itself was proof to the

Onqwanonhsioni that the body could never have withstood the rigorous lifestyle of the Mohawk. The old woman shook her head in dismay at the stark realization that only one child in thirty-five survived the first few weeks in camp. She was aware, however, that those who did survive were physically superior, possessed of inherent qualities and traits that elevated them to the rank of Indian of Indians.

It wasn't until she swept the infant out of the water that she noticed the right leg was slightly dangling. Praying to *Shonkwaya'tishson* that it was an illusion caused by her failing eyesight, hampered by too many moons of lodge smoke, she rubbed her eyes in an attempt to see more clearly. Again she glanced at the dangling leg and again she prayed. Perhaps her eyes were being tricked by the flickering lights of the campfires in the distance behind her, casting uneven wavering beams in the direction of her and the papoose. Her knarled hands moved timidly up the frigid limb of the newborn, probing, scrutinizing, until at last her greatest fear was realized. Grasping the hip, her experienced fingers sunk into flesh where bone should be. Retracing her fingers down the leg, she perceived the truant bone, foreign in its location. Her heart sunk. Where just moments before she had experienced a remarkable calm, she was now devoid of all hope. It was clear to her that *O-nes-sohn-ro-noh* had not yet finished with her. Though the leg would not be rendered useless, she'd surely suffer a permanent limp.

Binding the shivering infant once more in the fur pelt, she turned and slowly dragged her feet back in the direction of the camp, her legs heavy and her step faltering as one who is completely conquered. For the second time in her life she surrendered to her tears, allowing them to cascade down her shriveled parched cheeks. In the suffused light of the distant fires, she was a paradox of beauty. Her aged, crinkled face was completely veiled with the silvery fluid, an appearance both majestic and supernatural.

She was tired, very tired. The events of the day had been too much of a strain on her. She contemplated the many times she had been the bearer of sad tidings to the new mothers, expectant in their looks as she returned to the birth hut from her numerous trials at the edge of the temperamental river. As she retraced her steps back to camp clutching the little one in her arms, she considered over and over again what it is she must say, and worse yet, do. She knew from years of experience what must be said and done; it was law, and it was up to her to see that the law was honored. She was aware she had no right discussing these details with Dancing Leaf. Perhaps she should have heeded the other midwives when they tried to persuade her to retire from her duties. They could see she was becoming too soft to do what must be done. Crippled Sparrow had prayed their observations were not true, for she was well aware of the danger to the *Ongwanonhsioni* that misdirected emotions could foster.

An isolated ribbon of light thrust forth from the waning sun bathed the crown of the infant's head, prompting Crippled Sparrow to glance down at the swatch of raven hair peeking from within the pelt. She was instantly reminded of her first official role as midwife. She had been fourteen summers and it had been her own son she had reluctantly submerged into the river to test his vigor. It had been the season of howling winds. She had dunked him as quickly as possible but the shock of the icy waters had stopped his heart, even before she raised him back to her breast.

Returning to camp, she had wrapped his lifeless form in a soft deerskin robe, taking special care to leave the sides unsewn, for an infant that size would be unable to free his soul had the robe been stitched all around. Placing him gently in the crotch of a large elm tree, his miniature feet facing west, the young mother had fasted and mourned the allotted time – ten days.

The awakening of this long buried memory prompted renewed tears to the old woman's eyes, one of which found its place on top of the infant's head. As if signaled by some archaic bond, the papoose tilted her head slightly backward and stared full-faced into the moist eyes of Crippled Sparrow. Possessed of a depth that seemed infinite, the newborn's eyes were dark and luminous, like wet, black stones. Filled with compassion, understanding and tolerance they possessed a depth that seemed infinite. The old woman could barely gasp in awe. Her lashes were long and thick. She blinked, a long drawn out motion, almost purposeful in its intent, relaxed and sure. As if by osmosis, Crippled Sparrow had a momentary sense of being transformed into the child's psyche and the child, in turn, appeared to assume the aged visage of the ancient midwife. The experience was fleeting, but it stigmatized the old woman, leaving her perplexed, yet very much taken with this fresh little being that she squeezed even closer to her heart.

Once inside the hut she paused, allowing her tired eyes to adjust to the scattered lighting. The fire, still smoldering in the center of the dwelling, cast alien shadows upon the totems carved into the walls, causing the vividly coloured symbols to merge into one another. A stirring at her feet caused her to glance down. Recoiling at the sight of a snake, she watched in fascination as the image suddenly vanished. Symbolic of deadly enemies to her people, the snake's image, she concluded, was merely a result of her tired mind and still hazy eyesight. Directing her attention to the overall appearance of the room, she was satisfied to see that all was in order. Dancing Leaf had dutifully executed the task of disposing of the birth remnants; the birth pad had been removed and burned and there was fresh wood laid out beside the fire. The young mother herself was meticulously clean after having literally dragged herself to the river, where she thoroughly bathed before washing her hair with sand from the river bottom. After grooming her hair with a turtle shell comb, she'd carefully braided it in a single plait down the back of her neck. She then massaged her aching body with oil of pine before slipping on her fringed deerskin skirt and beaded moccasins. Since it was still the season of falling leaves, she remained bare breasted. Around her neck she retied the narrow doeskin thong from which hung a chunk of raw amethyst, a gift from her husband Black Whirlwind. She had then buried the infant's umbilical cord, returning it to Mother Earth in thanksgiving for her new daughter, and to ensure that the child would remain free in spirit, in this life, as well as the next. Making her way back to the hut, she had taken time to gather fresh wood for the fire.

Upon her return she had been delighted to find that one of the other women had placed a generous helping of fresh, raw liver beside the beaver skin, during her absence. The *Onqwanonhsioni* knew that freshly killed meat retained more goodness and vitamins before cooking, and new mothers were encouraged to consume as much as they could following delivery. Squatting on the fur beside the fire she had hungrily reached for the bark bowl before scooping up the warm meat with her fingers. She delicately placed the nourishing staple in her mouth, chewing slowly and deliberately, wishing to savor every succulent piece. Finishing the last morsel, she lifted the bowl to her lips, drinking the fresh blood that lay in a scarlet pool at the bottom. Ignoring the stinging sensation on her arm caused by an amber spark exploding from the hissing fire, she then lay back on the beaver mat, anxiously awaiting the return of Crippled Sparrow and her new daughter.

Her acute sense of smell told her the old woman was in the hut seconds before she actually heard or saw her, as Crippled Sparrow bore a distinct, though not unpleasant scent, a mixture of earth and pine needles blended with the piquant odor of cherry bark upon which the old woman had taken to chewing, in hopes of appeasing a cough, aggravated by many moons of smoking the sacred tobacco.

The women's' eyes met. Crippled Sparrow, attempting to hold her gaze firm, strode hesitantly across the ground toward her niece. Standing over the new mother, with trembling voice, she said,

"The child must die, she is imperfect."

Every primitive emotion in Dancing Leaf had wanted to scream out, protest, but since she was the result of a culture so adverse to weakness in any form she allowed herself no more release than a slightly muffled moan as she lowered her head in sorrow. The truth then hit her like a thunderbolt! The old woman had broken all rules by returning to camp with the infant still alive. A great spark of hope shot through her. Taking instant advantage of the midwife's apparent indecision, she held her arms upward. "Allow me please to delay her a little longer from the spirits."

Pausing for a moment, the confused midwife reluctantly lowered the papoose into the arms of her mother. Taking hold of the left arm of the baby, Dancing Leaf reached under the folds of the beaver mat and retrieved a tiny soft deerskin strip she had fashioned for the child. Tying it onto her daughter's wrist, she watched as it slowly disappeared between the creases of bronze fat. The *Onqwanonhsioni* knew that newborns are able to converse freely with the spirits, and if for some reason they should choose to call the infant back, the baby can then say, *"I am tied to earth by my mother's love."*

Cupping the oval-shaped face of her daughter in her hand, Dancing Leaf looked deeply into her eyes, the windows of her soul. In that split second she intuitively knew her copper-skinned miracle would live.

She named her *Onekwenhsa Karonya* – Blood Sky.

CHAPTER THREE

September 19, 1665, 4:30 p.m.

"Laisse allez de mon bras vous hybride! Let go of my arm you bastard!"

The young, green-eyed breed cursed the man beside her and attempted to tear her frail arm from his grip. Other than the sporadic twitch in his left eye, Claude La Belle's face was devoid of emotion. He gave the scrawny arm a powerful yank in an attempt to set the broken bone, releasing a fresh flood of obscenities from his young patient. It had been a sloppy break and Dr. La Belle had to call on every bit of medical knowledge he could muster if he was to right it. He very much doubted the arm would ever be of use again. This bit of information he kept to himself.

Bending down, he grasped the neck of a half-filled bottle of brandy and a battered tin cup that lay partially hidden under the straw-filled cot covered with a squalid bearskin upon which he sat. After pouring the amber liquid into the receptacle, he raised the girl's head with one hand and gently placed the cup to her parched lips with the other, his soft brown eyes silently coaxing her to drink. Like two pieces of chipped green ice, her slanted emerald eyes met his gaze with defiance. She couldn't have been more than seventeen, yet she gave the impression of being much older. Tiny web-like lines crept around her jaded eyes. A single snow-white strip initiating from her right temple contrasted her dirty, unkempt black hair, and her narrow nose looked out of place on a flattened pockmarked face.

Mentally weighing her defiance toward the doctor against the acceptance of the brandy, better known in these parts as *'English milk'*, that would surely numb her pain, she opted for the latter, allowing Claude to trickle the welcome relief down her throat.

"Bonne fille, bonne fille, good girl, good girl" he whispered paternally, "Soon you will sleep."

The initial strains of a *grivoise,* or bawdy song crept from behind the striped blanket hanging from the crudely constructed doorframe of the stuffy room, a type of the music favoured by the reckless coureurs-de-bois, frequent clientele of the infamous establishment

14

where the good doctor had been called earlier in the day to mend the limb of the young prostitute whose head he now supported.

A brothel and gambling house, the *St. Tropez* was unique in that it specialized in half-breed women, or as the French called them, *Bois-brules,* or "bits of brown". Considered a novelty because of their mixed pedigree, these women were growing in numbers as intermarriage was fast becoming a common occurrence.

The log dwelling was located several miles outside the barricaded confines of Ville Marie, the village where Dr. Claude LaBelle resided alone since the death of his wife Kathryn.

The most common customers of the St. Tropez were the hotheaded, passionate, half-breed coureurs-du-bois, whose habit it was to drop in following their trading sessions at the Ville Marie trading post. The sum amount of livres received for their pelts determining the length of time spent in pleasurable debauchery at the infamous establishment. Operating in secret and choosing to cast off all semblance of civilized attire, these men had adopted the customs and weapons of their Indian heritage. Generous to a fault with both their *livres* and their lovemaking, the hearty voyageurs had a well-deserved reputation for being more barbarous, noisy and ferocious than their pure native companions. The taste for danger inherent in them, and lacking the inhibitions that controlled the self-conscious of the Europeans, these men were bound to the women of the *St. Tropez* through their joie-de-vivre. Shunned by society as a whole, they shared an extreme loathing for convention, a loathing surpassed only by their love of excess in all forms. Alas, it was this unnatural love of excess that led to the badly mangled arm of the young prostitute; her overly amorous partner of the moment too drunk to heed her painful cries.

Having drained the contents of the cup, the girl lay her head down on the curly bearskin, surrendering to the brandy's effect. As Claude prepared to leave the musty room, he glanced over his shoulder at the tranquil figure lying on the cot. The crimson sun in its death throes penetrated the lace curtain covering the sole window in the room, casting fragile, ruby-tinted designs on the sleeping girl's worn face.

The only available exit from the log dwelling lay at the opposite end of the main parlour, blocked now by a group of laughing men. With gunpowder pouches slung over their shoulders and bearing long barreled muskets, it was difficult to know if they were coming or going. Entering the crowded area, Claude attempted to draw as little attention to himself as possible, a difficult feat since he stood at least a head higher than the other occupants of the smoky room. On the floor, a ragged homespun blanket had been spread out, surrounded by a boisterous group engaged in a game of dice. The men played for high stakes, the highest, not uncommonly, being the life of one of the unfortunate participants who, in a fit of rage, failed to draw his knife as quickly as his opponent.

It was quite possible that Claude could have made it across the room unnoticed since the men's full attention was focused on their game of chance; however, just as he approached the door, a familiar voice greeted him.

"Claude, bonjour!"

Swinging his head around he recognized the face of Jacque Langevin who stood leaning against the stone fireplace, one hand hidden in the pocket of his fringed buckskin coat, opened in front to reveal a colourful *fleshe* wrapped around his visible paunch, the tasseled ends hanging below his leather knee britches. Sporting the high moccasins he'd fashioned from the skin of a dead Mohawk, his free hand held a pipe from which he had just taken a hearty puff, the nebulous gray smoke encircling his touqued head like a misplaced halo.

A regular patron of the St. Tropez, Jacque Langevin was an inveterate gambler. His constant losses, however, far outweighed his paltry gains. A carpenter by trade, he was an excellent craftsman, his earnings more than adequate to sustain he and his wife Jeanette, as well as their cherished domestic Marjolaine. A devoted husband, he never engaged in the specialty of the house, choosing instead to limit his strength and efforts to gambling, however elusive the rewards.

"Bonjour Jacque, how goes it?" replied Claude. "Has Jeanette seen to it yet that you are a father?"

"I think she is taking care of that right now!" Jacque answered with a proud grin. "When I left home this morning she was having the baby pains. I couldn't wait to get out. Babies are women's' work eh Claude?"

"There has been time enough for her to have three babies already Jacque. Why don't you join me in the walk home. Less chance that way of some renegade Mohawk making off with our scalps."

Uncrossing his leather-clad legs, Jacque pondered a moment, the grisly aftermath of the last local ambush flooding his mind. Tilting his touqued head to one side, he shrugged. "Why not, it's a long walk back without company, besides, that bearded bastard on the floor has the last of my hard earned *livres* tucked away in his flea-infested pocket."

Leaving together, the two men walked side by side in the dusky evening shadows, Claude La Belle towering over the slightly built Jacque, who chopped the air unnecessarily with his hands as they strode across the high grass toward Ville Marie.

Formerly named *"Hochelaga"* or "At the Beaver Dam" by the Huron who'd occupied the village, Cartier, in 1535 had renamed it, *Place Royale,* and so it remained until 1600, until *Paul de Chomedy sier de Massonieve,* first Governor named by *Louis XIV,* dubbed it *Ville Marie*. From 1642 until the present time, hundreds of emigrants from France had settled here. However, the wrath of the Iroquois was upon them and although the village was fortressed, it was to no avail, for the Indians would hide in small groups for hours on end behind trees, bushes and rocks, noiselessly creeping from one area to another before ambushing, and today, despite the soaring birthrates, there were now fewer than three-hundred and fifty residents left, only fifty-nine of which were heads of families.

Jacque often reflected on the odds of surviving a raid in *Ville Marie*, and wondered why he and his family had been so fortunate, unlike poor Claude. Glancing sideways at his companion, he felt a sudden rush of pity stir deep within his gut. He marveled at Claude's inner strength in the face of his wife Kathryn's untimely and gruesome demise. He wondered as well why Claude continued his dangerous pilgrimages to the *St. Tropez,* risking his life from a surprise ambush just to administer care to the resident whores who, as far as Jacque was concerned, asked for what they got and got what they deserved.

As they walked in silence the late afternoon sun cast deep green shadows beneath the trees. An explosion of fireflies erupted before them. A red-tailed hawk drifted majestically beneath the wispy clouds before swooping down to disappear into a thick stand of trees in the distance. Blinded to the surrounding beauty, Claude's thoughts were filled with his beloved wife Kathryn, her cherubic face and wistful eyes fixed, as usual, in his mind's eye. He recalled how happy his new bride been upon their arrival in New France, her happiness flowing over and touching him as always. Their life had been as idealistic as one could hope for considering their humble station, but it was not to last.

Just eighteen months before, Kathryn had been en route to *Trois-Riviere* to pay homage to her ailing aunt, when her group had been ambushed by a party of Mohawk. The search party made the grisly discovery three days later, and it was decided amongst them to eliminate the finer details of the incident while relating the news to Claude. In truth, the mutilated bodies of the victims were almost beyond recognition. The search party never did find Kathryn's head.

About to break the silence with some light conversation, Jacque turned to his friend, his mouth open in preparation of speech, but the sight of Claude wiping a tear prompted the carpenter to avert his eyes and gaze instead at the brilliant red and gold sumacs beckoning them from a stand of trees in the distance. A thicket of brambles snapping sharply under Claude's foot startled him back to the present. With a deep sigh he turned his eyes upward just in time to spot a shooting star descending directly over the area of Ville Marie. As seen through his still moist eyes, the blazing tail of the dying star appeared to be mistily surrounded by a ghost-like aura. In the distance, the scream of a goshawk shattered the stillness.

For no apparent reason, both men experienced a chill.

CHAPTER FOUR

September 19, 1665, 7:45 p.m.

Standing alone on a high grassy knoll two miles outside Ville Marie, Black Whirlwind restlessly shifted his weight from one foot to the other. As undisputed leader of the five war parties that now surrounded the village, his primal awareness assured him that surprise would not be lost tonight. On the rare occasions the enemy had been forewarned of a raid and surprise had been lost, the men had traditionally returned to their prospective camps to plan and await the next raid on the despised Frenchmen, or as the Onqwanonhsioni called them, O'seronni.

Ranging themselves with the Dutch and English communities in New England, the Iroquois had sworn everlasting hatred against the O'seronni, vowing to destroy them. As well, the Dutch introduction of firearms in trade for beaver skins was fast increasing the number of Mohawk victories.

Lifting his gaze skyward, the Chief extended his sinewy arms toward the sky, palms upright, and offered a silent prayer to Aireskoi, the War God, promising to sacrifice at least four of the Asseroni captured in tonight's raid. As he exchanged unspoken thoughts with his Creator, he listened, not with his ears, but with his soul. Great prism shaped tears slipped like quicksilver from the corners of his eyes, sparkling like shattered diamonds as they flowed down his face. He was suddenly overwhelmed with an acute sense of deep core distress, a combination of despondency and spiritual pain, emotions that had never before permeated his being. His melancholy state was prompted by the red rains that had fallen earlier in the day, for the legend of Wawnatta's vision, recounted to him many moons before, remained buried deep in his subconscious mind.

Standing over six feet tall and boasting no more weight than necessary, he was an imposing figure. Naked except for a soft deerskin breechclout and knee-high moccasins fringed in scalps, his walnut skin was hair free, a result of plucking with clamshells. His shaven head bore the Mohawk scalp lock, a strip of hair on top running down the back of his neck, stiffened with river clay and

19

painted red with ochre. An eagle feather, worn for keen sight, was attached to his hair. His moist black eyes, decidedly more slanted than his companions, were wide set and bore a purplish tinge. His nose was aquiline above a full and sensuous mouth. Broad shoulders tapered down to a slim waist and muscular legs, a result of running down the deer. Red and black stripes were slashed across his high cheekbones in preparation of war and a headband of snakeskin was wrapped around his forehead, the rattled tail trailing down his back. On each outstretched arm, encircling the bulging muscles, were multi-coloured tatoos. One ear displayed three conch shell earrings and his powerful neck was adorned with a necklace of claws from the ohkwari or bear.

It had been fourteen summers since Black Whirlwind last prayed at this site. That morning had dawned bright and frosty, the wisps of mist that moments before circled the giant evergreens had been spirited away by the rising sun. He recalled the eagle soaring high above, barely skimming the emerald pinnacles of the towering pines, its pinions flashing in the sunlight. In the distance he'd heard the muted sounds of hooves treading on damp autumn leaves as a great bull elk led his herd in a long procession toward their feeding ground.

By the fifth day he had carried out the mission that would initiate him as a warrior. At his feet lay the body of a giant grizzly bear; its herculean back sprawled across a dry, barkless stump, an arrow protruding from its thick neck. Straddling the trunk, Black Whirlwind had leaned forward over the dead animal, whose jaws remained apart exposing the once deadly fangs. Placing the stem of his lighted pipe into the great beast's mouth, the young warrior had blown into the pipe bowl, thus proceeding to make peace with the animal's spirit. As the smoke filled the cavernous mouth and throat of his victim, he began to pray, begging the departed spirit of the bear not to resent the injury done to its body and not to thwart in any way, the good hunting of the future.

Four days previous, Black Whirlwind had vowed to live in the venerable forest for five days and nights without food or drink in order to purge his a-tonn-hets or soul, from evil spirits and hopefully receive a vision of his totem. Lightheaded and weak from hunger he'd prayed for his patron animal to make its ghostly appearance in a dream vision during his five day vigil. By day he had sat under the

20

sheltering branches of a lush onen'takwenhton, red cedar, a tree the Onqwanonhsioni felt especially akin to as they were of the same hue, also it was known that smoke from the cedar had the power to chase away bad spirits. He willed himself not to hear the chattering of birds and animals, but to listen instead with his soul for guidance from the spirits. The melodious rustling of the branches had lulled the fasting brave to sleep at night, his head resting upon the large skull of a bear, half-buried beneath the mint coloured needles carpeting the ground. While he slept, the creatures of the forest had cautiously approached him, staring in awe. Beady-eyed mice playfully skittered across his an occasioned feet, and a red fox sidled up to him, her tiny nose delicately sniffing the air before disappearing into the looming shadows of her forest home.

He would later conclude that the spiritual influence emanating from the skull of the bear upon which he rested his head, had prompted the visions of the monstrous grizzly bear. The visions started on the second night, faintly outlined and sketchy at first. However, by the fifth night the enormous animal had gained complete precedence over his dreams, it's mammoth paws beckoning him. Standing erect, the huge and ponderous grizzly stood eight feet from nose to tail with claws five inches long. Black Whirlwind could only stare in veneration as the giant beast lumbered toward him with open jaws and outstretched paws. Crouching menacingly over the young brave, he'd bared his teeth before sinking them deeply into the rough bark of the tree to score his mark just inches from the warrior's head. Standing upright, the animal retraced his steps, faced Black Whirlwind, and with a thunderous growl, lifted his giant paws in the air.

Awakening with a start he had been about to raise his head when his keen eyes scanned the fresh scoring near the base of the tree. A tremor passed through him, and he sensed, rather than saw his prey standing but a few feet from him. Reaching for his bow he uttered a silent prayer, a prayer that was soon to be answered. And so it was that Black Whirlwind's totem was the bear, and he called him brother.

The rustling of leaves in the distance behind him prompted Black Whirlwind's thoughts back to the present. Trained as a hunter he swiftly identified the intruder as a small fox scurrying across the forest floor. About to continue his prayers, he glanced down from his vantage point, spotting two men walking in the direction of Ville Marie. The shorter of the two wore the O'seronni's strange hat and had an odd way of walking, his arms swaying back and forth in the air. As he studied the men, the Chief's body became taut; his black eyes narrowed like a panther about to spring on its unsuspecting prey. As if on cue, a fiery arrow slashed its way across the azure sky; the direction of the spiraling smoke behind the burning weapon, a signal to Black Whirlwind that the time for surprise was right. Right on cue, the Mohawk signal of a goshawk scream echoed from the clump of trees behind him. He turned and headed toward his band of warriors.

Having discarded all clothing save their breechcloths, moccasins, and cedar wood breastplates covered with interwoven thongs of hides, they stood at the ready. Their bodies had been suitably painted and they all sported their amulets and feathers in their scalp lock. Standing before them, Black Whirlwind raised his arm. "Onen, now is the time."

"Chagon, Feel no sorrow." These words were uttered by Dancing Leaf to the old midwife who sat huddled in the corner of the hut; her frail body all but hidden from view by the fur cape she clutched around her. Despite the warmth emanating from the fire that permeated the confines of the hut, Crippled Sparrow was shivering violently; the spastic trembling of her bones accompanied every few moments by a low, mournful cry. Placing the slumbering infant on the beaver skins, Dancing Leaf knelt before the pathetic woman and placed both hands on her frail shoulders.

"Now is the time for strength, not weakness, old woman! It is only through our courage that *Shonkwaya'tihson* will afford us a solution. You yourself have taught me that weakness serves no other purpose than to shrivel the spirit and numb the mind."

Crippled Sparrow dropped her head even lower in shame for she was unable to meet Dancing Leaf's eyes, eyes that bore strength and promise, eyes that were reminiscent of her own, many moons ago. Dancing Leaf's silver bracelets tinkled as she gently grasped her aunt's chin, tilting it upward, compelling their eyes to meet.

"My eyes show me your heart is heavy my mother friend. Your guilt over my child's misfortune seeps from your pores and surrounds you in gray, murky mist. Where is your spirit now, old woman? I defy you to challenge *O-nes-sohn-ro-noh*. Decrease your fear of his power, and in doing so your inner strength will return! I beg of you; help me to save my child!"

A small glimmer of light shone from deep within the clouded eyes of the old woman. Her young ward had fanned the last dying spark of hope within her. A surge of vitality flowed through her veins; she would not retreat; she would fight this one last battle for her beloved niece and the unfortunate papoose. Dancing Leaf watched as her red-rimmed eyes gradually crinkled into deep creases. When at last she spoke, it was with the old tone of authority.

"It will be done!"

They spoke far into the night; their voices hushed and low, as the spitting fire gradually died down to reveal the waning life of a few glowing embers. The infant's imperfection could be kept secret from the others until the time of the First Fruits ceremony, or eight or nine moons. She would be constantly encased in a cradleboard, removed only to be bathed or to reline the carrier with dried moss. It was unlikely that anyone in camp would be aware of her defect until such time Blood Sky made her first attempts to walk. In the meantime, both women would take turns massaging the afflicted area at regular intervals, a treatment, according to Crippled Sparrow, that may well alter the severity of the dislocated socket and in turn, the severity of the child's limp.

Expert at relieving dislocations, the old woman's knowledge of anatomy was far greater than that of even the most educated white man. Dancing Leaf herself had been witness to one of the braves in camp being treated by the old woman for a dislocated hip joint. After securely tying his foot to a tree, he'd been instructed to yank the leg backward with a powerful thrust and the hip socket had settled neatly back in place. She was also known to massage movement into a stiff limb in record time. If the expert manipulative and constant massages failed, the next step would be to invent a mishap by explaining to the others that Blood Sky, in her initial attempts at walking, had suffered a bad fall, dislocating the hip joint as a result. Both women prayed this drastic measure would be avoided for the *Onqwanonhsioni* knew that to purposefully distort the truth was a very bad thing as the penalty for *onowen,* or lying, was to risk having one's ghost remain earthbound for eternity.

Although it was too early to tell just how severe Blood Sky's injury was, if it caused her to be severely crippled for life, there was little, if any chance of marriage for her. Despite this, she would live a rich, full life, for although the Mohawk were known to the outside as the cruelest and most savage of Indians, within their own circle they were the opposite. Hospitable, charitable and never abandoning their aged or infirm, they chose instead to find a suitable place in their society where the unfortunates could be of use, thus maintaining their sense of pride and inherent dignity.

Their plan complete, the women made a pact that the matter was never again to be discussed lest one of the other women overhear and report their conspiracy to the great Sachem Chief, White Thunder. Satisfied that all details were foolproof, they placed their left hands over the other's heart to signify the love and trust between them, while in the center of the room, unseen by their eyes, a tiny smile crept over the face of the still sleeping newborn.

Thus done, Crippled Sparrow stoked the fire before returning to the *Ka-nonh-sehs* – longhouse, for a much-needed pipe of tobacco and bark.

Alone now with her baby, Dancing Leaf suckled her for the first time, her emotions encompassing those of all mothers, primitive and civilized. A sister to every woman, she experienced the full and complete satisfaction of motherhood. Her thoughts turned to her husband, Black Whirlwind, justly named for his sudden bursts of unbridled temper, however infrequent. The time would be chosen carefully before the details and aftermath of Blood Sky's birth would be revealed to him. She was sure in her heart he would understand her desire to protect the child, for he was a kind and gentle man, despite his occasional flares of anger.

With a smile on her lips and the tiny warm body encircled in her arms, she prepared to sleep. Far off in the distance a wolf lifted his head toward the sky and howled four times in succession.

"Four times," she thought, "the sacred number. The howls of my brother the *okwaho,* tells me many changes will be wrought this night."

As she slept, her dreams revolved around a female infant, but as the dream unfolded, she was confused as to why the papoose who lay cradled in her arms had skin the colour of snow and hair like corn silk.

CHAPTER FIVE

Bolting upright in bed, Jeanette trembled with fear. The beads of sweat escaping from her brow left moist transparent speckles on her white muslin shift. Marjolaine had been alerted to her bedside just seconds before, startled by her mistress's moaning.

"Madame, it was only a bad dream. Calm yourself!" So saying, the agitated domestic withdrew a small, embroidered handkerchief from her pocket and proceeded to wipe the damp forehead of the shivering woman. But Jeanette would not be calmed. Her fingers were digging painfully into Marjolaine's arms and her glazed eyes stared at the poor girl in mute horror. Speaking soothingly to her as one would a frightened animal, the domestic helped her change into a fresh gown after sponging her body with the violet scented soap the women had made together last fall, one of the few luxuries stocking the oak shelves in the Langevin household. She then coaxed the anxious mother to sip on a hot cup of chamomile tea, known for its relaxing qualities.

Easing herself gently beside Jeanette, she lowered herself onto the multi-coloured quilt covering the crude bed. Constructed with a rope lacing to support the palliasse covered in ticking, a featherbed, woolen blankets and sheets, Marjolaine thought she'd never been more comfortable. Her eyes grew heavy and she balked at the thought of having to prepare Jacque's evening meal. With the infant now sleeping, the silence in the room acted as a hypnotic and twice she nearly dropped the scalding tea onto her aproned lap. Jeanette remained silent. She had not uttered a word since emerging from the dream that had been so terrifying. Staring blankly, she was trying to recall the contents of the dream.

"I can't remember *Souris,* I just can't remember what frightened me so much. I have to remember!" But try as she may, she was unable to recall even the slightest detail of the grisly nightmare. Gradually the sedative effect of the chamomile took hold and she lay back on the plump feather pillow and fell into a deep and dreamless reverie.

The infant stirred in her maple cradle. Marjolaine's stomach lurched and she was sorely tempted to ignore the sound, opting instead to lift the babe from the confines of the lilliputian bed to change the soiled napkin. Gingerly hoisting the tiny legs to replace the fresh diaper, she perceived the contour of a birthmark under the left thigh.

"Strange," she thought, "I didn't notice this mark before; it looks like a snake. How odd." On closer inspection she was able to make out a definite serpentine shape, the minute outline of a forked tongue barely visible. She pondered as to how she could have overlooked such a curious birthmark, recalling with a shudder the adverse reaction she'd experienced during the initial contact with the infant's flesh; a reaction that had induced her to rush through the newborn's preliminary care. Placing the infant back into her cradle she strode toward the fireplace. Too wound up and over-tired to sleep herself, she proceeded to prepare a fresh pot of tea. Employing one of the many devices the residents of *Ville Marie* adopted from the Indians, she suspended the tarnished water pot on a green hardwood hook over the fire. The familiar chirping of a housebound cricket soothed her. Spotting the intruder last week under her old birch broom propped against the fireplace, she'd placed tiny mounds of sugar and breadcrumbs in the area to nourish her quarantined friend.

Retrieving her bobbin lace that lay in a colourful grass basket by the hearth, she sat in the large rocker with a deep sigh. She was momentarily soothed by the exquisite fragrance of yesterday's blueberry pies pervading the area, but it wasn't long before she realized the futility of trying to concentrate on the intricate pattern. Dropping the work on her lap she closed her heavy lids, but was still too jittery to relax. The cricket chirped once more. Replacing the bobbin lace in the basket, she vacated the comfort of the rocker. Walking sluggishly across the room she absentmindedly grabbed a large slice of cold venison from the scarred maple coffer guarding the kitchen door before helping herself to some cider she had made last fall. Retrieving the flickering oil lamp from the sideboard, she slipped through the door into the summer kitchen. Reaching upward to free the handle of her large woven basket from where it hung on the wall, she stepped outside, making her way to the far end of the expansive fenced-in area where she and Jacque had planted the beans together in June.

The fence, constructed to ward away animals and wind, retained the sun's heat, a necessity since the gardening season spanned just three months. Like the majority of gardens in Ville Marie, cabbages, turnips, corn, tobacco, oats, sorrel and parsley had been planted, though Marjolaine and Jeanette had expressed their desire for decorative plants as well but Jacque's response had simply been, "Let's just leave the luxury of decorative plants to the more illustrious families."

She had walked but a few feet before she perceived the eerie stillness. Cocking her head to one side she listened, wishing for the comfort of even the slightest sound. The remote echo of the sluggish clip-clop of oxen and cart reached her ears then vanished. Her nerves were getting the best of her and she trembled. In a thwarted attempt at humour, she tried to make light of the situation by uttering, "The brat's squeals have probably injured my eardrums for life." Cautiously, she made her way to the end of the garden.

Appearing a decade younger than her thirty years, she stood just slightly less than five feet and was possessed of a plump, sturdy frame; her moon-shaped face displaying pale skin despite the hours spent tending the Langevin's garden. Tendrils of light brown hair peeked saucily from her linen cap, trailing over her forehead and down the nape of her neck. Enormous gray eyes were contrasted by a tangle of jet-black lashes and brows. Her diminutive nose complimented a delicate, rosebud shaped mouth and tiny white teeth.

Born in Anjou, France, Marjolaine had been orphaned at the age of two whereupon she was placed in a convent under the strict discipline of the nuns until age five when the local butcher, a Gabriel Poisson, along with his wife, adopted her. The Poissons had been less than suitable parents for the shy child, administering arduous chores and punishment with equal fervor. According to convention, she'd returned to the convent at the onset of school age to further her formal and religious studies. She enjoyed school and was well liked by her peers and teachers alike. However, at the age of fourteen, nagging doubts concerning her future began to plague her, a future that threatened to be most dismal indeed.

Her destiny revolved around two sole options. She could marry, thereby gaining some semblance of control over her life; or she could remain in the convent. Although she reasoned that marriage would be preferable to a lifetime in the austere convent, she was unprepared to enter a union in which she would have little or no say as to the choice of husband, for surely her greedy adoptive parents would hastily accept a dowry from the first interested suitor with little or no concern for her feelings. She was inclined to shy away from marriage for yet another reason. The majority of husbands in France had a tendency to preach obedience to their wives, while assuming for themselves, the greatest amount of personal freedom.

This quandary as to her life's direction took a surprise turn when, on the fourth day of June in 1649, her fifteenth birthday, she had been duly informed by Mother Superior that there was indeed another option open to her in regard to her future.

Marjolaine, along with seven hundred and seventy-five other females, most of them widows and orphans under the protection of *King Louis XIV*, had been handpicked by the crown to emigrate to New France. Making the proposal more attractive was the statement casually uttered by Mother Superior during their discourse. "All females who comply with the King's wishes are assured upon their arrival, the finding, and hopefully the securing, of a husband best suited to their station in life. An easy task if I may say so myself, the men outnumbering the women two to one."

What Mother Superior failed to mention however, was that the majority of *Les Filles Du Roi*, ' The King's Daughters,' had been orphaned or otherwise unsupported and in a society with strict rules regarding female conduct, young, unprotected women were extremely vulnerable, a situation that no doubt had encouraged the majority of the *Les filles du rois* to seize the chance of an arranged marriage. For ten years, as many as one hundred and thirty women a year abandoned their hazardous existence in France for New France and marriage.

This information, coupled with the young girl's awareness that the colonists in New France were known to treat their wives with far more equality than their homebound brothers, piqued her interest even further.

"The unmarried officers, soldiers and colonists are in dire need of wives." Mother Superior continued. "Many of them have expressed their willingness to remain in New France once released from service, provided they can find wives. From what I've been told, the availability of the native women is non-existent as many of them are jealously reserved for the Chiefs of their prospective tribes."

Marjolaine, who up to this point had hung on to every word uttered by the elderly nun, suppressed a giggle when all of a sudden Mother Superior jumped upright from where she sat, a look of horror on her face. Seconds later, the culprit in the form of a tiny mouse, skittered from under the heavy skirts of the matron. Freed from her attacker, Mother Superior attempted to gain some semblance of decorum by frowning at Marjolaine's obvious amusement.

"You are an extremely fortunate young lady my dear, since you have been selected for your amiability, your ability to work hard and your honorable character. Special emphasis however, rests on your intense religious education. I would advise you my dear, to accept the challenge."

And accept the challenge she did. Her dowry from the King's purse compensating for any misgivings she harboured. Along with forty-four other King's Daughters who were eager to comply with *King Louis XIV's* wishes, she received fifty *livres,* ten of which was for recruitment, thirty to be spent on clothes and the remaining sixty to be used as payage for the voyage to New France. In addition she received a gift of one hundred *livres,* some ordinary clothing, a hood, a small money box, one taffeta handkerchief, shoe ribbons, one hundred sewing needles, white thread, one thousand pins, a comb, one pair of stockings, one pair of gloves, scissors, two knives, a bonnet, four braids and two *livres* in silver.

They had set sail from New Rochelle on a blustery March morning in 1651, the twin emotions of sorrow and melancholy prompting untold numbers of tears to be shed among the women as they clung together for comfort and reassurance. Marjolaine however, was void of all sentiment as she stared impersonally toward the diminishing shoreline of France. On the contrary she felt exhilarated and adventurous.

The eight-week trip was long and tedious. Two of the women met early deaths from sickness while a third girl, frail and blind in one eye, who'd talked incessantly to herself since leaving New Rochelle, opted for suicide by throwing herself overboard during the night. Morale was low among the passengers, causing Marjolaine many a sleepless night, as the sobbing of her homesick companions became a nightly ritual throughout the sleeping quarters. The overall dismal mood however, was about to shift dramatically.

On the day of their arrival in New France, the women had spotted a number of over-zealous colonists jumping into their bark canoes at the first sight of the French frigate. Unlike the town's aristocrats and well-to-do merchants, these men numbered among the majority of villagers who were, by early spring, half-starved and often forced to eat cats or rats in order to survive until the ship's arrival. Starving as well for female company, the young swains had raced out to meet the ship, hoping to proclaim for their own the healthiest or most comely female. As well, Intendant LaValle had recently issued an ordinance compelling bachelors to marry the King's Daughters within fifteen days of the arrival of the vessels bringing the women or face the penalty of being prohibited from fishing, hunting and trading for furs. Added to this was the fact they'd all been taught that it is God's will that whoever is born subject should not reason but obey.

Their efforts were to no avail however, as upon disembarking, the women were put under the authority of a monitoress, a Madame Boureau, who had been delegated by Royal warrant. The first three days in New France was spent in the care of local nuns before Marjolaine, along with the other women, was transferred to the *Chateau of Saint Louis,* the Governor's mansion known as 'The heart and soul of the social world," where a ceremony was held in their honour.

Arriving at the mansion Marjolaine felt oddly acquainted with the landscape surrounding the circular carriage drive. As she stepped into the enormous marble foyer, an overpowering sense of *deja vu* engulfed her and she felt certain that she had inhabited the manor at another time. The atmosphere was wrought with subtle familiarities. She experienced the acute awareness of knowing beforehand, the exact location of the myriad of rooms. Unable to rationalize the experience, she tried to ignore it for the time being, occupying her mind instead with the excitement of the evening's festivities.

Never before had she witnessed such an impressive assemblage, the most impressive by far being the Governor's guests from Louisburg. The women, decadent in dress and cosmetic, frolicked about the ballroom exchanging the latest gossip with local dignitaries, their fluttering silk fans wafting a pot pourri of sensual parfum into the atmosphere. Even their shoes, considered a necessary evil to

Marjolaine who preferred to run about barefoot, were decorative in colour and buckle.

So staggering was the opulence that Marjolaine balked at the realization she'd have to take leave for a few moments to attend the *cabinet de toilette.* Dropping a slight curtsey to the small group she'd been chatting with, she made her way to the powder room where she happened upon one of the Louisburg women adjusting her petticoats in front of the ornate mirror. Chagrined, Marjoline apologized for her untimely entrance and was about to leave when the woman, an elderly matron with extremely pointed features, bade her remain, introducing herself as Madame Estelle Benoit. Responding in kind, Marjolaine couldn't help but comment on the number of damask crinolines worn by the woman, eleven in all. With a shrug Estelle blithely commented,

"*Oui,* I suppose I am fortunate, considering the price of just one such petticoat is sixty *livres,* half again," she remarked, "the wages my servant makes in one year."

With a forced smile, Marjolaine glanced down at her own shabby frock that, until this moment, she'd considered rather charming. Feeling absurd, she managed a slight curtsey, leaving Estelle primping in front of the mirror, the awkward incident causing her to forget why she'd entered the *cabinet de toilette* in the first place.

Incorporated into the evening's celebration was a ceremony in which the Governor himself presented each of the King's Daughters with a gilt envelope bearing the name and station of her prospective employer. Less than a week later Marjolaine was in the employ of the local carpenter, Jacque Langevin, a compassionate soul with an unusual bent for bawdy humour, and his wife Jeanette, a timid girl who aspired to nothing more than caring for her husband. Life looked very bright indeed for Marjolaine until, one by one, the vast majority of immigrant King's Daughters secured suitable husbands. Marjolaine however, hadn't been that fortunate; thus fifteen years hence, on the morning of her thirtieth birthday, she'd relinquished all hope of ever marrying.

Finding herself at the rear of the garden, she tossed her basket on the ground and burrowed a hollow in the soil in which to place her

lamp. Stooping over, she plucked the ripe vegetable from its vine, slowly filling the basket. Standing upright, she threw her head back, the palms of her hands pressed against her arched back to relieve the stiffness. Her gray eyes widened in astonishment at the colourful tail of a falling star shooting across the vast expanse of the evening sky.

CHAPTER SIX

The serene cloak of security that overlay *Ville Marie* was instantly shattered by the eerie, guttural whoops of the dreaded war cry. Resounding from all sides of the village, few residents were spared the primitive warning. It is said the war cry, once heard, is never forgotten. And so it was this night that Roy Henri, an elderly cobbler and survivor of two Iroquois raids, died at the first howl of the Indians. His bowels involuntarily emptied and within minutes he lay slumped over the side of his makeshift cot situated at the rear of his shop. Pure fear had stopped his heart.

Not so fortunate was Father Arter. Strolling through the opulent gardens behind the rectory, relishing his final smoke of the day, his attackers were upon him seconds after the initial cries. Dropping silently from a mammoth elm where he'd lain in wait, a half-naked warrior pounced on the priest's back, the sudden impact forcing the air from the old man's lungs as he collapsed to the ground. Within seconds he was dead, his bald head fiercely severed from his shoulders by the tomahawks of three painted braves who leapt from their hiding place on the roof of the now burning rectory.

One of the Mohawk warriors, Tall Elm, so named for his height, which was close to seven feet, bent down to retrieve the bloodied head of the *O'seronni* witch doctor before unceremoniously skewering it to a wooden stake, which he firmly implanted into the ground. Standing back he observed the other braves.

"Now is the time for revenge!" he screamed.

Less than a year ago, Tall Elm's village, *Tionnontoguen,* had been raided by the *O'seronni;* his mother and sisters brutally raped and slaughtered before his disbelieving eyes. The evil white-man had destroyed all winter supplies before torching the camp. Emblazoned on his mind was the sight of the large wooden cross the *O'seronni* had stabbed into the frozen ground as the defilement and carnage abounded. He would never forget the cries of *"Vive le Roy",* the *O'seronni* war cry.

The raid on Tall Elm's village was a result of concerns surrounding the numerous Iroquois uprising against the French in Canada. It had been the newly appointed *Viceroy Alexandre de*

Prouville de Tracy, by military order, who'd led the six hundred troops from France into New France. Many members of the *"Carignan Salieres"* regiment, as they were called, refused to embark as they had been informed beforehand that they were going to a hostile land to fight 'wild savages.'

In January of 1665, the regiment, along with five hundred Canadian militia, was ordered into densely snowed forest to fight the dreaded Iroquois. Unused to the frigid winters and walking on snowshoes for the first time in their lives, the men were required to carry their militia packs weighing no less than fifteen kilos. Paying little or no heed to their native guides, they suffered terribly; watching in horror as their fingers, ears and noses which were numbed by the cold, dropped off, leaving sporadic imprints in the snow. They'd been cursed with snow-blindness, the blue-eyed men suffering the most; their food supply was fast exhausted and in order to stave off starvation, they hastily adopted the native way of chewing on the deer sinews that made up their snowshoes.

Those who succumbed were left unburied, prey to the starving wolves and foxes. The survivors were beyond exhaustion, many of them being carried on the backs of their native guides. They were, however, successful in burning to the ground, Tall Elm's village, along with three others, destroying all winter supplies. The cries of *"Vive le Roy!"* could be heard among the screams as the Natives were slaughtered and raped. The handful of Native survivors succumbed shortly afterwards as a result of the white man's legacy – smallpox.

The French then claimed the land through right of conquest. They had lost seventy-five men. The Mohawk tribe had lost two hundred and fifty. Although Tall Elm had managed to escape with a handful of others, the mutilated bodies of his French victims from that day forward bore witness to his scarred soul.

Recognizing their survival as an obligation to seek revenge, the small war party had traveled a great distance to execute their sworn retaliation. The trip had been perilous with many portages and the chance of ambush from their enemy, the Huron, but the sight of his companions rallying around the headless remains of the old priest more than compensated for the 1280-kilometre journey.

Joining the throng of men, Tall Elm crouched beside the violated corpse of the *O'seronni* witch doctor. Deftly slashing open the breast with his scalping knife, he thrust his large fist into the cavernous torso, ignoring the gushing protest of the lifeless body. With a powerful yank he ripped the heart from its hold, his bloodied hands placing the obsolete organ between his strong, even teeth. Gnawing off a small piece of the heart, he tossed the remains to the others who followed suit.

"Raweryahsiyo!" they cried out. "He has a good heart!" Bloodied spittle trickled down their chins and bare chests causing narrow streaks of the priest's vital fluid to mingle with the crude totems painted on their skin. The giant native then initiated the war dance around the skewered head of Father Arter whose features in death appeared wildly rapturous. One by one the others joined Tall Elm, their feet shuffling and pounding the earth. As they danced, scarlet flames licking the wooden innards of the rectory cast a reflection on the men, bathing them in a soft veil of misty blood. The live green garter snake threaded through Tall Elm's ear lobe recoiled from the heat of the fire.

"Courier, courier – run, run!" Claude screamed out to Jacque who'd fled in the direction of his home and family. Claude had no one waiting at home, and since any attempt to make it safely through the village would be suicidal, he turned and cut back through the chaos, making his way through the rioting crowd toward the mammoth gates of the fort hoping to find some protection. Enclosed by pointed stakes and measuring at least a hundred yards along its sides, the fort contained lodgings for the missionaries and colonists, a magazine, soldiers' barracks, a rudimentary chapel and temporary lodgings for the Governor.

Spurred on by the thick stench of fear in the air, he ran, as never before, the beginnings of a feeble cry lay strangled in his parched throat. Like the beating of drums, his heart resounded deep and full in his ears, his vision was clouded by droplets of sweat. Stumbling over the body of a trampled dog, he lost his footing and fell headlong onto the jagged remains of a discarded wheel. Disoriented, he clambered to his feet as a crowd of rioting villagers, maddened with terror by the unanticipated onslaught, bolted in front of him. Raising his hands to shield his ears from the screams, he staggered forward, and stopped, frozen in his tracks.

Crawling toward him with pleading eyes, a member of the militia who'd been struck down by a tomahawk, reached out to clutch his leg before collapsing under the weight of a Mohawk warrior who'd ghosted from behind to grip the head of the bawling soldier between his bare legs before relieving him of his scalp. Transfixed in horror Claude was unable to avert his eyes from the hideous sight of the scalpless man, his skull sheathed in a slimy covering of blood, his cheeks, separated now from their hold, sagging grotesquely.

With lurching stomach, Claude turned on his heels and bolted toward the stockade, only to find the area crawling with Indians. Half-crazed with fear, he sought refuge in a narrow alley separating the officers' quarters, but the smell of smoke and crackling of dry, seasoned wood forced him back to the street. They were on him in seconds, six painted braves brandishing spears, knives and tomahawks, their black eyes glinting with hate. Trembling, Claude tried to keep them at bay; his arms, like impotent weapons, thrashing and flailing in the air; the hoarseness of his screams betraying his show of courage. They circled round him, cruelly taunting their *O'seronni* prey. Like cats, they pounced forward, stabbing him with their knives and tomahawks before leaping back. Exhausted to the point of fainting, his clothes saturated with blood oozing from his wounds, Claude fell to his knees, closed his eyes and began to sob. Closing in for the kill, the warriors halted at the sound of a loud guttural cry, their heads collectively turning toward the source.

"Tekta's – Stop!"* Stepping from the shadows, their leader, Black Whirlwind, uttered a few words to one of the braves who then approached the bloodied prisoner before grabbing him roughly by the arm to lead him away.

Jacque, in his terror at the onset of the war cries, had immediately begun praying for the safety of Jeanette and his newborn. As he ran, he cursed himself for having settled in this God-forsaken village, this advance post on the way to the east, condemned to the merciless warfare of the Indians. A great chilling scream echoed from somewhere in the distance. Confused and dazed with fear, he failed to recognize his surroundings. Convinced he'd taken the wrong direction, he slowed his pace, scanning the area for some semblance of familiarity when suddenly he realized he was less than a hundred feet from his home. Taking a deep breath, he picked up speed, crying out Jeanette's name.

He heard them before he saw them. A band of Indians surrounding his house, shouting and howling, their weapons thrust toward the sky as they leapt victoriously in the face of death and destruction of the enemy. Some archaic force prompted Jacque to lift his head toward the heavens and let loose a chilling scream, a scream that was short-lived by the war club shattering his skull. Brandishing a scalping knife, a young warrior straddled the brained carpenter, and bending down, retrieved the discarded toque that lay on the blood soaked ground. Tossing it haphazardly on his head with one hand, he reached out with the other and, with lightning speed, deftly slashed open the stomach of the dead *O'seronni.* Dropping his knife, he cupped his hands in spoon fashion and proceeded to scoop the warm blood into his mouth. Another brave stepped in to rid Jacque of his scalp, and as a final indignity to the desecrated corpse, proceeded to slice a circle around the upper arm before stripping it down to the wrist and severing it. This he would use for a tobacco pouch.

Inside the blazing structure, the hands and feet of Jeanette, hacked off prior to her being scalped, lay strewn on the floor beside the bed where she lay. With bloodied hands her assassin had then reached into the cradle of the newborn before gingerly raising the infant to his breast. Supporting the tiny back with his left hand, he ran the fingers of his right across the delicate white forehead and cheeks, leaving faint traces of Jeanette's blood on the babe's translucent skin. He had never seen a white baby before, and the sight of this papoose bearing mock traces of war paint from her mother's blood delighted him. He tossed his large head back in resounding laughter.

"You shall be called Corn Child!" So said, he'd set fire to the bed upon which lay the remains of the infant's mother. Satisfied that the flames were enveloping the room, he left the house, Corn Child held securely in his large murderous hand.

CHAPTER SEVEN

Blood Sky stood at the entrance of the birth hut, her doeskin cape fluttering like a bird's wing in the morning breeze. Secured around her forehead was a deerskin trumpline connected to the cradleboard where Blood Sky slept contentedly. She'd been swaddled from chin to toe before being securely lashed to the board, her minute feet resting against a block of wood that had been placed between her feet, molding them inward, a tradition common to the females of the tribe. Lavishly decorated with beadwork and laden with shell trinkets, the creation of the cradleboard had been a labour of love for Dancing Leaf.

The pungent scent of burning pine needles swept in her direction by a sudden gust of wind told her the women of the lodge were long since up preparing the morning meal. She mentally thanked *Shonkwaya'tihson* for sending this subtle reminder that life as she knew it remained comfortably intact. A trio of squirrels scampered across the dewy grass in front of her, their bulging cheeks filled to capacity with nuts. This sight, when coupled with the *Onqwanonhsionis'* concern about the unusually thick and heavy cornhusks of the season, prompted her to exclaim,

"So, little Blood Sky, your first season of the Howling Winds will be long and severe."

Lifting her face toward the sky, she savored the exquisite warmth of grandmother sun against her dusky skin, an experience she likened to a fragile butterfly emerging from its prison of silk. Perceiving a spark of newfound strength taking root in her soul, she freed all memory of last night's dream, allowing it to spirit away like soft mist at daybreak. She'd dreamt of a suckling, a foreign looking papoose with white skin, while the contorted face of Crippled sparrow loomed above her in the dark.

"The infant must die; she is imperfect. The infant must die; she is imperfect," repeated the ghostly image of the old midwife. Forcing herself awake, she'd clutched Blood Sky tightly to her breast. Trembling, she'd pressed her face to the infant's head, massaging her cheek against the fuzzy down of her sleeping daughter. A puny sneeze escaped from the babe's mouth causing Dancing Leaf to breathe a sigh of relief. Placing the warm bundle to her milk-laden breast, she'd reflected upon the dream and its hidden message, for the *Onqwanonhsioni* knew that dreams were to be respected; the messages therein were guidelines and warnings to the dreamer, guidelines to be followed and warnings to be heeded. The dream had left her feeling slightly agitated, more puzzled than anxious, but these emotions had been short-lived and all negative thoughts vanished the moment she'd placed Blood Sky to her breast.

Walking toward the elm bark longhouse a few hundred feet away, she was intercepted by her cousin Little Current, skipping toward the river to fetch a fresh supply of water, her arm extended to balance the tightly woven basket upon her head. Dancing Leaf's heart was near bursting with pride even though she feigned modesty as her cousin expounded on the newborn's elegant facial characteristics before scurrying off in the direction of the river.

As if trying to escape from its hold, a quivering buzzard's feather, designed to ward off evil, beckoned to her from the sole entrance of the longhouse. Beside it, a carving of the Clan's totem, the wolf, identified the dwelling. A small group of children interrupted their game of Basket and Dice to view the new arrival, their excitement pleasing Dancing Leaf who allowed them to take turns holding the little bundle. Lifting aside the mammoth fur covering, she entered the place she called home along with one hundred and seventy-four members of her maternal lineage; old women, female descendants, unmarried sons and husbands of married daughters, all members of the Wolf Clan of the Mohawk tribe.

Each tribe was divided into four or more Clans bearing animal names, and since each Clan was enogamous it was necessary for members to marry outside of it. The individual Clans were distributed over several villages and Clans bearing the same name, whatever the tribe, formed a single unit. As they were matrilineal, descent was recognized only through the female line.

The longhouse was overheated, causing Dancing Leaf's eyes to sting from the smoke. Glancing upward, she was relieved to see the slots in the ceiling had been reopened following the violent rains of the previous day, curious rains that had been red as blood. She watched the curling puffs of smoke writhe up through the muted light of the dwelling before escaping into the chilly morning air. Curing tobacco leaves hung from the rafters over the fires. She smiled at the realization that the Thanksgiving Ceremony was almost upon them as it was her favourite time of the year, the time when the *Onqwanonhsioni* bid the corn rest for the winter while the people hunted.

The children were awake now, running to and fro; their rings of laughter were contrasted by the solemn, almost stoic expressions of their mothers, most of whom were leaning over the cooking fires, readying the morning meal. A young girl, impatient at having to tend the meal for her mother, sang a charm to make her food cook faster; the small babies felt their hunger pangs, a few of them wailing tearfully from their cradleboards that were slung from the various joists throughout the lodge. The air was deluged with odors of fish, venison, corn and fowl, aromas that piqued Dancing Leaf's appetite and caused her mouth to water. As if sensing her thoughts, Reason-For-Life tugged at the hem of the new mother's fringed skirt, her tiny brown hand extending upward to offer a warm biscuit from which a hearty bite had been taken.

"N*yawen ki' wah* – thank you very much," Dancing Leaf said, graciously accepting the child's gift. Reason-For-Life, a Huron captive, smiled in acknowledgement, for even though she was deaf and mute, her eyes spoke clearly and her heart heard all. Placing what was left of the warm crisp biscuit into her mouth, Dancing Leaf luxuriated in the taste. Made from flour of the grass-seed, water and bear grease, it was one of her favourite foods and the taste of it whet her appetite for something more substantial. Gazing in the half-light down the long broad corridor of the longhouse, where cooking fires smouldered every fifteen feet or so, she spotted a group of women taking full advantage of their men's absence. With the males gone off to battle in Ville Marie, there were fewer meals to be cooked and more time for idle gossip. She smiled to herself as she observed her small niece Singing Goose attempt to stoke her fire with a stripped willow stick while her lazy mother, Sunflower, slept soundly on the fur-lined bunk opposite the feeble blaze. Reaching down to retrieve a handful of pitch that lay on the ground, Dancing Leaf threw it onto the waning embers, causing the flames to vigorously renew themselves. Sitting in a circle, a small group of women busied

41

themselves chewing and gnawing on large sections of moose skin, rendering it supple prior to fashioning moccasins for their families.

Heading toward Crippled Sparrow's bunk, she was met by *Taraktarak*, her closest and dearest cousin, and to whom Dancing Leaf had never kept anything from, until now. Like the cricket whose name she bore, the timbre of *Taraktarak's* voice had a distinct chirping quality, never more endearing than today as the excited girl reminded Dancing Leaf of her precognitive dream just nine months previous.

"I told you there would be an increase in our family in nine months, I told you so!" she chirped. *Taraktarak* had dreamt of a mother gathering eggs, a dream indicating an increase in the family within nine months. Dancing Leaf had rarely seen her so exhilerated.

Glancing over her shoulder at Blood Sky one of the women joked, "You'd almost think *Taraktarak* alone was responsible for your conception!"

Chuckling, *Taraktarak* begged permission to show the infant around the lodge and began removing her from the cradleboard even as Dancing Leaf nodded in agreement.

"*Nia:wen* – *T*hank you Dancing Leaf. I will take good care of her."

Dancing Leaf watched as her friend strolled happily in the direction of the old people huddled together at the far end of the lodge. The sight of the newborn would cheer them, briefly erasing from their thoughts and conversation, the implications of yesterday's red rains, rains that sustained their belief in *Wawnatta's* premonition. They would bless the infant after taking turns holding her, a ritual that delighted them.

Dancing Leaf found Crippled Sparrow resting on a bearskin, the head of a scrawny dog resting on her lap as she sat puffing on her pipe and staring pensively into her cooking fire.

"Good morning my mother friend," she said.

Raising her eyes to meet Dancing Leaf's own, the old woman nodded her head in response, as yet not trusting her voice to be heard among the others, lest it tremble. She was still unnerved from the intensity of last night's occurrence and the deceitful role she'd agreed to play was weighing heavily on her mind. Studying the face of her grandniece, Crippled Sparrow couldn't believe the uncanny resemblance she bore to her deceased mother, Fragrant Grass. Dancing Leaf was possessed of the same moon-shaped face and blue-black hair; the corners of her mouth slightly turned upward and her widely spaced eyes brimmed with the sensitivity of a deer. Her straight nose and tawny skin was like velvet to the touch. She had long, slim legs and when she walked, it was as Fragrant Grass had walked, the movements sure and unhurried.

Forgetting herself for a moment, Crippled Sparrow's mouth opened as she began to relate the striking resemblance, but just as quickly clamped her jaws shut. The old woman shuddered at the thought of what she'd almost done, for the *Onqwanonhsiono* must never speak the name of one who has gone to the spirit world. To do so would be to disturb their spirit, and the love for her niece, Fragrant Grass had been great.

Placing her pipe on the ground and leaning forward on her crossed legs, she filled a bark strip with squash that had been simmering over the fire. Ripping a chunk of bread from the fresh loaf she'd just made, she handed it to Blood Sky who eagerly bit off a good-sized piece.

"Yawekon kiken' kana' taronkhonwe, Wakekahonh – This bread tastes good!" she said in an attempt to make small conversation. "I like the taste of it."

"Tekatakhonha – eat up, eat up, you must nurture your baby." Placing a hearty portion of squash onto a bark vessel for her niece, she closed her eyes and lowered her head, a gesture signifying silence.

Three servings of squash later, Dancing Leaf excused herself, anxious to reclaim her daughter. Retrieving a long slender willow stick and extending it into the fire, the old woman ignited it from a burning ember, and relighting her pipe, mumbled, *"Ona* – I will see you later."

That evening, following many congratulatory comments and offers of food, Dancing Leaf slung the cradleboard in which Blood Sky lay sleeping, against the joist beside the *onenhste*, or braided corn, above her own bunk. Resembling the other bunks in the lodge, it was doubled, six feet wide and twelve feet long, with one bunk on top of the other. The lower section, lined with bearskins, was where she slept with Black Whirlwind. The upper bunk was used for storage, the wall beside filled to capacity with clothing, traps, hatchets, knives, cosmetic paint, wampum, food tobacco and other necessities.

Too excited and exhausted to sleep, she sat on her fur-lined bunk with the intention of completing the beadwork she'd applied to a new tunic she'd made for herself. As she sewed, she pondered as to how she and Crippled Sparrow were to carry out, unnoticed, the necessary massages to Blood Sky's ailing limb. Privacy was not easily secured in the longhouse as the people were always coming and going and the fires burned night and day. Placing the unfinished beadwork beside her, she absent-mindedly clutched the chunk of amethyst that lay partially hidden between her milk-laden breasts. Closing her eyes and ears to the confusion that surrounded her, she prayed to *Shonkwaya'tihson* to deliver her husband safely to her side.

A white dog, reserved for sacrifice upon the men's arrival, nuzzled his cold nose against her leg and with a soft whine settled down quietly beside her moccasined feet.

CHAPTER EIGHT

The charred trap door concealing stairs to the dank cellar slowly opened as Marjolaine cautiously emerged from the confines of her underground shelter. Muffling an involuntary scream with her fist, she stared in disbelief at the destruction surrounding her, the events of the previous day flooding her mind.

She had been at the far end of the garden when the first strains of the war cry resounded in the distance. Horrified, her hands flew to her mouth, causing the freshly plucked beans to scatter from her basket onto the rich black soil. Forced into action by the adrenaline charging through her veins, she'd turned and fled toward the house when her foot made contact with a knarled root, its exposed tentacles extending a few feet beyond the enormous oak tree from which it projected. Lunging to the ground, her fall was cut short as her head struck a large meadow-rock, rendering her unconscious.

She had no idea how long she lay there, but when she came to, the sky was orange with fire and the ghastly yelps of the war cry resounded in her ears. Too disoriented to struggle to her feet, she'd crawled toward the house on her hands and knees, the occasional sound of musket shots exploding like firecrackers in the distance. Reaching the back door of the dwelling, she'd managed to pull herself upright, her breath emanating in short sporadic pants. Her right knee felt like it contained a piece of ice, cold and stinging. Reaching down, she flinched with pain as she touched the exposed area where her stocking had torn. Swollen and slippery with blood, the knee had been slashed open by a jagged piece of glass lying disguised in the soil under the huge oak where she had fallen, left there, in all probability, by Jacque or one of the soldiers hired yearly to assist in the ploughing of the expansive garden.

Unlatching the back door leading to the summer kitchen, she entered. The familiarity of the area lessened her anxiety somewhat. She swiftly observed, as if for the first time, Jacque's tools neatly hanging from the large hooks he'd set into the walls. Releasing the hook on the inside door leading into the house proper, she entered, and then halted, frozen in her tracks. From where she stood, she was able to make out the figure of a gigantic savage looming over the lifeless form of Jeanette. Unable to tear her eyes away, she watched in horror as he raised his bloody hatchet high in the air before swiftly driving it down to sever the forehead of her mistress. Like a vermilion fountain the blood spewed forth, spattering the Indians belly and herculian arms with crimson dots.

Knowing how defenseless she'd be if the intruder spotted her, she crept noiselessly toward the fruit cellar at the back of the house. Although she felt certain the newborn had been slaughtered along with Jeanette, she was unable to assuage the overwhelming sense of guilt as she lifted the heavy trap door before climbing down to her safety, a feat requiring every bit of strength she could muster. The egg-sized lump on the side of her head throbbed incessantly. Clawing a handful of cold, moist earth from the wall of the cellar, she fashioned it into a ball and pressed it firmly against the aching protuberance in an endeavor to gain momentary relief. She then applied it to her bloodied knee. The queasiness in her stomach heightened, and try as she might, she was unable to quell the violent spasms of vomiting.

She remained huddled in the dark corner of the cellar all night and most of the following day, her back firmly pressed against the dank, earthen wall, her knees drawn up to meet her chin; her trembling hands clutching to her soiled linen cap.

Now, on this the following day, she stood on the blackened flagstones in front of the mammoth fireplace, the sole suggestion of what was once her home. A great crash resounded behind her causing the poor girl to nearly jump out of her skin. Glancing around she realized the area that had housed Jeanette and Jacque's bed had given away, collapsing downward into the cellar, sending forth an enormous puff of coal-black from the gaping cavity in which it fell. Sections of the demolished floor were still smoldering.

Her head pulsated with agonizing pain, causing her vision to blur. Alerted by voices in the distance, she cocked her head to one side. The voices were anguished and mournful, brimming with grief and sounding more animal than human. She knew they were the primal cries of her neighbors following last night's raid. Swinging her head around to examine the source of the moans, she was overcome by vertigo and grasped onto the fireplace in an effort to steady herself. With disbelieving eyes she found herself gazing past where the familiar log wall once stood, out into the great expanse of countryside, the wall having been consigned back to earth in the form of ashes.

"Ashes to ashes, dust to dust," she muttered, as if presiding over a burial. Her bottom lip trembled as she surveyed the devastation of the garden and the wreckage of the extensive fence Jacque had so lovingly built around it for protection against the animals and wind.

She had identified strongly with the garden, taking great pride in the plants as they flourished under her tireless attention. As she observed the rape of her hard labours she perceived a chord of anger beginning to swell within her soul. As immaterial and irrelevant the loss of the garden seemed in light of the overall chaos, her train of thought was dictated by her shocked state.

Teetering on the edge of insanity, her conscious mind was merciful, releasing only the information she could handle without causing her to go over the edge; thus she occupied her thoughts, not with the slaughter of Jeanette and her newborn, but with the more mundane topics such as the loss of her beloved garden. "Ashes to ashes, dust to dust. No more hops for Jacque's brew, no more bouncing beth for Jeanette's favourite soaps." she mumbled, her temporary madness believing her employers would still require such luxuries.

"Ashes to ashes, dust to dust, no more tansy for bruises and inflammation." She unconsciously stroked her injured knee, angry red with caked blood. She had only to apply her herbal remedy acquired from the tansy plant and the swelling would subside.

Confused, her eyes scanned the room for the maple coffer in which she'd safely tucked away her precious medicines concocted from various herbs. Again, her eyes met with the landscape outside. Her head involuntarily lowered slightly to the right, her forehead wrinkling in perplexity, much like a first-grader attempting to solve an arithmetic problem.

"Ashes to ashes, dust to dust," she murmured again, the religious connotation of the phrase allowing her a sliver of comfort. "Winter is almost upon us and there will be no yarrow to cure the grippe and sneezes. My medicine has disappeared. So important to have medicine, medicine for my head, medicine for Jeanette, for the baby, my strong medicine made from angelica roots to stop the babe from crying, her crying hurts my head. Ashes to ashes, dust to dust."

She was incoherent and completely oblivious to her neighbours' plight, their ghastly situation echoing her own. Her ears were suddenly deaf to their cries. She placed her hands over her eyes, too frightened to confront any further wretchedness, but it was to no avail as the stench of burning flesh assaulted her nostrils. Without warning, the gruesome details of Jeanette's demise at the hands of her giant executioner gushed into her mind. She wretched uncontrollably, each spasm accompanied by white-hot searing pain behind her eyes. Unable to cry, she stood in front of the fireplace for what seemed an eternity, until finally with a great sigh, she lowered her head and crouched down. Reaching out with her trembling hand, she retrieved her scorched bobbin that lay on the charred floor. As she stared at the tiny object, a sense of acceptance and finality deluged her, allowing the floodgates of despondency to give way at last. She broke down in tears and began to wail.

In sympathy, the dark menacing clouds that loomed in the sky throughout the day burst open and spewed their moist innards onto Ville Marie as if to purge the defiled settlement. Nebulous, upward swirls of smoke, induced by the union of raindrops with the still smoldering walls, silently conveyed her anguished prayers to the heavens above.

CHAPTER NINE

His prayers to the war god *Aireskoi* had been answered. The Iroquois remained victorious once again.

The sun peeked cautiously through the murky curtains of rain clouds as if indecisive as to whether or not it should grace Black Whirlwind and his party of men with its golden splendor. After a moment's hesitation it burst radiantly through, wrapping the canoe-bound men in an invisible cloak of warmth. A rainbow, or "mark of life," as the *Onqwanonhsiono* called them, gradually arched its back across the horizon like the spine of a multi-hued cat, its delicate colours possessing such clarity that Black Whirlwind felt he could almost reach up and grasp this miracle of nature with his bare hands.

On this the final day of their watery trek toward home, Black Whirlwind and his party of seventy-four warriors would be arriving at camp soon. Their brothers, the Seneca and Cayuga, had since veered off in various directions from the St. Lawrence making their way back to their prospective camps. Followed by four large elm-bark canoes that seated approximately twenty men each, Black Whirlwind's vessel was visibly distinguishable by the array of scalps hanging from the bow, and invisibly distinguishable by the delicate cargo tucked safely beneath the wooden plank upon which he sat.

Lying quietly upon a bed of animal pelts, protected from the sun by a handful of mint-green spruce boughs placed atop two plank seats, the newborn captive slept soundly. Her captor, Tall Elm, sharing the great love all *Onqwanonhsioni* held for children, had proudly presented the infant to his cousin Black Whirlwind the night before. Barely able to contain his excitement, he'd approached the Chief as he'd sat cross-legged around the campfire, a sudden breeze prompting the single *akweks* or eagle feather attached to his scalp lock to flutter upward in an attempt to free itself. There had been an air of exhilaration as the victory feast commenced. Looming over the solemn warrior, the young giant had noisily cleared his throat before squatting beside him. Lacking the social grace of initiating even the simplest conversation, he clumsily thrust the fur-bound souvenier into Black Whirlwind's folded arms, his large face breaking into a shy, almost cautious grin. Aware of Tall Elm's social inadequacies, Black

Whirlwind accepted the mysterious package graciously, presuming it contained a quail or rabbit his young cousin had captured for him, a delicacy in which to top off the main meal of human flesh.

"What is this my cousin, a gift? There is no need of tokens on this victorious night. You have given all there is to give for the people of the Iroquois nation. You led your men well."

The more accolades Black Whirlwind directed toward him, the wider Tall Elm's smile became until it could stretch no more, taking on the appearance of a grimace. Black Whirlwind suddenly flinched as the contents of the pelt stirred. Thinking the small game had been merely stunned instead of killed, he laughingly joked to his benefactor, "I pray your *O'seronni* victims remain in the land of the dead longer than your animal prey." Still chuckling he unwrapped the fur.

She was staring up at him, wide-eyed and unafraid. Her shock of white hair was tousled from where the pelt had been removed, leaving a few strands of ivory silk pointing upward on either side of her head. To the Black Whirlwind, she looked like a tiny horned owl. Unfamiliar with Christian symbols, her eerie resemblance to the devil escaped him.

"*Ho, renhnakenra*, a white papoose! I have seen but a few; the first when I was but ten summers when my father brought him back to our camp following our victory in St. Louis." He hesitated and glanced down at the infant whose stare remained fixed upon him. "But that white child had hair the colour of fire and was very bad luck for the *Onwehonwhene*. He died after few seasons with the white mans' disease, smallpox, taking with him many members of our people. But this one, so white, so pure; this one might bring luck to our people. I am ever in your debt cousin. I will bring this little one back to camp as a gift to Dancing Leaf to suckle along with our own who is to be born soon. It is a very good day!"

Corn Child was then placed in the custody of Broken Knife, a young brave who would serve as her guardian until they returned to camp. A mooncalf, the *Onqwanonhsioni* term for those among them whose sensibilities were limited, Broken Knife was honored to be given the duty of caring for the baby. Unlike the Algonkians whose practice it was to abandon their aged and infirm, it was the way of the *Onqwanonhsioni* to allow certain responsibilities to members of their tribe who were so afflicted, thereby instilling in them a sense of worth, and consequently, an attitude of pride which was undoubtedly the cornerstone upon which the Iroquois nation flourished.

Broken Knife took his obligation most seriously. Placing his finger into a large container of fresh cow's milk seized from the property of a family slaughtered during the raid, he gently placed it into the suckling's tiny mouth, thus nourishing her until a wet nurse could be found back at the village. Preposterously absorbed with his tiny ward, he held his head a little higher than usual as he strutted around the temporary campsite, eager to display her. More red-skinned than copper, his lanky legs moved with their knees slightly bent like the smooth gliding slouch of an experienced woods runner. He strode as if his legs were somehow disconnected from his torso, which was lean and straight. Square shoulders gave him an air of confidence bordering on arrogance as he milled around the warriors in his loose fitting robe; the sole feather attached to his braid caressed his back. With obvious pleasure he drank in the numerous accolades passed his way for a job well done.

In the shadows beyond the campfire, hands tied behind their backs, sat Claude and the other four captives. They were circled round the base of a large pine tree, firmly secured deerskin binding their hands which chaffed painfully against the scabrous bark causing small fissures in their skin, evidenced by the ring of blood trickling to the ground upon which they sat.

A small cluster of warriors sauntered about them, laughing and joking. A lad of sixteen or so that was seated next to Claude, had been convulsively sobbing since his capture the previous night. An Oneida brave the others called *"Onawatsta Ohsita"* or Muddy Foot, approached the crying boy and thrust a turtle-shell cup to his trembling lips, holding it securely as the thirsty captive lunged his tow-head greedily toward the cup, his mouth agape, his teary eyes bulging from their sockets.

Smiling deviously, Muddy Foot withdrew the cup just beyond the reach of the boy's mouth, breaking into laughter and shouting to his companions, "Look what we have here my brothers, a gasping fish out of water!"

"More like a minnow out of water!" retorted the others who'd been observing from the sidelines.

All laughing now, the natives moved in closer to the prisoners, eager for a little harmless fun at the expense of the freckle-faced captive. Basking in the attention of his peers, Muddy Foot crouched down to face the boy and began to mimic a panting fish. His small black eyes protruded as he opened and closed his pursed lips from which emanated short gasps. Several of the men joined in by assuming the attitude of floundering fish, rolling and jerking their bodies sporadically on the ground, causing Muddy Foot to break into toothless gales of laughter.

Ceremoniously raising his free hand to silence the others, Muddy Foot spoke, "It saddens me to see such a puny minnow die for want of water when the Creator has provided more than enough for all. Do my brothers agree with me?"

Unanimously voicing their assent, the warriors threw their clenched fists upward several times to verify the validity of Muddy Foot's statement. Grasping the back of the boy's head, the toothless Indian jerked it roughly downward toward the lip of the cup. Claude winced with pain as the boy's arm bunted coarsely against his own, causing his bloodied knuckles to scrape deeper into the jagged bark. The habitual twitch in his left eye became more pronounced and he clenched his jaw for fear of crying out. Quaffing an enormous gulp from the cup, the parched captive jerked his head sideways in horror, and gagging loudly, spewed the watery contents onto Claude's face, dousing him with a liberal amount of urine. With blackened gums exposed, the smiling Muddy Foot pulled himself upright and proceeded to pour the remainder of the foul-smelling liquid over the gagging boy's head. Tossing the cup to the ground, he clenched his fists together before landing a well-placed kick between the boy's splayed legs causing him to faint, his tousled head hanging like a discarded rag doll.

Tiring of the amusement, the men drew sticks to determine who would stand guard over the prisoners until the festivities began. The two losers having drawn the shortest sticks mumbled their disappointment as the others made their way back to the campfires with much camaraderie and good-natured backslapping.

The rhythmic beating of drums resounding from the campsite conveyed their primordial message throughout the verdant forest. A lone deer, taking refreshment from a mirror-surfaced stream deep within the forest, shifted its slender neck in the direction of the swelling drums, its large black eyes visibly saddened by the desecration of serenity within the virgin woods.

The cream-coloured moon climbed high in the sky.

From where the drums beat, the tribal leaders sat around the great blazing fire heatedly discussing the politics of their nation. Completely independent in domestic matters, it was they who delegated authority in councils representing them all. As they spoke, a number of painted young braves served them great platters of raw bear meat, venison, mounds of wild foul, speared fish and sagamite, a staple of corn that had been ground between two stones prior to being boiled into a mush-like substance. According to custom, the men partook only of meat foreign to their prospective Clans, as the *Onqwanonhsioni* knew that the bear, wolf, deer and other animals or totems representing the Clans were related to them. Only in extreme cases of hunger or in error would it be eaten, lest they die.

Uneven slivers of light wavering in the background lit the area where a cluster of smaller fires burned, each one hemmed in by an assemblage of warriors. The victory feast, a tribute to *Aireskoi* the war god, was about to commence. Black Whirlwind shifted uncomfortably as the familiar pain that had mysteriously pursued him during the last few moons lashed once more against the inside of his skull, momentarily clouding his vision. Unable to concentrate, he glanced toward the roaring inferno a few yards in front of him.

As if seen through a veil, he could barely comprehend the outline of an enormous water-filled pot hanging ominously from the crux of a large sapling spit. The heat emanating from the fire subdued his headache somewhat and he raised his eyes toward the star-splashed sky, his true vision gradually returning, evoking memories of his *Totah* or Grandmother telling him, "Never count the stars, for you will lose all your winters. Dare to count those little suns above your camp circle and you will surely die."

"Why do my thoughts turn to death?" he wondered out loud. Concentrating on the constant star, the one that stays fixed to provide light to those in pain, his thoughts turned again to his beloved Totah. It had been she who had honored him by passing the charcoal-covered sinew under the skin on his arm with an awl to fashion the permanent representation of a bear, the totem of his Clan. The pain had caused the young boy to flinch but he dared not cry out for one day he would be a great warrior and great warriors don't cry. Rewarding him with a puff from her soapstone pipe, his *Totah* had then discreetly left him alone to shed his small tears in private.

The droning of voices shifted his focus to the other Chiefs. On the opposite side of the small fire before him the Seneca Chief, Half Moon, placed an ember in the bowl of the sacred pipe and with outstretched arms extended it toward the four corners of the earth.

"The pipe, symbol of truth; the bowl and stem, heart and path to the center. The pipe, earth and holding earth, truth and holding truth. My brothers will speak truth this night into the pipe and the pipe becomes sacred." He then puffed four times on the pipe before handing it to the Onandaga Chief beside him, Rain Cloud.

Gradually the pipe was passed around the circle to all the Chiefs and the time for the address of Screaming Owl, Chief of the Oneida tribe, was upon them. Majestically occupying the ground beside Black Whirlwind, the Oneida leader's chalk-white pendant suspended from his nostrils contrasted dramatically against his dusky skin.

Raising both arms to signify silence, the drumming abruptly ceased; the crowd was hushed and Screaming Owl spoke, his voice powerful and filled with clarity so that all could hear him. "Brothers, it is the will of *Areskoi,* our War God, that we are here together this day, victorious in battle. We have once again brought the enemy to their knees, but for how long? No longer are we the hunters of the bear and deer!"

He paused, and a rumble of agreement flowed from the crowd.

"They steal our land, our game and our forests. They kill our women and children; they destroy our winter supplies, leaving us no sustenance. We cannot weaken brothers, for as I speak, the *O'seronni* hunters are crouched in wait, preparing to spring upon the Iroquois nation and devour it."

As he spoke, he pumped his great arms up and down to better emphasize his words, causing the fire's reflection to dance like molten amber upon his wide beaten silver bracelets. An eagle-feathered fan, dyed red, was clasped in his hand. Black Whirlwind studied him pensively. He was a large, angular structured individual whose massive barrel chest bore numerous tatoos depicting his Clan's totem, the turtle. The wavering lights from the fire combined with the rising and falling of the Oneida's chest, gave the impression that the breath of life had entered into the inanimate turtles, as they appeared to glide back and forth across his expansive breast. A small silver disk attached to his right temple held three white eagle feathers that hung over his shoulder. A deerskin loincloth and moccasins completed his outfit.

He continued, "Like maggots, they eat away at our furs, taking more than they need before destroying the rest. They wish to eat away at our pride and self-respect. They treat us as children and old women! Brothers, they seek to eat away our very existence upon our grandfathers' land."

He halted for a moment, refreshing himself with the fan before sweeping it arch-like in the air for all to see.

"Like the great sacred eagle who survives freely within the arms of the Sky Spirit, so must the Iroquois nation survive freely and in harmony within the bosom of the nine great spirits: Sky, Sun, Wind, Thunder, Moon, Star, Earth, Plant and Animal. Our people cannot survive freely and harmoniously with the spirit of the white man. This we have painfully learned. Never will we be united with the *O'seronni* as we'd hoped, for they are filled with deceit. These past hopes are now crumbled as the dirt crumbles beneath our moccasins. Like the sun, let the truth shine upon us. Be prepared brothers, for soon many more of the *O'seronni* war canoes will travel up the big river of the lakes and they will try to strike our nation into the earth, but we will be ready brothers. Again, we will destroy them!"

A thunderous roar of approval peppered with high-pitched war cries allowed him to pause for a few moments before continuing.

"Let your ears hear well what I now say to you. *Wawnatta's* vision of the Red Rains has come to pass! Never will we share the pipe of peace with the *O'seronni;* never will we share hopeful words or lend our ears to their empty promises. Instead, they will lend their ears to the war-whoop of the Iroquois. We have fish and game in plenty; our forests teem with stags, moose, deer, bears and beavers. We must protect them, but first we have to drive away the *O'seronni* hogs!"

Screaming Owl completed his oratory by whipping out his tomahawk and holding it high in the air, broke into a screaming war cry. The crowd followed suit, stamping, shrieking, thrusting imaginary knives into the cool night air as the beating of drums, louder this time, and more frenzied, commenced once again. Screaming Owl had successfully stoked their fire of hatred for the French invaders. Their hideous screams cut through the atmosphere like the howls of crazed banchees.

Witness to Screaming Owl's oratory, Claude, along with the other captives, had been untied from the base of the tree and roughly dragged to the site of the main campfire. The Frenchman was amazed at the clarity and refinement of the Oneida Chief's recitation for he knew these people had no written language. He noted as well, the superiority of the native's stature as opposed to most Europeans and concluded this was a result of better diet. Stepping in front of him, a young brave clad in deerskin leggings fringed in scalps tossed a handful of pitch onto the fire to make it hotter. If Claude had any misgivings about what was to happen next, the sight of the over-sized pot brimming with angrily boiling water eliminated them.

A sudden breeze carried the bittersweet melody of a whippoorwill in Claude's direction. He cocked his head to one side and listened intently. The bird repeated its lament.

"According to Indian legend," thought Claude, "someone is about to die."

As if mirroring his thoughts, the bird released its final cry just as Jordy Favre, bachelor and schoolteacher of Ville Marie, was silently approached from behind by two ochre-painted warriors who swiftly stripped the stunned captive of all clothing before dragging his naked, thrashing body toward the fire.

Most of the captives instinctively averted their eyes from what they knew was going to be a macabre scene while a couple of them observed with morbid curiosity. Limp now with fear, the ill-fated schoolteacher was hoisted in the air before being unceremoniously tossed into the bowels of the pot. The flesh, boiled from his bones, visibly bubbling on the water's surface with alarming rapidity. The lad standing next to Claude attempted to avert his gaze from the repugnant sight of his nude schoolmaster being plunged into the scalding cauldron, but a bronzed hand reached from behind him, and clutching a handful of hair, forced him to witness the atrocity. He collapsed to the ground in a dead faint leaving the astonished native with a fistful of coppery red hair.

Lurching toward the fainting boy in a thwarted attempt to assist him, Claude too was felled by a strategically placed foot that sent him flailing chin first to the ground.

Although the warriors would consume Jordy Favre equally, Claude found some comfort in the knowledge that savages would never force a man to eat the flesh of his brother; hence, he and the other French captives were to be spared this final indignity. Jordy Favre had met his death with a dignity that awed even the Iroquois who highly regarded all acts of bravery. The schoolteacher's final act of bravery didn't go unnoticed by the warriors, and had it not been too late, his life would have been spared, and another, less courageous captive sacrificed to appease *Aireskoi.*

Surveying this gruesome scene with smoldering eyes, yet somehow strangely detached, Black Whirlwind experienced the same obscure emotions he'd been feeling off and on since the previous evening whilst studying the massacre of Ville Marie. Oddly enough, he perceived a profound sense of loss and sadness for the captive who'd been randomly chosen to serve as sacrificial lamb.

"Such a brave warrior deserved a more triumphant death." he mused. Vexed at to the source of his distress at a time when he should be jubilant in the knowledge of his people's recent conquest, he concluded the gloom may have sprung from the terrible realization that man can be truly capable of such grotesque and inhumane acts toward their brothers. It was a strange revelation for the young Chief who, until this moment, had accepted such atrocities as commonplace.

Pondering this insight, his mood darkened. He was fully aware that Indians alone were not the sole offenders of such heinous acts. With a shudder, he recalled his father's account of an incident that occurred in Staten Island in the white man's year of 1622. According to Long Claw, a Hackensack Indian had been tortured in front of a laughing Dutch Governor in a manner that equaled the Iroquois at their cruelest. Going one step further, the Hackensack victim was made to eat his own flesh. As a child, Black Whirlwind's father had recounted the story many times, however, it wasn't the torture of the Hackensack that disturbed him, as it was common practice among his own people. It was the idea of eating one's own flesh that terrified the young boy causing him to suffer from the occasional nightmare in reference to the incident. As well, white settlers agreed to pay bounty on dead Indians, and scalps were proof of the deed, being easier to handle than whole heads.

His somber thoughts were interrupted by *Koo-koo-sint* – Man Who Looks at the Stars, who held a flat bark tray upon which held the boiled remains of Jordy Favre. Gravely acknowledging *Koo-koo-sint's* presence, the Mohawk Chief automatically reached out as he had so many times in the past and retrieved a sodden piece of human flesh before bringing it to his mouth.

Suppressing the beginning of a smirk, Dr. Claude LaBelle observed the natives devouring the carcass of Eli, a patient of his who had, just moments before, been spared a slow agonizing death caused by the malignant growth in his stomach.

"Bon appetite mon enemie le savauge," he murmured silently before saying aloud, *"Bon voyage bon ami* – goodbye Jordy my friend."

Lying on a pallet of furs a few yards back from the main campfire, Corn Child stirred, the aroma of human flesh pervading her tiny nostrils. A semblance of gratification brushed fleetingly across her wizened features before she surrendered once again to sleep.

CHAPTER TEN

He found her the next morning. She was kneeling in the gray sooty ashes among the tombstones at the burned-out site of the rectory. Oblivious to the swarm of flies buzzing listlessly around her slumped shoulders, she stared toward the overcast sky, her eyes mad with fear. Thunder rolled in the distance.

He paused at the gate, observing her and feeling her pain. With a heavy sigh he lowered his head, raking strong calloused fingers through a mass of tousled blonde hair. The painful sting of a black fly on the back of his sun-burned neck caused him to jerk his head upright, his china-blue eyes focusing once more on the pitiful domestic.

Studying the morose scene, he was reminded of a picture in the religious catechism his class had studied when he was a child in France. The faintly coloured sketch had been opposite the page of the Ten Commandments; of this he was sure. He recalled with clarity and pride that he had been the first student to master the memorizing of the commandments, giving him ample time in which to ponder on the sketch of the praying saint while waiting for the rest of the class to commit to memory the cornerstone of Christianity. Although he was still acquainted with the commandments, he could not for the life of him recall the name of the peasant saint he'd so religiously admired.

"Saint Marjolaine," he uttered quietly, "Perhaps her name was Saint Marjolaine."

Still unmarried at age thirty-one, Henri was content with his lot. His decision to remain single was contrary to the majority of males in Ville Marie who procured wives out of a sense of duty to the King's express wish that the colony be populated in direct proportion to a colony of rabbits. He'd had his share of light dalliances with a number of local girls whose moral fiber was less than tightly woven, however, such experiences had left him feeling empty and morally bankrupt. His ideal mate could be nothing less than virtuous. His lofty standards in terms of wife-material were, no doubt, a sub-conscious memory of his unrequited boyhood attraction to the nameless saint in his well-read catechism, Marjolaine, being by far the closest he'd found to that ideal.

During his checkered visits to chapel he'd attempted a number of times to strike up conversation with the Langevin's domestic but her obvious shyness made such moments awkward for both of them and he eventually contented himself by admiring her from afar. He'd thought about her often, thought about how good it would be to know her, talk to her and laugh with her. Often at night, just before sleep, her image would vaguely materialize behind his closed lids and he'd gaze at her sweet face until sleep overtook him.

The Governor's Estate, where Henri resided, was located on the outskirts of Ville Marie and as such had been spared the Iroquois wrath of last evening. Alerted from their beds by the bone-chilling screams echoing from the village, the occupants gathered one by one to the main parlour, rosaries in hand, to pray in unison for their neighbours' safety. The grand latticed windows of the room received images of the blood-red flames soaring skyward from the broken heart of Ville Marie, bathing the kneeling worshippers in a soft, diffused scarlet glow. Henri could think only of Marjolaine and he had silently prayed for her life alone, leaving the survival of others to the prayers of the Governor and his staff. They prayed until a silent blanket of death descended over the village transforming the crimson sky to a pale gray.

Excusing himself, Henri slipped quietly from the back entrance of the looming mansion into the cold dawn. Shivering, he'd run toward the Langevin residence, bracing himself against slashing winds that bore the unmistakable stench of death. A mile or so from his destination he'd spotted her in the old graveyard behind the rectory.

Walking quietly toward the frightened girl so as not to startle her, he whispered, "Marjolaine, it's going to be alright. I'm here now."

Obviously confused, her eyes, void of all reason, mute and lifeless, appeared to have sunk deep into the bone. She glanced over the length of him as he stood above her, his leather-clad legs spread wide. He could feel the pent-up emotion that lay tightly coiled behind her eyes, like a poisonous snake preparing to spring forth in misplaced rage, its venomous tongue madly lashing out in raw fury. He shivered. A mass of wild curls tumbled haphazardly around her face and forehead giving her the appearance of a mad waif. Her soiled linen cap lay strewn on the ground beside her. Removing his fringed deerskin coat and placing it lightly upon her shoulders, he placed his hands under her elbows and gently lifted her to her feet.

He led her, as he would a lost child, through the defiled churchyard in the pouring rain. The handful of local residents that lived in the immediate area of the church had been hardest hit by the raid, and the survivors were too preoccupied with salvaging what little they could from the rubble to notice the Governor's gamekeeper guiding the dazed Marjolaine in the direction of the stately mansion situated on the far end of the village.

"You crazy if you think you can get away with this Henri. The Guvn'r gwan find out and we all be out on the street!"

Removing the large wooden spoon from the soup she'd been stirring, Ruby emphasized her statement by vigorously shaking the utensil in front of the Henri, splaying tiny droplets of scalding chicken soup on his face.

"If she be crazy she belong wif the other crazies. This here place crazy 'nuff already. Who you expectin to nurse her? The Guvn'r? I gots my hands full 'nuff as it is what wif my cookin and overseein to the lazy good-fer-nuthin chars what the Guvn'r hisself hires. Don't need no more duties boy. You ought be ashamed even to ask!"

Ending her speech with a smart whack on Henri's muscular thigh, he was unable to suppress his laughter as the spoon snapped. Reaching out, he grasped her plump waist and hoisted her in the air while attempting to duck the playful punches she pretended to throw.

He knew he had her. Such was his familiarity with the woman who raised him from a boy in the Governor's mansion. "Mama Ruby" as he called her, could never say no to him, at least not with any seriousness. Then again, being of a most considerate nature, he asked very little.

Gently lowering the hefty woman to the immaculate floor of the stark-white kitchen he said, "Mama Ruby, she's not crazy; she's just in shock. I can't take her to the asylum; she might never come out. It'll only frighten her more and besides, after the last raid, they won't have room for any more patients."

Turning her back to Henri she busied herself at the butcher's block in the center of the spacious room. Carving large slices of wild fowl, she mentally calculated the length of time the Governor was to remain in Albany.

"Six mo' weeks," she thought. "Time nuff to help the poor soul."

With a resigned look, she turned her bandana-clad head toward Henri who was restlessly pacing the floor in mock anticipation of what he already knew would be, Ruby's agreement; his anxious look designed solely to humour his beloved nanny.

"Where is she now?" she asked.

"Out back, in my cabin. She's just sitting there staring into space. She won't talk and I don't think she recognizes me. I made a fire and tried to coax her to have some tea but she sits there like a statue. I bolted the door from the outside so she can't wander out but I can't leave her too long." With these words he adopted the best 'pleading' look he could summon up.

With a great sigh Ruby placed the carving knife on the butcher's board before sweeping the back of one hand across her furrowed brow. Turning to face him, she placed both hands on her ample hips.

"Gwan then boy; fetch the poor soul and bring her home to Mama Ruby."

CHAPTER ELEVEN

Black Whirlwind lay contentedly upon the fur-lined bunk, reflecting on the wispy ribbons of smoke from his pipe of *kinnickinnick* that wafted ghost-like to the ceiling of the longhouse. Made from *oyen'kwa'onwe, a* traditional Indian tobacco, crushed willow leaves and pulverized dogwood bark, this evening's smoke had an especially relaxing quality due to the marijuana he had added. The melodious strains of a cedar flute drifted through the great lodge and the scent of apples being baked in ashes whet his appetite. Through half-closed lids he studied Dancing Leaf sitting at the edge of the bunk suckling the infants. He wondered at the paradoxes of life. Where just a few moons ago he had been an active participant in the slaying of countless *O'seronni*, here was a mere woman sustaining the life of two infants from such an insignificant source as her breasts.

Securing the still-famished Corn Child with one arm, she placed Blood Sky on her father's tattooed chest with the other. Black Whirlwind caressed his daughter's tiny back with his large hand as he studied his wife through half-closed lids.

In his euphoric state he thought he'd never seen a woman more beautiful. Her long silky hair freed from its braid cascaded over her bronzed shoulders like an indigo waterfall. Instantly overcome with an immediate desire to physically possess her, he reached out and began to stroke her naked back. Outwardly she didn't respond, but the act had quickened her blood causing the milk to flow more freely into the delicate mouth of the *O'seronni* babe. Feigning indifference to his wife's aloofness, he felt a stab of pain in his gut. Blood Sky stirred. Sighing, he diverted his attention to his new daughter, studying her minute features for the first time.

"Yohskats," he whispered, "She is beautiful."

From the corner of her eye Dancing Leaf saw him attempt to unravel the striped red blanket she had swaddled the infant in. Fearing he'd detect the impaired limb she gently removed his hand from the blanket.

"Yah ki' nonwa – not right now husband. Don't disturb her; she sleeps so soundly. Tomorrow is time enough to examine her."

"Hao ki' wahi," he whispered, "Okay then." With his large hand shielding his daughter's head, fell into a deep sleep.

Dancing Leaf reflected on Corn Child feeding at her breast, tender now and beginning to bleed. Like a tiny rodent the infant nibbled and sucked, oblivious to the young mother's efforts to assuage her discomfort by rocking to and fro, the exaggerated movements a far cry from the instinctive maternal gesture designed to comfort suckling babes. Satiated at last, her tiny lips pulled away from Dancing Leaf's aching nipple and she began to whine. Placing the sniveling infant in a quill embroidered cradleboard suspended from the wall beside the bunk, Dancing Leaf sprawled out beside her husband and prepared to rest. Within seconds Corn Child slept as though pacified somehow by the presence of Black Whirlwind's scalp-garnished belt hanging beside her on the wall.

As she relaxed, Dancing Leaf's thoughts revolved around the day of her husband's arrival from Ville Marie. That morning she'd been weaving her way through the vast cornfield her people had cleared from the great oak forest, heading for the dense woods in the distance hoping to secure fresh roots, berries or plants to augment the evening meal. She'd spotted a crow perched atop one of the highest stalks and was thankful this year's harvest had been so outstanding. Uttering a short prayer of thanksgiving to the Creator, her thoughts then turned to her beloved *Totah.* Deceased now, she and her grandmother had toiled side by side in the cornfield since she could remember.

On one occasion, when she was but four summers, her *Totah* lifted her off the ground, securing her with one arm while harvesting the corn with the other. Pausing, she'd stroked her tiny forehead and Dancing Leaf knew she was about to hear something very special. Speaking slowly so the child could fully comprehend her words, she'd placed a luscious fresh cob of corn in Dancing Leaf's tiny hand.

"Always take special care at harvest time my child, for if the corn is barely higher than you are now, you must gather all you can and store it safely, for the last famine is at hand and the end of time has come."

Her words had frightened the child, compelling her to compare the growth of the stalks against her own height, and causing her to breathe a great sigh of relief each year when their height surpassed hers. The creaking of a large tree jolted her back to reality and she paused, feeling compelled to glance back at the three-tiered palisade of thirty-foot tree trunks that enclosed her village, hiding from view the forty-nine longhouses that lay within. Her eyes scanned the structure. As she studied the fortress, her intuition, or as the *Onqwanonhsioni* called it, her "familiar voice," told her that when she returned, her life was to change dramatically. Glancing up at the intervalled galleries upon which were piled an abundance of large stones to be used in case of enemy attack, her skin bristled. Rather than viewing the stones as protection against the enemy, her familiar voice was telling her they might well serve to prevent the enemy from leaving the village. Sensing her mother's intense emotions, Blood Sky had whimpered softly from the cradleboard. Turning back toward the forest, Dancing Leaf crooned the infant to silence once more.

As if heralding the arrival of mother and daughter, the drumming of a partridge reverberated through the heart of the forest where Dancing Leaf stood at the foot of a towering oak tree. Kneeling beside a fast running stream, she cupped her hands in spoon fashion to scoop the clear, sweet water to her mouth. Her thirst satiated, she lavishly splashed some of the liquid relief upon her flushed face. Glancing up in time to catch the playful antics of two saucy chipmunks on the far side of the stream, she reflected on the beauty surrounding her.

Ablaze with fiery colours, these lush woods had always soothed her and today was no exception. There was however, a sharp nip in the air, a subtle reminder that the season of Howling Winds would soon arrive, freezing the ground and rendering the digging of roots impossible. With a slight shudder she recalled the last winter when birds dropped from the trees as the intense cold froze their wings. With a deep sigh she shifted her attention to the awesome majesty of the blood-tinted leaves, the sight of which quickened her heart and filled her with a sense of well-being, a contentment marred slightly by her dire concern for Black Whirlwind's safe and victorious return from battle.

Though he had been gone a relatively short time, his absence left a great void in her soul. She often wondered if the other women in camp felt the same physical attraction toward their husbands as she. Somehow she doubted it.

Although conversation between them was a rarity, their physical closeness proved more than adequate communication. When they made love, which was often, their mutual desire allowed them a lusty, almost violent union.

Happening upon a cluster of ginseng, she placed her basket on the ground and, in *Onqwanonhsioni* fashion, she circled the plant counter clock-wise before facing east to dig for the root. Scooping up a handful of pine cones she'd spotted half-concealed among the giant ferns carpeting the forest floor, she broke them apart to find the nuts at the base of each hard petal. As she relished their taste she'd all but forgotten the grim thoughts that had besieged her just a short while ago. Lowering her eyes, she was delighted to find a clump of moss beneath her feet, the sight of it whetting her appetite for the delicacy *awerahs* or moss soup. Scanning the south base of a large oak tree where the vegetation grew heaviest, she chose a healthy mound of velvety moss. Her task completed, she'd dipped her hands into the frigid water of a nearby stream and nursed Blood Sky.

She was about to retrieve a handful of hearty bull rushes with which to reline the cradleboard when she'd been alerted to the commotion surrounding the camp area. Sensing her husband's nearness, she flung the plants aside and fled back toward the village.

Having spotted the war canoes from where they'd been fishing at the water's edge, a group of young boys scattered through the village alerting the people. All tasks were forgotten. Two old women with snow-white hair shakily assisted each other to their feet, leaving the moccasins they had been applying shells to, strewn carelessly upon the grass; a small girl, pounding corn in a hollowed tree trunk, tossed aside her pestle and scurried off to the riverbank, ignoring the pleas for guidance from an aged man who sat cross-legged beside a meager fire, an opaque film covering both of his eyes; a woman, heavy with child, joined in with the others, vacating the small pile of bone splints she'd been sorting.

Threading her way through the mass of villagers, Dancing Leaf was the last to arrive at the shore. Jostling to the front of the crowd, she raised her hand to her forehead to block the bright rays of sun; watching intently as the war canoes glided closer, her eyes straining in an attempt to spot Black Whirlwind's vessel.

The crowd was hushed, anxious to see if the warriors bore their war paint, a sign of victory over the despised O'seronni.

With keen eyesight, Running Panther was the first to spot the vermilion colour. He quickly let loose an ear splitting cry. The others joined in, laughing, yelling and whooping. A great shudder of relief swept through Dancing Leaf as Black Whirlwind's canoe came into view. Uttering a prayer of thanks to the Creator for his safe return, she removed Blood Sky from the cradleboard so that he might lay eyes on her before the vessels came ashore.

Drifting ghost-like from the canoes, the mournful repetitious death chant was repeated a number of times for the warriors who had died, followed by four loud yelps indicating the number of prisoners. Fearing the loss of their men, a few women began to wail. A group of overzealous youngsters ran into the frigid water waving their thin copper arms toward the oncoming dugouts. Having left for Ville Marie with four canoes, the men had returned with five, the latter having been hastily constructed from elm bark, the ends laced with deer hide to accommodate the O'seronni captives.

From the moment he'd set foot in the crude vessel, Claude, along with the other prisoners, felt confident it would capsize. The natives themselves harboured no such fear as they'd had the foresight to appease the great water serpent beforehand by placing sacred tobacco on the rocky shore before departure. Nevertheless, just to be on the safe side, Claude occupied himself during the tedious voyage by continuously crossing himself. The other prisoners satisfied themselves with simple prayer.

On shore at last, Claude and the others watched in bewilderment as the warriors' families greeted their heroes with all the emotions of a sphinx; the poker faced men in turn, acknowledging their families with the same impassive stare. Once within the confines of the lodge however, the silent warriors would shower affection and love upon their families. It was beyond native comprehension that, to the white man, silence proved embarrassing, even intolerable.

Stumbling from the makeshift craft, Paul, a captive youth whose flaming red hair glistened in the sunlight, became at once the center of attention. White-faced and visibly trembling, he raised his glance toward the assemblage of villagers only to become painfully aware that their gasps and whispers were directed toward him, a realization that caused the lad to blush uncontrollably. Frozen with fear and apprehension, he spotted a young woman making her way toward him from the density of the crowd.

Tsiktsinonnawen, so named for the butterfly, brazenly sidled up to him. She was so close he felt her breath caressing his cheek. A stunning maiden known primarily for her boldness, she was taller than most of the others with long legs and full breasts. She wore a white doeskin tunic and he noticed she'd fastened hawk bells in her long black velvet hair. Reaching up she ran her slender fingers through his tousled mane, all the while gazing intently into his awestruck blue eyes. Grasping his quaking hand, she raised it to her head, guiding it slowly and firmly through her own thick hair before guiding his trembling hand to her breast, gently and rhythmically kneading their linked fingers into her exquisite softness, her midnight black eyes searing into his very core. Mixed emotions of fear and desire caused his head to spin. He thought he'd faint. He dared not pull his hand away for fear of offending the girl who was, after all, the enemy. After what seemed an eternity she released his hand, which he promptly employed to wipe his profusely sweating brow. A wave of tittering swept through the onlooking crowd as a handful of older women, obviously relishing the *O'seronni's* discomfort began making, what appeared to be obscene gestures. In reality, they were just having fun.

"*Oyeri nihati Tsiktsinonnawen* – There are five men *Tsiktsinonnawen,*" a woman called out. "Why waste your time with the baby prisoner with hair like a woodpecker?"

The women roared with laughter.

A sickly smile escaped from Paul's lips. Though he didn't understand the language he thought he'd better feign a smile to humour the women. He'd heard enough about the natives to know the decision-making power of the tribes' females.

Tsiktsinonnawe however, wasn't amused. Angrily running toward the woman whose comment reduced her red-haired hero to the status of a redheaded woodpecker, she loudly berated her. The more she yelled, the louder the women laughed, until, with a final act of defiance, Butterfly slapped the palm of her hand smartly against her stomach before raising her head proudly and stalking back to camp.

A dark-skinned warrior then led Paul, Claude and the other prisoners up the hill toward the village. Scrawny work dogs growled and leapt toward them nipping at their heels. The children, taught to suppress laughter and not show a trace of curiosity among strangers, scolded their younger siblings who were hurling small stones and dirt at the O'seronni. Fearing the worst, the captives shuddered to think of what horrors awaited them upon reaching the village.

As for Paul, he was unable to erase *Tsiktsinonnawe's* image from his mind. So preoccupied was he with the memory of their brief encounter, he failed to spot a girl peeking at him from behind the giant oak, a girl with hawk bells in her hair.

CHAPTER TWELVE

Season of Almost Mature

The warmth of Grandmother sun felt luxurious against Dancing Leaf's moist skin as she stood waist deep in the medicinal waters of the river. Swirling about her were the small plants, twigs and russet-coloured leaves from the plant family that *Shonkwaya'tihson*, the Creator, had given the *Onqwanonhsioni* as healing agents. Though the great healing ceremony was over, the villagers continued to bathe as much as possible during the Season of "Almost Mature" or October, to prevent sickness and prepare them for the long winter.

Choosing a secluded area away from the other bathers she'd placed the twin cradleboards among the lush pussy willows lining the shore before submerging into the frigid river. Late each afternoon she sought refuge from the other women's constant chattering and prying eyes by taking her laundry to the river where she'd wash her tunic and the infant's leggings before hanging them to dry on a spruce branch.

Pausing to watch a group of naked children, she recognized Crippled Sparrow heading in her direction. Tight-lipped and somber, the midwife strode directly to Blood Sky's cradleboard where she proceeded to massage the tiny limb, the soft cooing sounds emanating from the little one making her smile. She began to croon the Mohawk Growing Song, thus ensuring the infant would be straight of limb and strong of body and heart. The therapy complete, she dipped the baby into the healing water for a few seconds and placed her back inside the cradleboard after relining it with fresh moss.

It had been just one moon since Black Whirlwind arrived back at camp bearing their adoptive daughter Corn Child. A demanding infant, she required more care than Blood Sky. Dancing Leaf was determined to stay strong. She found however, that it was only when she suckled her true daughter that she experienced a sense of serenity. Like the other mothers in camp, she was solicitous, nursing the babies whenever they cried, and Corn Child cried a lot. Although she had ample milk for both she chose not to nurse them simultaneously as Corn Child nursed for an intolerably long time, causing her nipples to ache and bleed, leaving the young mother physically and emotionally drained. By feeding Blood Sky last she was able to regain most of her stability, but her constant fluctuating moods were beginning to play havoc with her nerves. She'd become short with the other women during the day and had trouble sleeping at night.

Stepping from the water at the sound of Corn Child's eerie cry, she hastily dried herself before reaching down to retrieve her buckskin skirt upon which a black raven's feather had settled. She smiled, grateful for the gift from the Creator. She raised it high in the air.

"Niawenkowa Shonkwaya'tihson – Thank you Creator. I will weave it into Blood Sky's headdress to give her good luck."

Tucking the feather safely inside her medicine pouch, she lifted Corn Child from her cradleboard and began to nurse her. Jeering sounds drifting from camp told her the prisoners were being prepared for the ceremony of Running the Gauntlet. Finding the ritual abhorrent, she wanted no part of it, and she hoped her absence wouldn't be noted. The jeers became frenzied prompting the young bathers to scurry out of the water.

"Oksa sasahtent – run home quick, they're going to start without us!" they screamed to one another as they ran up the hill to join the villagers who'd formed a double line. Crippled Sparrow decided to tag along after them leaving Dancing Leaf to nurse her child. The swelling cries of the natives resounded in the air; the delirious timbre of the voices proof that a captive was being prepared to run the gauntlet, an exercise designed mainly to relieve the monotony of the people's lives at the expense of the captives' suffering. The rite had never seemed entertaining to Dancing Leaf who was extremely adverse to acts of violence.

"When Blood Sky and Corn Child have reached the summer of understanding I will sing to them gentle stories and pray to *Shonkwaya'tihson* that they might never wish to inflict pain on another living creature, for it saddens my heart," she said aloud.

As if rebelling against her words, Corn Child let loose a loud howl, obliging the young mother to nurse her once again.

⊞

Planted firmly in the ground just outside the council lodge, uniformly painted red in times of war, the post was a place of refuge for prisoners whose lives were spared if they succeeded in completing the run. Stripped naked, his eyes lowered, Claude was led to an area about fifty feet from the blood-covered refuge post. Though he was numb with horror, his professional demeanor during the past month of captivity had led his captors to believe he was in many ways superior to the other prisoners, thus he had been selected to serve as an example of endurance by initiating the ceremony. An icy wind violated his bare flesh yet failed to cool the burning anxiety stirring in his bowels. He was not ignorant of the ritual that lay before him and for this he was thankful. Although he gave credence to the old adage, "forewarned is forearmed", how he was going to arm himself was another matter entirely. Without warning he was roughly shoved from behind.

"Tewakeka – run!" screamed the crowd.

Sucking in as much air as possible, he took off, eyes focused on the post in the distance, his peripheral vision taunting him with snatched images of yelping women and children armed with clubs, firebrands, stones, briars, and knives with which they pierced the air on either side of him. Compelled to pass between them with as little injury to his person as possible, his mind raced in an effort to recall all the information he'd ever acquired pertaining to the running of the gauntlet. Seldom did anyone survive this torture without the loss of a hand, eye or finger, if in fact they survived at all. He knew that even if he did make it to the post alive, he needed to be claimed by someone or he would likely be tortured and killed.

He winced as small splinters of stone pierced his feet causing him to stumble awkwardly forward, slowing his pace long enough to allow the smaller children breaking from the line to slash his legs with their stinging switches. Gaining speed, he felt the cold blade penetrate deeply into his upper leg. His assailant, a young boy, who was so excited by his victory, neglected to yank the blade from Claude's flesh; leaving the knife's handle jutting from his thigh as he continued to run. From the corner of his eye, he spotted a large club whirling angrily toward him. Instinctively raising his arm to shield his head from the crushing blow, a great hollow crack resounded in his ears as the blunt instrument came in contact with his forearm, breaking the bone in two.

Still he ran, the frenzied yells and whoops swelling as he neared the final trek of his bloody run. Blinded by tears and sweat he was barely able to see the refuge post and though his senses were failing, reason cautioned him not to falter as his dispatch with a hatchet would be swift and sure. Reaching out to grasp the post with his one good arm, he collapsed to his knees. The last thing he saw before fainting was the grotesque sight of a woman with two scarred gashes on her face where her nose should have been.

Claude now belonged to Coyote. As the first woman to toss a wolf-hide at the feet of the debilitated prisoner, she'd claimed her right to do with him as she pleased. A few of the other women, hoping to have claimed Claude as their own, hid their disappointment and congratulated the winner as a group of young boys struggled to lift him from the ground.

One of the losers, Spotted Antelope, shook her head in mock concern as the boys carried their burden toward Coyote's lodge.

"The *O'seronni* prisoner will pray for death once he realizes why the noseless one adopted him," she said with a sly grin.

The other women chuckled for they too had heard stories of Coyote's sexual exploits.

Spotted Antelope blushed at the memory of tripping over Coyote and two young boys in the tall grass by the river a few seasons before. Shocked by the unexpected interruption, she fled, but not before she saw that the boys were naked. Sensing she'd come upon an unhealthy situation, a spark of anger flared in her as the bawdy lilt of Coyote's laughter had followed her back to the village. She'd been only eleven summers then and the situation had seemed very serious. Older now, and more compassionate, she understood Coyote and truly liked her, as did most others in the village. Aside from her infamous sex scandals, which made her more of a comic figure than anything, she was generous, warm and extremely kind-hearted. The women watched as Coyote, bearing a lascivious grin, turned and made her way to the longhouse where she hoped to acquaint herself with her new mate as quickly as possible.

Once an extremely handsome woman, Coyote's disfigurement was a result of an act of infidelity on her part. Her people, the Monami tribe from the south, had cast her out following the amputation of her nose, a common punishment practiced by some tribes in dealing with adulteress women. The *Onqwanonhsioni*, alerted by her wailing, had found her half dead from hunger and thirst. She'd been adopted into the tribe and given the name Coyote; appropriate they thought, for the woman whose howling cries had broken the stillness of the night. Her Monami name had been Dawn Woman.

Had none of the females claimed Claude as their own, he would have been assigned to the guards at the end of his run until such time his fate was decided by the council. Survivors of the gauntlet were sometimes spared, though more often than not their hands and feet were bound and they were severely whipped. In most cases they were condemned to death. It was common knowledge that some of the bravest captives intentionally slackened their pace as they ran between the ranks of the gauntlet so they might be beaten to death rather than face the much crueler fate awaiting them.

CHAPTER THIRTEEN

The gigantic crystal chandelier loomed majestically from the cathedral ceiling. A fire crackled merrily from the confines of the mammoth fireplace; its turquoise-marbled surface lavishly decorated with gold-coloured spruce boughs and pinecones draped luxuriously across and down the sides of the enormous structure. Platter sized bows of pink and turquoise velvet had been strategically placed among the gilded branches. A splendid fourteen-foot gilt mirror lay suspended above the fireplace, its illuminating reflection magically increasing the expanse of the great room twofold. Threads of sparkling light from the chandelier kissed ivory satin drapes and narrow sofas fringed in gold. An immense wall opposite the fireplace separated two large, arch-shaped doorways finished in red mahogany.

The wall was fully embraced by a sprawling tapestry of a highly speculative subject matter. Fastidiously woven by hand, the delicately coloured masterpiece had been ordered by Governor Mercier and imported from Bovai, the most famous tapestry center in France. It depicted hordes of angelic-looking rosy-cheeked cupids in various stages of undress and debauchery. A potpourri of creamy, dimpled buttocks and chubby pink limbs were entwined, one with the other, as they gleefully engaged in what appeared to be a sexual orgy. Most of the chubby little participants had the presence of mind to discard their bows and arrows before diving in, however, the runt of the litter, an extremely rotund, flaxen-haired cupid with a heart-shaped face, lay in the foreground, doughy legs askew and rosebud mouth agape, apparently strangled by the silken strap of his ornate quiver as he hastily tried to remove it before joining in on the sensual goodies abounding before his little blue eyes.

Pausing for a moment to reflect upon this handcrafted scene, Eli failed to suppress the beginning of an amused smile as he observed the unabashed revelers. As personal valet to the Governor, the black man was expected to carry himself with utmost dignity at all times and under all circumstances, never allowing his decorum to alter. By nature an obsequious, fun-loving innocent, he found the best way to adhere to his professional deportment was to constantly assume a dignified attitude, the only exception being when he was in the company of his wife Ruby.

An orphan, he'd been sent to New France at age fifteen whereupon he'd been adopted by a local family who, as was customary, considered all blacks to be pagan and untrained – equivalent to children. As a result, young Eli was immediately christened, the ten-year old son of his adoptive parents acting as Godfather. Shortly after, his adoptive father; personal friend of Governor Mercier's manservant, arranged for him to become a houseboy in the large mansion until five years ago when he had been suddenly elevated to the position of personal valet to the Governor, a promotion he'd acquired as a result of his predecessor's sudden death.

It had been a tasteless affair in which the gentleman in question hung himself from the rafters in the dining room just moments before Mercier and his guests entered the spacious room in anticipation of a hearty meal. Although the victim had not neglected to don the required lace collar and white gloves of his station, he was otherwise naked, and had the enormous carved dining table been two inches higher, his feet would have rested comfortably inside the china soup tureen thereby foiling his own demise. As it stood however, his big toes merely skimmed the surface of the chilled vichyssoise. Two chairs stacked together beside the tureen were assumed to be the necessary implements in which to complete his swan song.

Upon entering the dining hall, Governor Mercier had glanced up at the corpse, and without batting a lash, addressed Ruby who'd just entered the room from the kitchen.

"We'll dine in the parlour Ruby, preferably something light." So said, he turned on his heel to head off his guests who were making their way toward the dining area. From that day forward, vichyssoise was never again served at Mercier's table.

"Eli, get that lecherous grin off'n yo face and see to your duties! You want both of us kicked outa this here mansion? Whatcha gonna do then man? Join the whores at the St. Tropez and sell that big black body o' yours?"

Tearing his gaze from the delightful tapestry scene Eli turned to face his wife Ruby, who stood inside the mahogany framed doorway leading to the main foyer, wiping flour from carmel coloured hands onto her starched white apron. Eli recognized the impish flash in her large black eyes.

"Why not woman?" he retorted. "Seems that way I can make a lot o' woman happy instead o' just makin one so miserable!"

Throwing her bandana-clad head back, Ruby broke into gales of hearty laughter, her ivory-white teeth exposed like so many piano keys. The pleasant scent of cooking vanilla she dabbed behind her ringed ears every morning sweetening the air.

"Seem to me you too tired last night to make any woman happy!"

Lurching forward with a wide grin, Eli playfully patted her ample, gingham-covered buttocks with one large hand before jumping back in mock terror lest the plump woman retaliate with a well-placed smack.

Ruby returned to the kitchen leaving Eli with the tedious chore of unpacking the latest shipment of finery the Governor ordered regularly from France. Running low on wig-powder, the Governor had been more than a little upset to hear the shipment was late again, the difficulties of the St. Lawrence making it necessary for the French ship to stop at Louisburg on the way to Quebec. He was however, delighted to hear they'd arrived, having been dispatched to the smaller, locally owned vessels of Ville Marie.

As he emptied the contents of numerous barrels and bins chock full of exotic colognes, powders, snuff, liqueurs, various bolts of coloured silks and fine lace, Eli pondered as to how an ordinary mortal could find use for such an enormous amount of frippery during the course of one lifetime. But then, Governor Herbert Mercier was no ordinary man.

Born to privilege, Mercier's father had been one of the wealthiest men in Ville Marie. As part of the newfound Royal Government and a Knight of St. Louis, Mercier was as powerful as a Tudor monarch, standing high in colonial society, in charge of defense, government ceremonies and relations with the English and Indians, yet he survived almost entirely on artichokes, capers and champagne. A narcissist and extremist, he'd spend hours titivating in front of his mirror. Everything about him, from the top of his elaborately curled and powdered wig to the tips of his silver-buckled elevator shoes was over-stated. At first glance he gave the distinct impression of authority, almost regal-like in bearing and dress, though some might argue he showed too much lace at collar and cuff. Genetically speaking, there appears to have been some indecision as to the final coloring of his close-set shifty eyes, until nature, in her infinite wisdom, compromised by allowing him one blue and one brown. A pug nose, just a tad too small, accentuated a larger than average head, and sloping shoulders discreetly disguised by more than an ample amount of padding. His only redeeming feature was his exceptionally white even teeth, a small miracle in itself when one considered his ghastly diet and advanced age of fifty-three. He was possessed of an overt femininity, a trait from which flowed a swishing gait as opposed to the more accepted masculine stride. Any whispers of latent homosexuality, however, were soon quashed, as his numerous indiscretions with members of the opposite sex were legend.

An articulate man with an intimidating air, he refused to appear in public without aid of his high, powdered wig, unlike most other officials who did so with amazing frequency. Such unguarded moments, Mercier maintained, should be reserved for one's own personal valet, the sole individual to be privy to one's own toilette and the powdering of one's own wig. In short, mediocrity was a dirty word to Mercier, display being the bane of his existence.

Following the suicide of Eli's predecessor, the Governor had found the black man to be reliable, courteous and extremely discreet; indeed it had been Eli's bent toward discretion that prompted Mercier to elevate him to the status of concierge for prudence was, to the Governor, of utmost importance.

Rummaging through the Governor's decadent chattel, Eli reflected on his first day of duty as Mercier's valet, a recollection that never failed to bring a deep blush to his cheeks.

With a kiss for good luck, Ruby had reached up and straightened his tie for the fifth time that morning.

"Stop that fussin' woman, you makin' me all jittery!"

"Git movin' then, I nevah hauled all them buckets o' hot water all the way up them stairs so's they'd git cold. When you finish wif his Lawdship's namby-pamby dressin' and powderin' that fancy wig so's he look like one o' dem high-falootin' society ladies, his breakfast gone be ready."

Eli's attempt to snatch a hot pork sausage from the silver tray that lay on the butcher's block beside him was thwarted by a swift slap on the wrist from Ruby who roughly shoved him toward the door after adjusting his tie one last time. Turning back toward her butter churn she cautioned him, "Member now husban', you be the Guvn'rs personal man. No nonsense like ya knows how, and wipe that silly grin off'n yer face befo' you git up there."

If Eli was obliged to grin it was due more to nerves than happiness. Much as he relished the idea of his new position he had serious reservations as to how he would carry out the private duties required of him. As he climbed the circular oak staircase toward the Governor's quarters he began to chuckle involuntarily at the thought of assisting Mercier at his bath.

"Lawdy, he thought, that man wears too much stinky smellin' stuff. I gone be sneezin' all de time!"

Determined to make the best of a situation that could only behoove him, he straightened his face, adjusted his tie and with a deep breath, tapped lightly on Mercier's door before letting himself in as previously instructed.

The heavy damask drapes were still drawn. He paused for a moment, allowing his eyes to adjust to the room's ill-defined lighting.

"Well, don't just stand there boy, test my bath water. I have a busy day in front of me. Be quick now!"

Startled, Eli turned toward the canopied bed with no posts. Ruby told him the suspended canopy was reserved strictly for the beds of Governors, but to Eli it looked very strange.

"What on earth are you waiting for Eli? I told you I'm in a hurry!"

Eli's eyes searched the area from whence the brusque command erupted. At first glance he was unable to recognize the bed's occupant and was horrified to think he'd stumbled into the wrong room until further scrutinizing assured him the face scowling in his direction was indeed that of his employer. Propped upright on several pillows with satin cases bearing his blood-red insignia, Raymond Mercier was devoid of all bodily hair, a result of a serious bout of scarlet fever he'd contacted as a child in France. Separated from his meticulously coiffed wig, which held the place of honor on his Louis XIII dressing table, Mercier's once commanding height had dramatically diminished. Near speechless from shock, Eli managed to mutter something about a beautiful day though he hadn't a clue as to the condition of the weather. Tripping over the Governor's elaborate kneeling bench adorned with a cross of solid ivory, he lunged toward the concealed windows and grasping the gold-tasseled drawstring, yanked as hard as he could. To his relief it really was a beautiful day. The sun's rays spilled into the room, emblazoning the gold fleur-de-lis pattern on the garnet window coverings that had been tailored to match the canopy and down-filled counterpane.

"Yes suh, it sho is a beautiful day," he said, scrambling up from the floor, "Just beautiful!" he repeated, louder this time now that he was sure of it.

"Damn the day and the weather Eli. The bath, I want my bath!"

"Right quick suh!"

Heading toward the cabinet de toilette, a large room adjoined to the boudouir, he suspiciously eyed the Governor's hair on the gold-leafed table and wondered how familiar he was expected to become with it. This whole situation appealed to his childish sense of humour and it was all he could do to suppress his laughter.

Once inside the cabinet de toilette, he bent over the ornate lead tub and rolled up his sleeve before dipping his elbow into the water as Ruby had shown him. "He likes his water tepid, not hot, not cold, but tepid," she'd instructed him before proceeding to tell him what tepid was.

"Bath water is tepid sir!" he yelled, his booming voice magnified by the high walls of the clawed tub.

"No need to scream Eli. I'm right here for mercy's sake!"

Swinging his head around to face the naked Mercier who stood in the doorway, Eli hastily yanked his sleeve down and raised his big, black eyes toward the ceiling in an effort to avoid the sorry spectacle in front of him. All else was futile since every inch of space in the room, save for a fine china bidet with a seat of cushioned leather, was filled with elaborate mirrors. To his dismay he found the ceiling to be mirrored as well. It was therefore impossible to escape the comical sight of Mercier daintily mincing across the tiled floor before submerging himself into the water with a ridiculous arabesque gesture. Without the ornamental trappings of fleur-de-lis counterpanes and satin pillows, the man looked like a plucked chicken. As a last resort Eli lowered his eyes to the floor and prayed he should be spared the final indignity of having to bathe this rude, pink, little person.

His plea obviously got through for just then Mercier said, "You'll find ample powder in the chest on the dresser, and the puff is right beside it. Apply the powder liberally and don't be stingy. I like a well-powdered wig. Do you understand?"

"Yes suh, I understan', lots o' powder, yes suh!"

He barely made it back into the powder room when the laughing erupted. He began to prance nervously about the carpeted room, one hand slapping his knee and the other covering his mouth to stifle the mirthful sounds. To make matters worse, strains of a French ditty flowed from the cabinet de toilette. Mercier may have been many things but he failed miserably when it came to singing. His voice was high-pitched and squeaky, the feminine timbre causing Eli to sharply bite the inside of his mouth for fear of breaking down altogether. Unearthing the powder buried amidst copious pots of pomade, snuff boxes and parfum bottles, he had initiated the dusting of the dreaded tresses when he heard Mercier step from the tub, his wet feet making slapping noises as he walked across the tiled floor to stand next to Eli. With a great theatrical flourish, he swept up a gold-tasseled atomizer from the table before spraying the obnoxious scent onto his bald pigeon-chest. Eli's worst fears were realized when he found it impossible to hold back the sneeze. The white cosmetic that lay in the open chest in front of him splayed in all directions, masking both men's faces and torsos. He turned and fled from the room.

Moments later, a surprised Ruby found him racing down the stairs, laughing hysterically, his handsome ebony face and hair smothered beneath a thick layer of a white pulverized substance of unknown origin.

CHAPTER FOURTEEN

From the dining room came the sound of shattering crystal, followed by Henri and Marjolaine's muffled laughter. Ruby knew that yet another of the imported crystal goblets lay dashed beneath the legs of the great mahogany china cabinet, which served as the focal point of the spacious room. Proof that she was well on her way to recovery, Marjolaine's laughter had become one of the few pleasures in Ruby's daily secular existence. Unlike the melancholy waif who'd arrived at the mansion eleven months ago, there was now a welcome freshness in her attitude; a delightful contradiction to the atmosphere of sophistication and rigid social mores to which the older woman had been immersed for so long, a native quality the two women shared. In essence, Ruby had found a daughter in Marjolaine.

Even the Governor, who could never be accused of having a soft heart, took to the girl immediately upon being introduced following his arrival from a six-week trip to Albany. He'd found her to be exhilarating and delightful – her unpretentiousness a trait he'd almost forgotten existed. He couldn't deny that her naiveté and obvious innocence revived in him stirrings of a sexual nature. He sensed her shyness; her aversion to being the center of attention and couldn't help but compare her to the jaded and bejeweled ladies of his court.

Visually assessing her as one would a prized piece of stock, he determined that apart from her flawless complexion and magnificent bosom she was otherwise common; her mouth a trifle generous and her nose a fraction too tip-tilted. He concluded nonetheless that she would be a most welcome addition to the mansion's skeleton staff. As a result, the pleading words prepared beforehand by Henri and Ruby on Marjolaine's behalf proved unnecessary. To their surprise and delight, Mercier had insisted the girl be allowed a one-year trial period.

It had been a crisp September afternoon. Somber shards of light stretched lazily across the large pine table where Ruby and Marjolaine had just completed the preparation of a large sipaille; a fish casserole separated by thin layers of tender pastry. Mercier was entertaining in the parlour. His guest, a Madame Bertrand; one of the most elite citizens of Ville Marie, was frantically seeking the Governor's assistance to avoid becoming one of the most notorious as well.

As his personal manservant, Eli was generally privy to Mercier's most private affairs. These secrets he rarely revealed, unless he thought Ruby might garner some amusement from the situation, as in this case. With a twinkle in her eye, Ruby had related the story to Marjolaine and Claudette over a card game of belote one evening.

According to Ruby, Monsieur and Madame Bertrand, along with some of the best-known citizens of Ville Marie, had been found guilty of dealing in alcohol with the Indians. Automatically excommunicated from the church and condemned to thirty days in prison, the guilty parties were required to spend the last two weeks of the sentence daily exposed to public spectacle on the back of a wooden horse with placards round their necks bearing the words: "For having dealt in firewater with the Savages."

Having been involved in a clandestine tryst with the Governor several months prior to the sentencing, Madame Bertrand had solicited Mercier's help to avoid being publicly ostracized. Apparently, according to Eli, she hadn't been as apprehensive during the affair with Mercier considering the penalty for adultery in Ville Marie was immediate expulsion from the country for three years and loss of position, not to mention the hefty fine Mercier would have had to pay. As Ruby explained it, either he grant her an official pardon or she would go public with the sordid details of their secret affair, details which, according to Eli, were very sordid indeed.

The dinner bell rang from the dining room, its tone smacking of impatience. The staff had been given strict orders never to enter a room in which Mercier was entertaining as it was in extremely poor taste; in other words, he feared they might interrupt an intimate tête-à-tête should he be that fortunate. However, Ruby concluded he simply required more wine in which to assuage his frayed nerves. Fetching a bottle of Mercier's favourite year from the wine cellar, she walked briskly toward the dining room, Napoleon the cat playfully nipping at her heels. The hum of their conspiratorial voices were cut short as she entered the room.

"*Merci* Ruby; this will do us for now." uttered Mercier in his most stilted manner as he grasped the bottle from her hands. Turning to leave, she couldn't resist a fleeting look at the infamous Madame

83

Bertrand who sat fingering her wineglass, her eyes seemingly focused on the untouched plate of oysters and brie in front of her. Obviously well into her cups, the bright red lipstick, rouge and eye shadow did little to assuage her drunken demeanor.

Mercier, tipping the bottle over Madame Bertrand's glass, remarked in a most sarcastic tone, "I assume you'll be wanting more of this?"

Choosing not to ignore his boorish insinuation, Madame Bertrand, in a high squeaky voice, screeched out, "Who the hell are you to extol the virtues of restraint you sanctimonious bastard?"

On that note, Ruby swiftly vacated the room and headed back to the kitchen where later that evening, while fetching some kindling from the wood-box beside the fireplace, she spotted Mercier striding into the room, his usual intimidating air nullified somewhat by the ruffled scarlet dressing gown he wore. His visits to the kitchen were rare and the sight of him caused Ruby to drop the kindling at her feet, her eyes searching his face for unspoken clues as to an accident that might have befallen her beloved Eli.

Signaled by the alarm on Ruby's face, Marjolaine spun around to lock eyes with Mercier. "Such strange eyes," she thought. "...so remote."

During the rare occasions he'd addressed her since his arrival from France, his eye movements had been too shifty for her to grasp exactly what it was that puzzled her – until now. The distinctive whites accentuated what she realized was one blue and one brown eye. Her jaw dropped slightly.

Angered by her revelation, he lowered his gaze to the floor. "Ruby, I'd like to speak to you alone if you please. Marjolaine can wait in the dining hall."

Upon being dismissed Marjolaine was forced to pass in front of Mercier who stood blocking the doorway. Making no attempt to step back, he savoured the touch of her thigh brushing against his bare leg as she squeezed through. His instructions to Ruby, who stood brushing tiny chips of wood from her apron, were brief and precise.

"The girl stays. Certainly you could use more help around this place, especially now that the Christmas season is nearing. She seems healthy enough to assist you with domestic chores, especially the tedious ones that never seem to get done."

Ruby knew he was referring to the copious amounts of dust that gathered on his precious furniture, a sore spot with him. He continued,

"Perhaps now we'll all hear less complaining about the total lack of incentive from the part-time chars I've been forced to hire in the past."

This final statement made Ruby cringe, as she knew full well that the availability of competent servants in Ville Marie was overflowing. It was common knowledge that the chars Mercier hired were not handpicked for their dusting expertise, but rather their superior bedroom antics. Where he found these whores disguised as cleaning women she'd never know, though it had been speculated that they might be bored society women game for a kinky tryst with the Governor; a fete accompli of sorts perhaps. An imperceptible smile crossed Ruby's lips as she recalled the discovery of a diamond and ruby bracelet tangled in the satin sheets of Mercier's bed, left there no doubt by one of the hardworking domestics.

"See to it she is fitted for the proper attire and personal wardrobe in general, and by the way, I see no need for her to vacate the quarters on the second floor. From this moment on she is to be your total responsibility. Do you understand Ruby?"

"Yes suh, I understan' right well. She gwan be a big hep to me what wif all them parties and Christmas cookin' to attend to!" Then, as a mischievous afterthought she added, "Plenty o room down hea suh; no need fo' her takin up guest room space."

She was sorry she'd said it before the words escaped her. Nonchalantly she swung around to walk toward Napoleon, who lay curled up in front of the hearth. "Scuse me suh, I gots to feed ol' cat now."

With a burst of indignation Mercier turned and headed down the hall, Ruby's voice echoing from the kitchen, "Beg pardon suh, but dinner gwan be a little late."

Softly closing the paneled door to his book-lined study, he made his way across the lush oriental carpet toward the intricately carved server against the far wall. Pouring an ample amount of cognac into a

crystal snifter, he quaffed a generous mouthful, closing his eyes to better relish the burning sensation as it flowed down his throat. Reaching over the server, he parted the exquisite lace curtains and glanced outside. Despite the etchings of frost on the pane, he was able to make out the voluptuous figure of Ruby scurrying across the well-manicured lawn, Napoleon nipping at her heels. No one need tell him she was on her way to Henri's cabin in the back, eager to inform the gamekeeper that Marjolaine had been given permission to stay.

He was envious of the tall, well-built Henri whom he knew had designs on Marjolaine. Seeing them together it was apparent that Henri loved the girl, not lasciviously, but with the natural, healthy love of normal youth, the type of love Mercier could only guess at. His facial expression darkened as he dropped the curtain before emptying the contents of the snifter.

Seating himself at the large oak desk, he pulled open the middle drawer to remove the false bottom. He didn't remove the envelopes that lay there; he just stared at them as though their very touch would be painful. Rubbing his hand over his eyes he absent-mindedly toyed with the single lock of hair that fell loose from his powdered wig to find a place on his forehead. His troubled expression escalated as he eyed the opaque envelopes bearing the official wax seal common only to the Governor himself. They were love letters; all of them returned by the uninterested women he'd hoped to marry. He knew the letters should be destroyed before the depressing reminders of his failed attempts at true love destroyed him, yet for some deep masochistic motive beyond his comprehension he was unable to annihilate the visual proof of his lonely past. Replacing the hidden drawer he refreshed his drink and sank despondently into the plush velvet chair in front of the crackling fire Eli had put up earlier on. He closed his eyes and allowed his thoughts to wander.

Mercier had been elected Governor, as was the custom, by the Sulpican religious order, often referred to as "Aristocrats in cassocks". Chosen from the military, the title of Governor was bestowed upon him strictly to impress the natives, giving him no real power by royal decree other than the organization of the military. His oversized ego however, allowed him to fancy himself not just a representative of the King, but equal to the great Monarch himself. Since his election he'd lost no time in attempting to imitate the French Court by surrounding himself with an elaborate entourage of soldiers, officers, members of his council, rich trades people and distinguished personages from the courts of Europe. As well he was planning on gaining a fast reputation for entertaining Chiefs of various tribes, once they were at peace. This latter gesture was to be token, designed strictly for the amusement of the aristocracy rather than a true attempt at contributing to the foundation of a new nation.

Sly and arrogant to the point of being abrasive, Mercier could count no real friends among his aristocratic peers, who for the most part were of the same ilk; ambitious, shrewd social-climbing officials, more interested in personal amusement than politics. They loved to drive out in their fancy high-wheeled carriages for the express purpose of being admired and ogled by the less fortunate, rarely conspiring to the welfare of New France. Unlike Governor M. de Montagmy, Champlain's successor, Raymond Mercier was neither father, friend or confident to any man, and his basic snobbishness, a trait he chose to term "wordly sophistication," equaled that of the most socially pretentious. So taken with himself was he that he balked at performing even the most token of civic duties, failing to follow such protocol as greeting officials arriving from France at the shore, much less accompany them back to the quay upon their departure. The sole exceptions to this boorish behavior occurred only if there were a sufficient number of females arriving. At such times he'd appear surrounded by an impressive entourage of local dignitaries, dressed ostentatiously in his ceremonial robes and ever-present high, powdered wig.

Placing the empty snifter on the rug beside his chair he reached over and yanked the gold-tasseled servants' bell to alert Eli to his study. A few seconds later there was a light tap on the door and Eli stuck his head in.

"You called suh?"

"Yes Eli, bring me a tray in about two hours time. I'll take dinner in here." Turning his attention to the fire, he paused briefly before adding, "Eli wait. On second thought, have the new girl bring the tray and make it an hour. And fetch me another bottle of cognac before you leave."

With a knowing look Eli mumbled, "Yes suh. Right away suh."

Alone again, Mercier threw another log into the fire and refreshed his drink before settling back in his chair, the fingers of his free hand tapping irritably on his knee. Another drink and then another in quick succession until finally the cognac worked its magic, allowing him to relax and plan his unscrupulous strategy.

The prospect of bedding such a virtuous woman excited him. The others had been too easy, too eager to jump into bed with the Governor of New France. There had been no challenge and less reward. All whores were the same to him, but Marjolaine was of a different ilk; sweet, pure and untouched, much like the ones whose returned letters lay hidden in his desk. Overcome by a sense of excitement spurred on by visions of possibilities involving the girl, he leapt from his chair before breaking into a charming little minuet across the floor, glancing all the while into the ornate mirror suspended from the lofty ceiling. Never one to ignore his image in a looking glass, he danced closer whilst contemplating his reflection. Sweeping his brow with a little finger, he sucked in his cheeks.

"What more could a woman ask for," he said aloud. "And Governor of New France to boot!"

Adjusting his wig, which had tilted slightly during his theatrical solo, he literally skipped back to his desk to pour another drink.

CHAPTER FIFTEEN

The mournful cry of a whippoorwill greeted Claude as he slipped from the lodge into the frosty dawn air, the frigid November wind cutting through the feathered cape Coyote had fashioned for him. He recalled his good friend Jacque telling him that the Mohawk called the month of November *"yothore,"* or cold, and he'd responded with admiration at such a simple yet accurate description. The frigid weather had further aggravated his injured arm and he began to massage it in an attempt to soothe the dull ache that spread from his shoulder to the tip of his fingers. The shattered arm had been expertly set and splinted by Crippled Sparrow, and as a medical doctor he'd been genuinely impressed with her knowledge of the anatomy, primitive though her techniques might be. He felt his upper thigh where the blade had been embedded as he ran the gauntlet, running his fingers over the ridge of skin through his buckskin leggings. He could hardly believe it was nearly healed. How he'd cringed at the sight of the bloodied, rusty blade Crippled Sparrow had yanked painfully from the gash, for a wound that deep, inflicted with such a corroded implement could only mean infection and slow distressing healing. Too weak to convey the dire need for thorough cleansing before stitching the wound, he'd almost fainted from horror as she nonchalantly slapped a dour mixture of crushed sage and suet onto the gaping laceration before sewing it together with individual hairs from his head threaded onto an ominous looking bone needle. The *Onwehonwhene* knew that injuries healed free from infection if the victim's hair was used in place of sinew, but Claude, unaware of this custom, had prepared himself for the inevitable amputation of the leg, entertaining morbid visions of the limb prior to amputation, doubled in size from infection. He shuddered at the thought of his leg being barbarically separated from his torso by way of an archaic medical instrument such as a crude-edged stone. How wrong he had been. He had since learned not to underestimate the wisdom of his adopted brothers and sisters. Like most Europeans of the day, Claude had been puzzled as to how they survived at all, aghast at the realization that Mohawks always turned to magic when medical knowledge failed, their preoccupation with the supernatural far greater than all other tribes. He'd been concerned about being the subject of some obscure supernatural healing, and was relieved to find it wasn't necessary.

Scanning the frozen ground for the elaborately woven river-cane basket he'd discarded the previous morning, he chose one of the others piled against the side of the longhouse. Perhaps Coyote had stored his basket away somewhere but he wasn't about to risk waking her up. Indeed he made it his practice to leave the lodge very early each morning thereby avoiding her amorous advances; the woman was insatiable, keeping him up most of the night until he thought he'd swoon from exhaustion.

To make matters worse, by nature he was possessed of a lower than average sex drive. Coyote, upon recognizing this, had concocted an aphrodisiac in hopes of heightening his desire. The *Onqwanonhsioni* recognized the effects of herbs and sweet-smelling flowers, employing them in their puberty rites, courtships and marriages. Taken to increase potency, Coyote's love potion was the most sought after among the aged men and women of the tribe. The main ingredient was ginseng root, called *"garent-oguen"* by the people, or "man's thigh." Mixed with mica, gelatin and snake-meat, it was to be taken religiously four times a day until the desired effect became apparent.

Claude's rather strict European upbringing had led him to believe that the combustion of one's sexual desire was subject to one's whims and fortune, stimulated by most anything depending on one's past experience and the circumstances of the moment, yet there was no denying that within a week or so, during which time he dutifully ingested the odious antidote under Coyote's watchful and obviously wishful eye, a not so subtle change occurred. He found his sexual urges stirring from their usual sedentary state, and though pronouncedly more active, his aroused libido still failed to match that of his native wife. He had, in fact, become expert at feigning sleep, a deep sleep that even Coyote's pounding fists couldn't arouse.

Walking toward the jagged path leading to the river, he passed the lodge where Paul, his redheaded friend from Ville Marie, now lived with the family of Butterfly, who'd adopted him as her husband.

The other two captives hadn't fared as well. The first, a slight young man Claude knew only as Serge, had been felled almost immediately by a fierce blow to the temple as he set out to run the gauntlet and was ordered by council to be burned to the stake before nightfall. The other, a middle-aged shopkeeper who'd remained mute from fear since his capture, had succumbed to multiple injuries two days following the exhaustive run. He'd been claimed by Otter Woman, a widow who'd lost four husbands to the French, and was in dire need of a replacement; French or otherwise.

Tall blades of dewy grass brushed against Claude's leggings as he sauntered past the communal storehouse that had been packed to the rafters with foodstuffs from the harvest. Great sacks and baskets of food lay piled around the building for anyone in need. A buzzard feather, designed to keep witches out, stirred decorously above the main entrance. Claude thought he'd never understand the paradoxical complexities of the Iroquois psychology. On one hand they were like children, and on the other, renowned for their commanding attitudes. They'd succeeded in defeating the Huron and Tionontati nations as well as the Erie and Neutral. From what he'd gathered, it was just a matter of time before they overthrew the Susquehanna as well. It was common knowledge that warfare was so ingrained in the Iroquois personality, and their self-respect so dependant on personal glory, that individualism often outweighed their philosophy of peace. How they managed to raise such impressive warriors, however, was beyond his comprehension. In the two months he'd been living among the Mohawk, he'd not witnessed anything resembling a structured upbringing. Amazed at the indulgence of children, the most severe punishment he'd witnessed was a splash of cold water on the face of a misbehaving child or perhaps a quick dunk in the river, a far cry from the severe indignities he'd suffered as a boy in Paris. He'd once heard that suicide among native youths who'd been unduly punished was not unusual, the most common method being the ingestion of water hemlock or as the natives called it, "fatal root." At the time, the information seemed far-fetched, but now, having lived among them, it seemed not only feasible but also probable. As well, all sexual curiosities were allowed between youngsters of both sexes; the sight of their naked bronzed bodies engaging in general horseplay was a common sight, reminding Claude of a litter of innocent, rambunctious puppies.

The habitual twitch in his left eye started up and he knew it was caused from lack of sleep. Yawning, he gazed upward to find that the brilliant scarlet and golds of the maple and sumac had altered into various shades of dingy, muted browns. Most of the leaves had fallen, exposing naked tangles of grim-shaped limbs against a steel-gray sky. Reaching the rivers' edge he stood quietly, drinking in the surrounding beauty. He'd come to cherish these early reveries of solitude, the dim hours of mystery between the passing of night and the birth of a new day. For a few magic moments he was free, totally separated from the confines of the hub of activity that was now his home; his nostrils freed from the acrid scent of split-open fish and the long strips of moose meat hanging from the scaffolds over the simmering fires. The morning air bore a number of tonic properties that erased his dull headache aggravated by the continuous smoking of the *kinnikinnick,* or as the *Onqwanonhsioni* called it *"he mixes,"* a habit to all but the youngest inhabitants of the longhouse. His ears were freed from the perpetual droning of an ancient guttural tongue he didn't comprehend, the chopped-like words emanating from the back of the throat instead of the tongue as in most other forms of speech. Here he could move about freely without having to step over clusters of chattering women encircling the fires, their work-worn hands tirelessly creating pipes, fish spears, moccasins, bows and arrows, knife sheaths, necklaces and the ever useful root baskets colourfully decorated with porcupine quills.

Closing his eyes he breathed the perfume of nature's spoor, luxuriating for a moment in the arms of a freshly chilled breeze carrying the melodious song of a lone white-throat. He observed a pair of otters swimming in file toward the shoreline a few yards from where he stood. Gracefully scaling the bank they eyed him curiously before vigorously shaking the excess water from their glossy fur and slipping unobtrusively behind a tree trunk. The light was increasing, and wafer thin layers of fog rose slowly from the waters surface. A pair of whiskey jacks flew silently above him.

Alerted to the sound of water being suctioned, he cautiously stepped back and waited for the wolves to show themselves. Unlike dogs that lapped, wolves, like horses, sipped their fluids, and he knew there were no horses in the area. Timidly peeking round the curved edge of the shore, he spotted three of them sauntering back into the forest from whence they came. Slightly shaken, he glanced over his shoulder a few times before timidly approaching the river once again.

According to Coyote, the people of the Wolf Clan were able to communicate with the wolves as they were tribal ancestors, and from what he'd observed in the short time he'd been here, both wolf and man treated each other with a reverence of sorts.

Bending over the water he filled his vessel to the brim, one of the small contributions he was able to make toward his morning meal, at least until his arm fully healed. In the meantime however, his adoptive family had been more than kind to him, treating him with utmost respect and courtesy; even the small boys who ran in boisterous gangs would often present him with small game they'd caught with their snares and blowguns. It was obvious that the *Onqwanonhsioni* admired a man who could complete the gauntlet run and though the thought of escape had crossed his mind, reason cautioned him against it. Everyone knew that Iroquois captives had been known to be released after months or even years if they proved themselves worthy or were no longer useful to the welfare of the tribe. Rather than risk losing the respect he'd built up, he thought it wiser to bide his time, for no one knew better than he the uncanny twists of fate life can offer.

"Awiyo orhen'kene Iakwai - Good morning *Iakwa*i."

Startled, Claude swung his head around to find Black Whirlwind standing just inches away, a bear skin secured by a cord of dried intestine slung over his shoulder.

"Christ these people are sly," he thought. "Had I been an enemy, my scalp would be hanging from his belt by now."

Eyeing the mangy scalps displayed on the Chief's belt he shuddered before extending his right arm to shake hands in greeting. Hesitating, Black Whirlwind accepted his hand with his own left hand. The Frenchman had no way of knowing the Mohawks only shake hands with those who aren't friends, choosing to greet friends in a more intimate way such as hugging. On occasions where they were forced to adopt the white mans' strange custom, they never offered their right hand for it is the hand that draws the bow and yields the knife, in short, it is the hand of death. The left hand however, is joined to the heart and speaks of friendship. As well, it holds the shield of protection. It is the hand of life.

"You speak French!" exclaimed Claude, I'm surprised."

93

"I was raised with French captives. The music of their language comes easily to me. Not so easy was the language of the Dutch and English, for although they don't have the split tongue of the French, their words are difficult to master. Unlike the French, they keep their promises and speak always the truth. Soon the French and his despised brother the Huron will exist no more. Consider yourself lucky to have been adopted by Coyote for now you are one of us and your life will be spared."

"If I don't die from exhaustion first." Claude thought to himself. "One way or another these savages will be the end of me!"

As if reading his thoughts the Chief's rigid expression softened and a smile crept across his face. "Tell me *Iakwai,* how is Coyote treating you? From the dark circles under your eyes I would say she is treating you too well!"

"What did you just call me?"

"Iakwai."

"What does it mean?"

"It is a good name, and it is what you shall be called. It means White Bear." Turning to leave, he paused before adding, "There is to be a council meeting this day, perhaps *Iakwai* would find it of interest to sit in with the other men and hear a different story for a change."

Nodding his assent, Claude watched as the Mohawk disappeared into the woods. He knew he was gaining trust from the *Onqwanonhsioni* and the idea of being separated from Coyote for any length of time was appealing. He'd enjoyed his brief encounter with Black Whirlwind and aside from the fact he was a savage, he liked him. Either that or he was starving for male companionship, though he doubted that was the case.

He considered the name the Chief had bestowed on him. He liked it. Many times his beloved Kathryn had called him her "big, clumsy bear*"* for he'd always been awkward in her presence. How could it be that he felt a sense of kinsmanship with a man whose people had been responsible for his wife's death? How he'd cursed the Mohawk upon hearing of Kathryn's demise and now, he was living as one of them. How could this be? He found himself gradually being absorbed into the bosom of *Onqwanonhsioni* society, the bittersweet memories of his former existence fading into the distance. It had been weeks since he'd considered escape, and if he were able to free himself from the clutches of Coyote, he'd be more than content to remain. Something was happening to him, a transformation of sorts. It was as though he'd become a child again – filled with wonder and inquisitiveness. For the first time since his arrival from France he'd become aware of nature's majesty and was beginning to appreciate the enormous respect the *Onqwanonhsioni* held for this earth they call *"Ake'nihstenha"* – Mother.

CHAPTER SIXTEEN

Born in a Parisian gutter, sired by an unknown father, and deserted by his mother at the age of four, young Claude had been adopted and raised by his uncle, a Dr. Jean LaBelle, estranged brother of his runaway mother, Yvonne. Appointed Yvonne's legal guardian following the demise of their parents, Jean had steadfastly refused Yvonne's request to court Andre Bouchard, a man the good doctor knew to be morally and spiritually bankrupt, his reputation as a gambler being legend.

Angry and inconsolable, Yvonne had rationalized that she could, in time, wear down the resistance of her concerned brother, arranging clandestine meetings with Andre in the meantime. She had retained her virginity throughout these romantic liaisons, not for the traditional reasons of modesty nor the desire to remain chaste until wed, but for another more selfish end. Although Andre had never admitted as much, Yvonne had been intuitively aware that he was an avid womanizer. A handsome man, possessed of an endless source of income, it took little imagination to see that he aspired to take full advantage of the lavish attention the love-struck Yvonne bestowed upon him. His constant insistence directed toward her still-intact virginity fired her belief that it was the one treasure she possessed that would prompt the handsome young swain to sacrifice his cherished bachelorhood. This belief had been verified when he asked for her hand in marriage, but as Yvonne feared, her brother not only vehemently forbade the union, but kept Yvonne under close surveillance to prevent her from meeting with Andre again. Sick with grief, the love-struck girl fell into a deep depression compounded by news of Andre's death less than three weeks later.

Stabbed outside a gambling house located deep in the steamy bowels of Paris, Andre's corpse had been discovered the following morning. According to the owner of the establishment, he had been accused of cheating and it was assumed he'd been stalked by the irate loser who'd murdered him before relieving his pockets of their burden. Not completely without compassion, Jean had given Yvonne permission to attend the funeral. It would be the last time he'd see his sister.

Mad with desire for revenge against her brother, she had failed to return to his home following the somber ceremony, hiring a carriage instead to take her to the red light district of the *"Rue de Loc"*, where within less than two hours following the surrender of her adored Andre into the frozen, unrelenting earth, she had procured her first customer, a one-armed man with pocked skin and sadistic blue eyes.

Emerging from a smoke-filled tavern, he had reached out in an attempt to touch her arm. Startled, Yvonne had instinctively drawn away, her stomach lurching from the overpowering stench emanating from his pores. Her mind was suddenly deluged with the painful memory of her brother's constant denials to her repeated pleas to marry Andre, a memory that consumed her with hate and desire for retaliation. Brazenly meeting the stranger's steely eyes with her own, she parted her full red lips, revealing white, even teeth. Smiling seductively she relaxed her posture and leaned toward him. Understanding, he placed his arm around her slim waist before silently leading her to the first available room where she promptly, and without ceremony, surrendered her virginity against a filthy, plaster-cracked wall, her attention focused all the while on a lone cockroach scaling the mirror opposite her.

She had eventually found lodgings with two other whores of the *"Rue de Loc"*, Lucille and her scarred roommate Jocelyn, both of them taking her under their wing and teaching her the tricks of the trade. Eventually turning to drink, she sought solace from the bottle in an attempt to numb the increasing feelings of self-loathing and contempt.

Drinking more led to her working less, her once beautiful face now bloated and unattractive. It was during this period she was forced to ply her trade in the dark, hidden in the shadows along with the other less than attractive women-of-the-night, most of them well past their prime, victims of drugs and alcohol, many of them riddled by disease. These women sold their favours for the least possible sum; the transaction more often than not completed in or around some dark, debris-strewn alley, the acrid stench of urine pervading the damp night air.

It was in this degrading environment that Yvonne became with child. Her monthly cycle had long since become irregulated by copious amounts of cheap wine and lack of proper diet; therefore she was unaware of the pregnancy. Blaming her working conditions and self-induced decrepit condition for the termination of her menses, she continued her depraved lifestyle with frenzy, longing for an early release from her self-inflicted hell by way of death.

One sweltering August night in 1631, an elderly derelict climbed off her swollen, insensible body, adjusted his trousers and disappeared into the night, congratulating himself on his shrewdness in satisfying his lust without paying the fee. Through her drunken haze Yvonne was aware of a pain, the likes of which she'd never endured. Righting her disheveled undergarments she forced herself to sit upright. Disoriented, she placed her hands over her face in an attempt to halt the whirling sensation in her brain. Her alcohol-numbed body underwent another, stronger contraction. Great tentacles of searing pain tore through her. Frightened into near-sobriety she attempted to stand up but the cramps were too severe. On her hands and knees she sluggishly crawled out of the alley, making her way into the soft, orange glow of the gaslight bathing the street, praying aloud that someone would come to her aid. Another great spasm commanded her body causing her hand to slip on the greasy cobblestones sending her headlong into the squalid Parisian gutter.

She lay there moaning, the foul smelling dung of carriage horses a mattress for her tormented body. In the distance she was vaguely aware of a rig, the clip-clop of her mattress's benefactor echoing in her ears. Her moans graduated to urgent screams and the infant spewed forth, his puny head face down in the garbage-strewn gutter. The driver of a rig, alerted by her final shriek, had assisted Yvonne and her son. Raised for four years by Yvonne, young Claude had been dreadfully neglected, abused and finally, deserted.

It had been on a crisp, sunny April morning in 1637 that Claude had arrived unannounced on his Uncle's doorsteps located on the outskirts of Paris. He had been accompanied by an aging and grotesquely painted prostitute named Jocelyn, who bore a jagged scar down the right side of her face; the taut skin pulling her eye downward as a result of an inferior stitching job performed by the doctor who had attended her following a cat fight with another whore.

With a resounding echo, the mahogany grandfather clock in the hall struck ten as Madame LaBelle shuffled by on her way to the door, her ill-fitting slippers dragging forlornly across the rich Persian carpet. Hastily wiping flour-covered hands onto her crisp blue apron, she swung open the heavy carved door, fully prepared to give the insistent ringer of the obnoxious bell a tongue-lashing. Instead, the white-haired matron had been left speechless at the sight of a small lad peeking shyly from behind the wrinkled skirts of a heavily made-up woman.

The boy was emaciated. His sandy-coloured hair had the appearance of never having come in contact with soap or water. His sad, wizened brown eyes were underlined with bruised pouches from lack of sleep and nourishment, and his left eye twitched incessantly.

Nervously, Jocelyn had spurted out an introduction of sorts, prompting Madame LaBelle to show the scruffy duo into her husband's book-lined study. Excusing herself, the plump hostess returned to the kitchen to prepare tea while Jocelyn, having requested the whereabouts of the lavatory, freshened herself up before applying another coat of chalky powder in a futile attempt to cover her unsightly scar.

Left to his own, the young boy scanned the academic surroundings, drinking in every detail of the well-appointed room. He scrutinized the vast expanse of leather bound volumes, the intricately carved Louis IV desk upon which were scattered numerous *objets d'art*, the fine monogrammed stationary flanked by a solid gold letter opener and various sized quills erupting from a peacock-blue stand. Perched upon a well-worn dictionary was an exquisite miniature of, what appeared to be, Madame LaBelle in her youth.

Gingerly shifting his position on the emerald and gold settee to better view the far side of the library, his frail jaw dropped in awe as his eyes lit upon the greatest treasure of them all. Placed strategically under a gilt mirror that had been recessed into the wall, stood an enormous world globe. Suspended on an ornate stand, the wooden sphere's entire surface was sheathed with scores of multi-hued countries framed by turquoise bodies of water. It mattered little that he was totally unfamiliar with the function of a globe, the important thing was that the sight of it caused his little face to light up with joy, an emotion almost completely foreign in his life thus far.

Dr. Jean LaBelle's planned evening of studying had been thwarted by the unanticipated arrival of his estranged sister's son. Upon entering the house, he'd barely had time to catch his breath before his wife Marcella hastened him into the study to greet the boy. Late afternoon found them settled comfortably over large mugs of steaming cinnamon-laced cider. The warmth from the fireplace spilled out, shrouding the small group in a blanket of sharing and trust. And so it was that Jocelyn related the boy's history to Jean LaBelle and his wife Marcella.

As the story unfolded it was learned that Yvonne, for some unknown reason, had left the boy alone for an indeterminate period. Her landlord, a sleazy thief in the guise of a businessman, had dropped into the small flat where mother and son resided with intentions of collecting his overdue rent. Greeted by what appeared to be a vacant apartment, he made his way to the meager bedroom, half-expecting Yvonne to be hiding in attempt to avoid payment. The second he opened the door he was deluged by the unmistakable odor of stale urine and human excrement. From the corner of his eye he observed a family of cockroaches taking refuge in a crack of the rotted baseboard. Lying unconscious on the floor was the body of Yvonne's brat, his frail left foot tightly bound by a crimson scarf that had been secured to the leg of the tarnished brass bed. Beside him on the floor sat a large pewter cup half filled with curdled milk the colour of saffron. There were crumbs scattered in the area of the boy whose left hand still clung to a moldy chunk of bread, his lifeless face and exposed limbs bore witness to the gnawing of hungry insects.

Not wishing to soil himself by aiding the lad, the landlord had summoned Yvonne's neighbour, Jocelyn. Fearing involvement with the law he had offered her two months free lodging if she would, as he termed it, "quietly dispose of this inconvenience." Jocelyn, rendered speechless by the pathetic scene that lay before her, could only nod in agreement. Since she and Yvonne's working hours had been staggered, responsibility for the boy had often fallen on Jocelyn, and indeed she loved him deeply. He was her spiritual oasis, representing all that is good and pure, and in his presence, as if by osmosis, she too became good and pure as she had once been.

It was only in her company that young Claude received any semblance of maternal affection; something his natural mother was incapable of feeling. Had it not been for Jocelyn's excursions to the noisy flea markets to search diligently among piles of tattered second-hand garments, the boy would have little to wear. She'd often return home with sweets for the boy and once presented him with a doll, a replica of a Red Indian complete with feathers and hatchet. It mattered little that its former owner had ripped one of the tiny feet off for it became Claude's constant companion and symbol of security.

The setting sun cast golden slivers upon the concerned visage of Jean LaBelle as Jocelyn neared the finale of her account, an explanation of how it was she found the LaBelle residence. She revealed that since she and Yvonne resided in the same house and shared a common profession, they had on occasion, allowed each other sparse glimpses into their past, oftimes alluding to former friends and alienated families. Dr. Jean LaBelle had figured prominently during these tete-et-tetes and Yvonne's graphic descriptions of her estranged brother's residence, unique in structure, had led Jocelyn and Claude to his front door.

As Jocelyn neared the end of her account, visions of his cozy, well-ordered life flew out the window causing Jean to feel ashamed of his inner display of selfishness and he counted himself no better than his wayward sister, but the balding physician knew what had to be done, and with his wife's agreement, arrangements were made for the barren couple to adopt the boy.

Jocelyn had been granted visiting rights and the years spent under the guidance of his aunt and uncle had been filled with contentment and love. The boy would follow Jean whenever possible and as he became older, often accompanied him on his rounds of house calls. Despite a deprived background, he proved to be a shrewd observer, displaying a keen interest in the medical profession. He later attended medical school where he completed his studies as an honor graduate before returning home to assist his aging uncle in his practice.

Soon after, he met and married Kathryn De Jeaune, daughter of his aunt's brother. Less than two months later the young couple emmigrated to New France where Claude set up his practice.

CHAPTER SEVENTEEN

April 1674
Season of the Strawberry Moon

She was restless – tossing and turning in her bunk, the other children's taunts echoing in her head. *"Kentsyonk! Kentsyonk!* – You're a fish! You're a fish! Don't go near the water or you'll turn back into a salmon the colour of your skin!"

Corn Child knew the *Onwehonwhene* believed that twins were transformations of salmon and should avoid the water for fear of being retransformed, but she wasn't Blood Sky's twin and more importantly, she wasn't an Indian. Coyote's man, Claude, had told her she was French and came from a place called Ville Marie. He'd relate stories of the civilized village where he'd been the local doctor, answering her many questions about her true parents whom he'd known so well. As far as she was concerned it was just a matter of time before she got away from these red devils to return to Ville Marie where she belonged. She hated it here and she hated being a girl. She envied the boys who were allowed to do more or less as they pleased, whether it be playing at war or hunting with their small bows and arrows. Only the boys owned toy hatchets and competed in races, lacrosse and wrestling, but more importantly they could sleep all night in the bush if they wished.

Possessed of a perverse and sinister nature, coupled with an uncanny talent for stealing and lying, Corn Child was disliked by almost everyone in camp. As for the natives, they couldn't understand why she hated them so. Since the *Onwehonwhene* population had dwindled as a result of warfare, the white captives had been adopted to replace dead kinsman and were generally content with their life. The whole village had gone out of their way to help the rebellious youngster, but she rebuked their kindness, seeking only the company of Dark Shadow, her chosen mentor in the art of black magic. Though she was but eleven seasons, she was mystically connected to the evil woman. She ignored the others who warned her that in the eyes of the *Onwehonwhene,* black magic was a crime more serious than murder.

How little she cared when they pleaded with her to change her ways before it was too late.

Given that Corn Child's temperament was diabolical and self-absorbed to the extreme, it wasn't surprising she lacked friends. Jealous of Blood Sky who was tremendously popular among their peers, she took it upon herself to afflict the little savage with a curse taught her by Dark Shadow.

"Remember, the old woman had hissed, repeat the curse only three times – four times and it loses its power."

Her prescience being what it was however, Blood Sky was cognizant of the fact that Corn Child was up to no good. Once or twice she'd been awakened in the middle of the night to spot her scuttling away from the side of Blood Sky's bunk before climbing back into her own. She'd voiced her fears to Dancing Leaf and Cloud Woman and both of them advised her what steps she must take in order to protect herself from any curse Corn Child might be afflicting on her.

And so it was that twice a day, sunrise and sunset, Cloud Woman welcomed Blood Sky into her lodge where she'd immerse the young girl into a deep tub of cedar water, the healing qualities and spiritual power of cedar having been used by the *Onwehonwhene* since time immemorial.

"Fish, fish. Scaly, ugly fish with a white belly – look at your hair and eyes – bleached white from the sun. Were you lying on your back or swimming upstream Corn Child?"

Great rings of laughter broke out among the group of half-naked youngsters. Corn Child flung the turkey feathers she'd been gathering to the ground, and tearing off her woven grass headband, contemptuously tossed it in the face of a small naked boy who'd been making the caustic remarks. The children giggled, all but one little girl, standing half-hidden behind the others.

Cloud Kitten was the daughter of her adoptive cousin, Little Current. So named for her softness of heart, the child had large, almond-shaped green eyes, her grandfather having been three quarters French. It had been Cloud Kitten who'd tried so hard to become friends with the French captive, even presenting her with her favourite corn husk doll, only to witness Corn Child smash the tiny treasure against a large rock before laughing and ridiculing the girl for being a half-breed.

"I'll bet you don't know if you're a rabbit or a duck do you?" Corn Child scornfully hissed.

Immune to Corn Child's sardonic remarks, Cloud Kitten possessed the uncanny sensitivity toward others' pain that linked her to her cousin Blood Sky. The delicate-structured moppet couldn't bear the cruel taunts of the other children toward Corn Child, but her pathetic desire to be accepted had prompted her to at least give the appearance of joining in on their silly game. Wincing, she'd turned her small head to avoid watching the cluster of youths joyfully shove Corn Child to the ground before throwing dirt on her. Too occupied to notice that Cloud Kitten hadn't joined in, they would later hear her relate how she too, had hurled soil at the white-eyed witch. Cloud Kitten knew it was just a matter of time before the others discovered she was an imposter, but till then she'd try to be as much like the others as possible.

As a token gesture, she searched the gritty soil to find the tiniest pebble she could before slinging it sideways to avoid stinging the grounded prey.

Like a great buttery fan, Corn Child's hair lay splayed behind her on the black earth. Attempting to lift her head from the ground, her neck jerked backward as one of the older boys placed his moccasioned foot on the silky mane. How she hated the little heathens – hated their straight black hair and copper skin. They were nothing but slant-eyed savages and if it were up to her they'd all be dead.

'They never treat Blood Sky like this', she thought. 'They side with her because she's a savage like them, and a crippled one at that.'

Still pinned to the ground by her young tormentor, she spotted a jagged fist-sized rock lying within her grasp. With the keen analytical cunning of a person mad with hate, she feigned anguished discomfort by piercing the air with an excruciating scream. "Aaiiee, the pain – my back is broken. I can't stand the pain. Help me, help me please!"

Clever enough to understand the psychology of the native mind, she preyed on their weakest area, compassion. She knew only too well that they were engaging in what they thought was a harmless prank. Compared to the things she'd done to them, it was indeed harmless. She was also aware of the punishment that awaited them if they physically harmed the daughter of Chief Black Whirlwind, adopted or not. Black eyes agape, the youngsters froze with fear at her convincing screams of agony. Broken Feather, the leader of the group, gingerly removed his foot from her hair to eye her suspiciously. Sharp wits had elevated him to the position of leader amongst his peers and although he was almost positive Corn Child was faking, he was too intelligent to take any chances. Pondering his next course of strategy, he began to pace the area as the others, still glued to their tracks, looked helplessly on.

"Hurry! Do something! Help me please!" she cried out, writhing on the ground, in what appeared to be obvious distress. At her last cry the children huddled together, each one voicing their opinion on what should be done. Taking advantage of their momentary distraction, Corn Child deftly scooped up the jagged rock and feigning her most wretched expression, sought to meet the eyes of the child she hated most – Cloud Kitten. Their eyes locked, the empathy in Cloud Kitten's stare making Corn Child want to throw up.

'The pathetic little breed should know I couldn't move my arms and legs if my back was broken', she thought. She recalled the time she'd told Cloud Kitten she was dead. Not fully aware of the true nature of death but knowing it was a very sad occurrence; the tiny girl had sobbed her heart out for hours as Corn Child watched with great satisfaction.

She moaned once again, her eyes still fused with Cloud Kitten's. Barely had the sound escaped from her mouth before the softhearted girl broke free from the others to run to her side. Swift as a viper, the hand clutching the stony weapon slashed through the air finding its bloody mark in the tender flesh of her young savior's temple.

With beady, feral eyes the woodchuck skittered in front of Black Whirlwind's feet, which were firmly planted beneath the towering pine from where he observed the mourners. Leaning against the trunk, a fur robe slung carelessly over his bare shoulders, the distraught chief's vision was starting to clear. He stepped away from the pool of vomit that lay at his feet. It happened every day now, first he felt the sharp pain in his head followed by extreme nausea.

He'd slipped away from the others, the shrill keening of the mourners more than he could bear. With blurred vision he squinted, hoping he might view, one last time, the little girl he'd admired so much; but her body had already been placed on the platform set several feet above the ground. She would remain there for twelve years before being stripped of her small bones and placed in a common grave surrounded by her favourite foods and toys.

Irrevocably saddened by Cloud Kitten's death, Black Whirlwind had often likened her to Blood Sky; both of them possessed of an innate curiosity and compassion that could only make for greatness. Greater the pain was the fact that Corn Child, his adoptive daughter, was responsible for the girl's demise. Whether accidental or not, he knew she lacked any semblance of social conscience. Her hours spent in the company of Dark Shadow indicated a selfish desire on her part to acquire as much knowledge of the black arts as possible. Both he and Dancing Leaf had cautioned her many times about the dangers connected to witchcraft, but she closed her ears to their warnings.

"Sotsi teyoteryen'thara ne' eh yahonne – It is too dangerous for you to go there," they'd said. Having cautioned her, it wouldn't enter their minds to forbid her visits to the witch since they believed that all must seek their own path, however ominous or sinister that path may be.

He was tired, so very tired. Turning, he slowly shuffled back to the longhouse where he hoped to find some relief in sleep.

With a sigh of resignation Dancing Leaf studied her sleeping husband. His moods, mercurial at the best of times, had lately become very dark, his sleeping patterns erratic and fitful, almost non-existent as a result of his worsening headaches. Adding to his irritation was the fact he'd been too ill to attend the annual assembly in Albany, a momentous affair in which he sat in on council among the high English officials. Feeling fit enough to travel at the time, he'd returned to camp less than two days later, barely able to walk. Of little consolation was the fact that two of the men who generally assisted him in decision-making, had gone in his place. Adding to his misery was the nagging feeling he'd let Blood Sky down.

Accompanying him to Albany since she'd been old enough to talk, her interest and comprehension surrounding the politics of her people was staggering. Her frustration was alleviated somewhat when he promised to take her to the next council meeting at Lake Onondaga, a site central to the entire League, where matters of great importance were discussed among the tribes.

As for his illness, he'd rebuked Bright Star's offer to attempt a cure and she respected his decision much to her dismay. Involving the removal of a section of skull to release the bad spirits, the ancient surgical technique often succeeded as was witnessed by those people in camp whose neck amulet consisted of a chunk of skull from a survivor of the operation.

Lying beside her husband Dancing Leaf prepared to sleep but his constant tossing and turning made it impossible. She'd noticed the lines of fatigue around his eyes growing deeper by the day but when she'd expressed her concern he merely shrugged it off saying, *"Sewatyeren ahsonhtakwekon enwakye'on* – Sometimes I'm awake all night. I can't seem to sleep anymore."

"My husband, can I help you?"

Turning his back to her, he failed to respond but moments later she felt him slip quietly from the bunk and she knew he was sick again. The moment he stepped from the lodge, the nausea overcame him, his projectile vomit splashing the mangy dog guarding the entrance.

They found him at dawn; slumped on the ground, the whining guard dog, rank with the odor of blood and vomit, licking his face. The mournful cry of a loon filled the air

.

CHAPTER EIGHTEEN

He lay on a mound of wolf hides in the center of the funeral lodge, while outside a circle of women, faces painted black in preparation of his death, took up the terrible cries of the death chant. Swaying to the somber beat of the water drums, a number of women had ripped their tunics to the waist, and with exposed breasts and shoulders, slowed their pace, emulating the measured throb of a fading heart.

Dark Shadow, drawn from her obscure lair in the forest where she'd been frantically rising and crouching to the hypnotic rhythm of the drums' primitive beat, suddenly ghosted between Little Current and Cloud Woman, and grasping their hands, stared hypnotically into the raging fire burning within the circle of dancers. The dancing continued, more frantic now – the women's wailing reaching its peak, a sign to Cloud Woman, a Clan Mother, to notify the elders of the other Nations.

Black Whirlwind struggled to draw his final breath, the beating of Mother Earth's heart beneath the ground where he lay, a final comfort. The meager fire beside him cast flickering shards of muted gold onto his ruggedly handsome face, softening the angular features so obviously wracked with pain. A shard of moonlight peeked through the ceiling's smoke-hole, illuminating the masks set high on poles surrounding him, their grotesque misshapen visages frightening enough to ward away the spirits responsible for the dying man's disease. Ritualistic paraphernalia littered the earthen floor – gourd rattles, shiny with crushed shell paint; clay bowls filled with medicinal herbs; eagle feathers and strings of sacred beads.

Covered with a soft deerskin blanket upon which Dancing Leaf had embroidered in beadwork his crest of a bear, Black Whirlwind's impending death had been announced to the elders of the other nations by Cloud Woman, whose duty it was to pass the purple wampum made from quahog shells, over the fire. The elders, in turn, had made arrangements for a speaker to come to the village and comfort the people, Black Whirlwind's family and the Confederate Lords following the Chief's demise.

A string of black wampum lay at Black Whirlwind's feet, available for a Clan member to pick up upon his death before announcing his departure to the entire circle of Confederacy. The smoky atmosphere was pungent with fumes from the heady concoction the shaman blended into Black Whirlwind's feverish temples; the four sacred ingredients were a secret to all but the learned medicine men.

Her braids freed in deference to her husband's momentary departure, Dancing Leaf knelt by his head, softly chanting the death song. Her moist black eyes searched his face as she soothingly wiped small beads of sweat from his forehead with a square of dampened deerskin. Looking past the remote eyes sunk into hollow cheeks, she saw him as she always had – as she did when they first met. It was as though her great and powerful love for him had somehow masked the subtle alterations of age and illness. Absent-mindedly she clasped his gift of raw amethyst dangling between her breasts and closed her heavy lids, recalling with bittersweet fondness, the day he'd returned a full fledged warrior from his five-day fast in the forest to claim her as his bride.

Since she could remember she'd harboured a secret yearning for the handsome young man, but modesty prevailed, and unlike her peers in the village who were often brazenly forward, she felt compelled to cloak her powerful emotions. She behaved in a most demure fashion, particularly while in the company of Black Whirlwind's mother. Traditionally, it was the young man's mother who chose who her son would marry and although by nature Dancing Leaf was sweet and modest, these attributes were magnified while in the presence of the woman who had the power to change her fate.

She'd been more than a little concerned when two of her friends whom she knew adored Black Whirlwind, began to wear their beaded veil, an indication that they were ready for marriage. And during her monthly visits to the *Thundary* – a small hut where women gathered during their monthly flow – she'd overheard a few of the others singing the praises of Black Whirlwind. Even the elders had a great deal of respect for the young man.

"*Tokenhske tsi nihronkwe'tiyo.*" Crippled Sparrow had told her. "He is truly a nice man."

She counted the days until she was ready to don her beaded veil; at least then she'd have a chance.

She'd worn the veil but two days before Black Whirlwind's mother presented her parents with assorted foods and gifts, a gesture of goodwill between the families. She was ecstatic and according to his mother, so was he. A short time later, Black Whirlwind, accompanied by his father, brought more gifts and food for her family. How happy she'd been, her large doe eyes cast downward, afraid to meet his.

They'd been married during the season of Moon of Berries. That afternoon the young couple bid farewell to the crowd of wellwishers before starting out on their *First Time Alone*. Eager to find the perfect spot in which to spend a few carefree days in seclusion, they'd located an idyllic setting, a flower-strewn meadow atop a steep hillock. Making their way to the summit, the precipitous rocks seemed to present little or no problem for Dancing Leaf who bore the extra burden of a weighty backpack. Following close behind lest she lose her footing, Black Whirlwind admirably noted her well-developed, pigeon-toed gait that permitted her to conquer the hilly terrain with apparent ease. His eager eyes were drawn to the exquisite curvatures of her back and waist, visible through the white doeskin tunic as she climbed. He was fascinated by the sensuous rhythm of her buttocks flexing with each step, unable to tear his eyes from the sight of her long, powerful legs as he allowed himself to wonder at the secrets that lay between. Mesmerized by her fluid movements, he nearly lost his footing when a sudden gust of wind directed her scent toward him.

Reaching the meadow at last, he was overcome by desire, mad with longing to become one with the woman he'd dreamt of for months. He relieved her of the clumsy backpack and together they prepared a campfire. The languorous bronze sun ungrudgingly surrendered its spirit leaving a biting chill that failed to penetrate the young couple's heated flush. Spreading a woven rabbit-skin blanket on the ground, he silently beckoned her to join him. Accompanied by the song of crickets, she kneeled beside him and gazed lovingly into his eyes causing him to catch his breath at the sight of the woman-child gazing hungrily toward him.

It was there, cradled in the breast of Mother Earth, that he claimed her, gently and patiently at first, allowing her to be overcome by the great sweeping waves of desire he felt. He was pleased to find she was passionate and able to express her love freely and unabashedly. They made love all night, the small fire showering their bodies in an amber hue. Their mating instincts unfolded endless possibilities until; at last, they rode the highest wave together. As the sun rose, the couple drifted into peaceful sleep, shamelessly entwined by the smoldering fire.

The sole witness to their union, a spotted owl, flew away on silent wings.

The shrill sound of a wing-bone whistle swept her back to the present. Dipping the deerskin cloth into the clay bowl beside her, she wrung it out before placing it at the back of her neck, stiff from long hours tending to her husband's needs. The fire crackled, its puny light casting dancing shadows on the sorrowful couple.

Blood Sky stood at her father's feet, a look of sad acceptance in her large doe eyes. She too was chanting, keeping rhythm with her mother, the primal beat of the shamans' turtle-rattles accompanying their mournful song. Tied to their calves with a leather strip, the rattles had been fashioned from shells of dried box turtles, the plastron and carapace holding pebbles. Clad in a cape and headdress fashioned from the downy feathers of turkey breasts, Maskwa, oldest and most revered of the shamans, stepped forward to begin the recitations of the four prayers corresponding to the four steps of the death rites. Completing the first petition, he shakily crouched over Black Whirlwind before taking a puff from his pipe and blowing it directly onto his head, the seat of his illness. Repeating this act three more times, he consummated the sacred ceremony with four puffs of smoke blown onto the moist brow of the dying man. Bidding the other shamans to gather round him, he then initiated the opening verse of the fortieth and final death chant, a sign to Dancing Leaf that the tormented Chief would soon be at peace. Mother and daughter ceased chanting, and closing their eyes, lowered their heads in unison.

Black Whirlwind was floating, his spirit at one with the wind. All pain had been lifted – all cares and worries transformed like magic into delicate particles of silver that wafted into the ether before dissipating forever. From somewhere in the distance he heard the beating of a shaman's rattle, then, like his pain, it too faded into nothingness. He felt physically powerful and mentally alert; great forceful waves of comprehension swept through him providing him with all answers to every question he had ever pondered. Life's greatest mysteries unraveled before him revealing all manner of secrets. It all seemed so simple and so beautiful. He knew it was there before he saw it. The River of Death formed by the Great Mother's tears as she cries for the departed. All his ancestors before him had crossed it and now it was his turn and he was unafraid. Upon reaching the far side, he glanced down to see two baby turtles, symbols of life everlasting, struggling toward the water's edge. Crouching forward, he cupped them in his hand and gently placed the tiny creatures into the silver liquid. About to stand, he caught a glimpse of his reflection in the mirrored surface of the water. Staring back at him was a youthful warrior, a young man in his prime. Black Whirlwind understood and was content to make his way toward the lush forest in the distance, a forest he knew was filled with a multitude of game.

As custom dictated, the Chief's body, while still warm, was redressed in traditional buckskin garb prior to the ceremony of the *Taking Away of the Horns*, a ritual wherein a visiting Chief of another nation removes the horns of the deceased before hanging them on the wall. A symbolic emblem of power, the horns had been fashioned from antlers to be placed upon the head of Black Whirlwind upon his becoming chief. Decreed by the Great Spirit, *Shonkwya'tihson,* the importance of the ritual was so great as to have been stated in the Iroquois Constitution of Confederacy.

The message of the dead Confederate Lord was then taken across the fire, his sachem name adopted by the soon-to-be newly elected Chief.

Retrieving the small knife from the deerskin pouch, Dancing Leaf reached up and deftly grasped her long braid. Severing it at the nape of her neck, she solemnly placed it across her deceased husband's chest. Maskwa then placed a cold, flat rock in her hands, prompting her to vacate her position at the head of her deceased husband before carrying out the next phase of responsibility common to widows of the tribe. Kneeling on the ground a few feet away, she placed the rock on the ground, and wiping a tear from her eye, untied her medicine pouch to retrieve an angry looking jagged stone. Placing her left hand on the rock's smooth surface, she brought the stone down firmly with her right hand, the swift impact designed to sever her little finger from its hold. Wincing in pain, she realized the cartilage was still attached and with a deep breath, brought the stone down again and still again until the finger lay separate from her hand. Leaning forward with a glowing stick in his hand, Maskwa pressed the searing piece of wood against the open wound to stop the flow of blood, then picking up the lifeless finger from where it lay in a scarlet pool, tossed it carelessly into the fire before vacating the lodge to inform the waiting crowd of their Chief's death. A wolf howled in the distance, his sorrowful cry rising above the shrill yelps of the mourners.

CHAPTER NINETEEN

"Akwah ken' nikariwehs yakohententyonh – Corn Child has been gone a long time now. Where do you think she is?" asked Little Current.

Corn Child was nowhere to be found. As far as anyone could recall she'd last been seen stirring the fire in the lodge. It was uncharacteristic of her not to return to her bunk at night regardless of her whereabouts during the day. Fears of a wolf attack were ruled out following the reassurances of the designated search party. Unbeknownst to the people, the rebellious girl was on her way to Ville Marie in the company of Lucien LaRoche, an unlicensed fur trader with whom she'd been secretly consorting with since their chance meeting a few days previous.

The day had been born amidst distant rumbles in the sky; the reverberating threats of thunder reminiscent of a drumbeat. Attracted to the scent of the deer carcass suspended from a makeshift rack, a cloud of buzzing flies hovered above the grubby handful of men gathered by the river. The broad shoulders of Lucien LaRoche strained the back of his fringed jacket as he grasped the nape of the animal's neck before plunging the knife into the lower jaw, swiftly and deftly slashing forward. The dark red heart and liver would later be tossed into rapidly boiling water to which back fat had been added. A few of the men engaged in a game of dice while the others sat around whining about their empty stomachs.

The sound of a woman's voice prompted the men to turn their heads in unison. Grumbling loudly to herself as she returned from the river where she'd fetched some water, Corn Child lugged the tightly woven basket precariously in her grip. Empty stomachs forgotten, the men stared, mouths agape. It had been weeks since they'd seen a female and the sight of this young woman was a godsend. Whispering and tittering like young boys, they ogled the girl with ravenous eyes.

Without warning, Lucien broke free from the others and, hustling in her direction, sidled up to Corn Child to relieve her of her burden. Startled, she released her grip on the handle, dousing them both in a torrent of icy water, a scene that prompted his comrades to roll on the ground with laughter.

"That should cool you off Lucien!" yelled Normand, a lecherous fellow with yellowed teeth worn to a nubbin, giving him a most comical appearance.

"Bring her to me and I will dry her clothes by the fire," he cried out in jest.

Called *"coureurs de bois"* or *runners of the forest*, Lucien, Normand and their companions were unlicensed traders. The majority of them were half-breeds who made an illicit living bartering the vital suppliers of fur with the natives; an activity, according to the French government, allowed to be carried out by licensed traders only. Established merchants, Ville Marie authorities and royal officials frowned upon those colonists who chose to abandon the tight agricultural colony on the St. Lawrence to trade in native territory, and as a result, ordered them to be whipped and branded for a first offence, and sentenced to a lifetime of slavery on the galleys of the Mediterranean if caught a second time.

The majority of them, lured by the desire for adventure, exploration and wealth, had left behind wives and families. It was not unusual for them to have a native wife in every camp, hence the religious sector postulated that they were debauching the natives, as well as endangering their own souls. Intendent Benoit estimated that at least eight hundred men or forty per cent of the adult male population of New France had taken to the woods. The *coureurs des bois*, aware that the exceptional quality of the Canadian beaver was in great demand in the principal countries of Europe, particularly by those companies who secured monopoly over it, could barter a superb pelt from the natives for no more than a needle or looking glass. Their profits sometimes reached a thousand per cent.

Momentarily shocked into silence by the icy water, Lucien burst out laughing, a deep, throaty laugh emphasizing strong white teeth. Though by nature Corn Child was completely self-absorbed; as a female she found it difficult not to admire his good looks.

"Pardon moi." he uttered, half whispering, as he was so embarrassed.

She couldn't have been happier. He was French! She wasn't unfamiliar with the language having heard Claude utter those words from time to time. From as far back as she could remember, Claude had insisted she acquire the basics of her mother tongue lest one day she return to her people. He'd even told her that her real name was Eve, having gleaned the information from Jacque on their trek home that fateful night. If Jeanette had given birth to a son, he'd told her, his name was to have been Evan. Claude had been a patient teacher to the stubborn girl who, despite her complaints, had succeeded to master a number of French words. She never could have imagined how grateful she'd be for those tedious lessons.

Nor was she unfamiliar with fur traders, having seen them in the village bartering for pelts. From what she understood, the majority of them were from Ville Marie, her home. Her cunning mind raced with possibilities. This handsome stranger could aid in her exit from this mundane existence – perhaps even introduce her to the French society Claude had told her about. Though she'd been free to leave for years, the opportunity never arose until now.

Coyly gazing up at him, she made no attempt to continue her trek up the hill, choosing instead to remain where she stood. He turned his head, eager to see if his friends were still peeping at them through the trees. Almost effeminately handsome, his thick blonde hair was knotted at the nape of his neck in a queue. He focused his gaze on her then looked away. There'd been a hint of playful deviousness in his eyes and she couldn't help but notice his muscular arms and shoulders. As for Lucien, he was curious about this white girl dressed in buckskins. Ordinarily a cheeky individual, he found himself speechless, dividing his time between peeking over his shoulder to see if the others were still studying his progress and stomping on an imaginary bug beneath his feet. Tilting his head slightly, he looked directly into her green eyes, and was struck by the gold flecks sparkling from within.

"I am Lucien," he muttered, his voice barely audible. "What is your name?"

"My real name is Eve," she said proudly, "but the savages call me Corn Child."

And so it began. He walked with her toward the outskirts of her village. The short conversation was strained, particularly on Lucien's part, as he was smitten with her. Attempting to make small talk, he mumbled something about the beautiful white dogwood blossoms and was embarrassed when she didn't respond. The truth was, Corn Child was immune to embarrassment and cared little what anyone thought.

She did care however, if he was from Ville Marie. Acting as nonchalant as possible, she inquired as to where he called home. She could barely contain her excitement when he informed her he was indeed from Ville Marie and planned to return there as soon as possible.

"And what about you?" he asked. "Is this your place of birth?"

In a flash she poured out her story of captivity and misery in the village, resorting to a dramatic form of sign language when at a loss for the proper French word. While imparting her bogus existence of drudgery, disrespect and torturous days spent as a captive of the Mohawks, a stream of fake tears flowed from her eyes; a ruse she'd perfected as a young girl. Her towering fabrications moved Lucien powerfully. A man of compassion, he wrapped his arms around her in a display of comfort, the very gesture she'd hoped for. She had him right where she wanted him. Releasing his hold on her, he led her to a stand of trees just outside the village. Lying on a mat of enormous ferns, a once proud tree that had been felled by lighting caught his eye. Squatting upon the trunk, Lucien bade her sit with him. In doing so she rested her head on his shoulder, sobbing at various intervals for effect. Gently placing his hand beneath her chin, he raised her face to meet his own. Swept away by what he thought was her vulnerability; he placed a soft kiss upon her forehead, holding her even closer.

At seventeen, Corn Child was inexperienced in the ways of romance and though innately incapable of caring for anyone but herself, feigned attraction to entice him even further. Though most girls in the village had husbands by the time they were her age, she'd never entertained the idea of marrying a savage, nor would any of them have been interested. Lucien, at age twenty-six, had secured a couple of wives from different tribes. None however, had left him feeling so vulnerable as this white captive.

He playfully tugged on one of her beaded earrings causing her to smile despite herself. Her formerly pouting mouth had transformed into the most captivating smile he'd ever seen. Her small white teeth were perfectly even, complimenting a straight well-formed nose. Smitten, he brushed the side of her face with his large hand, his eyes locking with hers. Lowering his head to kiss her, Corn Child hesitated, her feminine wiles impressing upon her the necessity to hold back if she was to see him again.

Breaking free from his arms she exclaimed, "I must return now. They'll be needing the water."

"Will I see you again? Will you come back tomorrow?" Lucien pleaded.

'*Nothing could hold me back.*' she thought to herself.

"I'll do my best Lucien. If I can get away I'll meet you here at sunrise."

Once more he embraced her. She could feel him trembling. Breaking free she said quietly, "Tomorrow Lucien – I'll see you here tomorrow."

The fog was closing in on the shoreline as he watched her walk toward the village. He silently prayed she would hold true to her promise to meet him again. He didn't sleep that night, so powerfully drawn was he to revisit the area where he'd held her in his arms, as though her very essence permeated the atmosphere. He was completely absorbed by her.

Corn Child on the other hand, slept like a baby knowing that her time spent with her captors was to be short lived. It wouldn't be hard to convince Lucien to take her back to Ville Marie – that was obvious. As to what transpired after that she cared little as long as she was away from the people she so despised.

He was waiting for her at sunrise the following day after having spent the night in anticipation of her arrival. A column of smoke from the direction of her village told him the women were up preparing the morning meal. He saw her in the distance walking toward him. The very sight of her prompted his heart to pound deep within his chest. Closer now, he noticed she was barefoot and unlike the long skirt she'd worn the previous day, she sported a short doeskin skirt displaying magnificent legs. Her sandy-coloured hair fluttered in the gentle breeze as though beckoning to him. He was speechless and couldn't believe his eyes when she raised her arms toward him in greeting. Unable to control himself, he ran toward her, eager to feel her body against his. They embraced and she could feel his tears of joy on her cheek as he buried his face in her hair. Together they fell to the ground. He took her there, under the shadow cast by a big oak tree. So caught up in his own passion, Lucien failed to notice her silence and lack of ardor. She lay beneath him, scheming, congratulating herself for having snared the perfect vehicle for her trip back to Ville Marie. Only when he pierced her virginity did she cry out, a cry Lucien mistook for passion.

And so it was they met every day. She was overjoyed when Lucien asked if she would return to Ville Marie with him. *"Je prie de vous de reourner avec moi a Ville Marie ou vous appartenez. Je ne puis pas soutenir pour vous laisser ici. Parole vous reviendrez avec moi pour satisfaire* – I beg of you to return with me. I can't bear the thought of leaving you here!"

Feigning a thoughtful demeanor she hesitated a moment or two before agreeing to join him on the trip back to her place of birth.

"Oui – Yes," she said with more force than intended.

Tearing her gaze from his to lower her eyes for fear he'd read the deceit in them she whispered, "I too want to be with you forever."

As they planned their voyage together, Lucien cautioned her that although convincing the others to take a woman with them might be difficult he was sure they'd agree once informed she was a French captive.

"Once they meet you my love, they will be unable to reject you," he prophesied. And agree they did.

The following day Lucien brought her to the campsite to introduce her to his companions.

"Whoo-hee, regardez!" cried Lawrence; the youngest of the group at age seventeen. "Look at that!"

Lucien and Corn Child were treading cautiously down the hill toward the campsite. It was warm for late September, allowing Eve to wear only a skirt and leggings tied at the knee. When she came into view, the men, who'd been lounging about the camp, began to kiss the air in her direction. Sitting cross-legged under a tree several feet away, Normand dropped the whittling he'd been concentrating on to gawk at Eve. With slacken jaw agape; he was unable to tear his eyes away from her naked breasts.

"Mon Dieu." he whispered to himself, his jaw dropping even lower.

"Bonjour." cried out Corn Child, waving cheerfully to the group who were mesmerized by her blatant sexuality. One by one, Lucien

introduced her to the grimy lot, taking special care to establish her name as Eve. She had made it clear to him that, as far as she was concerned, Corn Child was dead and she was glad of it.

Quickly concluding these men were strangers to the art of bathing, she shook their hands, taking care to mask her distaste at being forced to come in contact with their filthy flesh. Inside she recoiled but outwardly she glowed, smiling and laughing with the group. Sensing Lawrence's adolescent crush on her, she sauntered over to where he was sitting on the ground, and bending down further than necessary to display her firm buttocks to the men behind her, tousled the love-stricken boy's greasy hair, her full breasts dangling inches from his disbelieving eyes.

The men's attention was diverted by Louie's uproarious laughter at the site of Normand who hadn't moved a muscle since Eve's arrival, oblivious to the fact his lap was sodden with spittle escaping from the corners of his open mouth.

They broke camp the following morning, heading directly for Ville Marie via the *Riviere de Iroquois.*

The landscape of her life was about to change forever.

CHAPTER TWENTY

Only through her intense yearning to reach Ville Marie did Eve suffer the voyage. Cautioned ahead of time that she'd be expected to carry her share of the load, she'd had no idea what that entailed. Soaked to the skin most of the time from dragging the boat, her feet and legs were cut and bleeding from her attempts to balance on sharp rocks. Not a day passed without suffering the wretched torments of horse flies, gnats, wasps, hornets and the most vicious of all, mosquitos. Her body was covered with tiny stinging bites and her arm ached from continuously waving a handkerchief in failed efforts to deter them from getting into her nostrils and ears.

She suffered terribly. The heat was unbearable at times and they were wont to adopt the Indian practice of protecting their foreheads with wet birch leaves, the soft, spongy texture of the leaves absorbing sweat and keeping them cool. And their incessant singing of French ditties handed down from their ancestors. The repetitious tunes echoed in her head long after the singing had ceased making it all the more difficult for her to sleep at night.

Calculating their distances by the number of pipes they smoked between two stops, they'd occasionally vacate their canoes for a short respite and nourishment. In order to save precious time they'd agreed that fishing was unnecessary, the dried beans, maize flour and biscuits sufficing.

Illiterates all, they left the keeping of the daily journal to Lawrence, who having a basic knowledge of letters, painstakingly attempted to record the day's events. Every evening following their meager meal he'd fetch a chunk of blackened clay burnt from the fire, and with wrinkled forehead and protruding tongue, scribble as best he could, the day's accounts onto a piece of birch bark while the men busied themselves sorting furs or repairing leaks in the boat with a mixture of spruce gum, animal fat and charcoal.

Lucien, sympathetic to Eve's apparent discomfort – the traveling conditions being what they were – was dismayed to find his words of understanding and encouragement being met with bitter evasion. Worse still, she began to balk at the suggestion of intimacy with him, citing weariness and poor diet as the source of her unresponsiveness,

121

an explanation he couldn't refute. Truth be known, she'd come to recognize within herself a natural aversion to the sex act yet fully realized how the mere hint or promise of sexual submission to the male animal granted her untold power, a power she intended to exploit to her best advantage, yielding to a man's desire when and if it could in some way behoove her.

As for unwanted pregnancies she was well armed with the knowledge of which herbs to ingest either to prevent or hasten pregnancy, common medicine to all fertile women in the village of her captors.

He'd known all along Eve was a woman without scruples yet it eluded him that she no longer needed him, her attachment to him merely transitory, a stepping-stone to her own end. Her sudden reticence left him puzzled, giving him the impression his feelings were irrelevant to her until he slowly realized he'd been a mere pawn, a vehicle in which to realize her dream of returning to Ville Marie.

Crimson and gold leaves whirled above the heads of Cloud Woman and Blood Sky while above, skeins of geese made their way southward. Despite the ineffable beauty of the day, Cloud Woman frowned, and with a deep sigh, reached forward to retrieve yet another moccasin from the pile in front of her. Glancing impatiently at Blood Sky who was obviously falling behind on the job, she broke the silence.

"Oksa Ok – Quickly, I want to finish these moccasins before the men come after them!" she scolded.

Her words startled Blood Sky who'd been daydreaming about *Kawera'shatste Karhakonha* – Wind Hawk, an activity she'd been indulging in more and more of late, particularly when involved in such an onerous task as curing moccasins.

Embarrassed, she quickly scooped another handful of lard from the elm container beside her and proceeded to smear the greasy concoction onto the moose skin footwear, a procedure carried out as a precaution against snakebites. The *kwes-kwes* or pig was a natural enemy to the reptile and as a result the men need not fear the chance of a snake biting them whilst wearing the treated moccasins.

The hunters would return soon from the river where they had assembled to paint images of the animals they were going to hunt, breathing life into the herds so there would always be food for the tribe.

It had been two seasons now since Corn Child disappeared and her whereabouts still remained a mystery, though intuitively, Blood Sky knew her adoptive sister still lived, for at night she assailed her in her dreams, laughing and mocking her with an supernatural clarity. At first the dreams occurred every night but lately they'd faded into the background, her dreams of Wind Hawk taking precedence. He not only walked in her dreams, his handsome image filled her day thoughts and she wished with all her heart to become his *tyekaniteronn* – wife.

She found it difficult to focus on the task at hand, particularly since the next pair of moccasins she retrieved from the pile, distinguishable by the simplistic yet eloquent beadwork, happened to be his.

'So like him', she thought. 'A man who seldom speaks unless there is good reason, but when he does, his words are powerful and true.'

Caressing the moccasins as though they were an extension of the man she loved so dearly, she began to reminisce again. As far back as she could remember, there'd been a feeling of reciprocal esteem between them; his very presence had soothed her and his quiet strength assured her all would be well. Compassionate beyond his years toward the other youngsters, he'd helped her immensely, soothing and balancing her emotions, particularly when she was dealing with the constant lies, trickery and deceit doled out by Corn Child. Taken with Wind Hawk as well, Corn Child had tried everything in her power to entice the boy to surrender to her charms. She despised the fact that he treated her with indifference throughout their formative years, going so far as to disregard her offer of pre-marital sex at the tender age of eleven. Despite her seductive failure, she'd recounted, step by step, the details of her supposed sexual romp with Wind Hawk to Blood Sky. Extremely perceptive, even at the age of eleven, Blood Sky knew Corn Child posed no threat, her monstrous little nature too far removed from his ideal.

A band of laughing boys chasing a hare broke her reverie. Smiling to herself, she knew it was just a matter of moments before she'd see him again and her heart beat a little faster.

As for Wind Hawk's feelings toward Blood Sky, at times they were almost stronger than he could bear; her copper-skinned beauty and inner strength drawing him like a magnet. She stood out from the other eligible females in the village, most of them obviously taken with him, their constant flirting and sexual invitations a far cry from Blood Sky whose demeanor was shy to the point of being restrained. He knew he'd have to make his feelings known to her soon lest she be swept away by another, a consideration unfathomable to him.

The sun had almost set by the time they stuffed the last clump of dried moss into the moccasins to keep the men's feet dry. Rubbing her hands into the dewy blades of grass to cleanse them, Cloud Woman lit her carved stone pipe, all the while studying Blood Sky. She knew her young friend was in love. She knew all the signs for she too had once been a young woman in love. Smiling, she reached out to smooth Blood Sky's hair from her eyes.

"Why are you smiling," Blood Sky asked, "Does my hair look that funny?"

"*Kehayarehkwe,*" she responded. I was remembering when I was young and beautiful and so much in love just as you are now." Just then, a boisterous chorus of male voices signaled the men's arrival.

Quickly combing her fingers through her hair, Blood Sky piled it on top of her head before fastening it with a wooden comb she kept in a deerskin pouch tied around her waist. Shaking the bits of earth from her skirt she hastily began to pack the moccasins into the large sack the men had provided.

"*Sago* – Hello, I have come for the moccasins. Are they ready?"

With a start, she spun around to face Wind Hawk who stood there smiling. Riveted to where she stood, she trembled and lowered her eyes for fear he'd see the love in them.

Finally trusting herself to speak, she whispered, "Yes, they are ready."

He was compelled to reach out to gently cup her chin in his hand. Lifting her face upward, he stared deep into her eyes – eyes that spoke of love. In that moment all pretence of mere friendship between them was erased. Words were unnecessary as he wrapped his arms around her and held her close. She buried her face in his bare chest to hide the tears of joy. From the corner of his eye he noticed Cloud Woman gazing in their direction.

Winking saucily at the older woman, he silently mouthed the words, "*Khenoronhkwa* – I love her."

Grasping Blood Sky by the shoulders he stepped back to face her once again.

"*Teyotonhwentsyohon ne aonkyo'tensha,*" he whispered, "I must go to the hunt now." As he leaned forward to kiss her generous lips, Blood Sky glanced nervously toward Cloud Woman. With a knowing smile, the old woman took another puff from her pipe and turned her eyes away.

With unfulfilled longing, Blood Sky watched Wind Hawk walking off among the bending willows until she could see him no longer. She felt as though she were walking on the clouds, so ecstatic and filled with anticipation following the romantic interlude with him. His eyes had spoken of many things his mouth dared not, yet his message was crystal clear, purer somehow. She could think of nothing else. If he'd dominated her thoughts before, he now dominated her very essence. She was speechless, breathless and oh so very, very happy. She had a glow about her, a gentle radiance that failed to go unnoticed by Little Current as they were preparing the evening meal.

"Your soul is smiling my cousin. What wonderful things are you thinking about?" she'd asked with a sly grin.

As though she'd been caught doing something untoward, Blood Sky responded a little too quickly, her tone of voice bordering on guilt.

"Nothing, nothing really. I was just thinking of what a glorious day it is. You know the season of falling leaves has always been my favourite time. I love the colours and gentle breezes. It is surely the most wondrous season of them all, don't you think?"

Feigning a quizzical expression, Little Current replied, "Perhaps it was your meeting with Wind Hawk that brings the smile to your lips. Morning Star and myself were returning from the river when we saw the two of you embracing. She couldn't wait to tell the other women. It appears your love for him is no longer a secret, but tell me Blood Sky, why did you wish to keep it from us in the first place?"

Blood Sky remained silent. How could she tell Little Current it had been for fear of inciting jealousy within the circle of unmarried females in camp that had prompted her silence in regard to Wind Hawk. Had not his name dominated their conversations throughout their adolescent years? She knew full well that every one of her peers had hoped to claim him as her own. As well, she needed time to let the day's events sink in as it all seemed too good to be true and discussing it might, in some way, debase their blossoming relationship.

A calamitous racket followed by a shrill cry cut short their conversation, alerting them to gaze toward its source. The site of Crippled Sparrow sitting amidst a heap of wooden bowls, one of which sat precariously upon her frail head, sent them into uncontrollable gales of laughter. It seems the old woman, wanting to be of assistance, had been carrying the utensils toward the cooking pot when she slipped on the damp grass and fell. Rushing over to help the poor woman up, Blood Sky was grateful the old woman hadn't fractured any bones but even more grateful for the interruption of the conversation she'd been having with Little Current.

Lying in her bunk that night she found it impossible to sleep even though she was mentally exhausted. The sun was rising on the horizon when she finally surrendered to a deep slumber yet, rather than dreaming about Wind Hawk as she'd hoped, she was once again brutally invaded by the image of Corn Child, laughing, taunting and threatening her throughout the night. Weary as she'd been before losing consciousness, she'd had the presence of mind to shift onto her left side, the side that invites dreams of recent and intelligent content as opposed to the right side, guaranteed to conjure up dreams that are inconsequential and ridiculous. Yet somehow during the night she'd shifted onto her back, a position invoking nightmares, and sure enough Corn Child was at the ready, welcoming her with the evil, unearthly laugh she'd become accustomed to in her dreams of the French captive, a cackle that made Blood Sky's stomach churn with fear every time.

As far back as she could remember she'd suffered from night terrors involving Corn Child, but the dreams were somehow different then. In a strange way they now appeared to be morbid extensions of her daily existence rather than condensed snippets of childhood fears and apprehensions as they once were. Following these nightmares, she was compelled to dwell on the content and being proficient in dream interpretation, deemed it futile to seek advice from the elders.

When she concluded her problems with Corn Child were far from over however, she sought counsel from Cloud Woman who verified her interpretation. Together the women had burned sage and praying to the Creator for the soul of Corn Child whom they knew was inevitably doomed by her own hand, made a pact never to mention the dreams again lest the attention afforded them nourish and keep them alive. Blood Sky was at peace with this as she adhered to the creed that evil, no matter how devious its intent, will never overcome good. It was this powerful belief that allowed her to remain strong and virtuous.

Unbeknownst to her however, was the amount of strength she would require throughout the next few years.

CHAPTER TWENTY-ONE

Marjolaine was exhausted. She'd spent the better part of the day scrubbing, dusting and polishing the Governor's formal parlour. Satisfied that all was in order, she'd set about gathering up her cleaning paraphernalia in preparation of vacating the lavish room when her eyes gravitated toward the plush burgundy velvet settee located invitingly beneath the ornate leaded windows. Bathed in a soft glow from the umber sun, the plump cushions beckoned her to rest awhile. With a thud, she let go her cleaning supplies, and making her way across the room, literally dropped onto the warm velvet. Within seconds, she was asleep.

Life had been difficult for her since Ruby's demise some four years previous, Eli having discovered her lifeless body sitting in the old wicker rocking chair in the kitchen, her hand still resting on Napoleon's furry body as he slept. Obligated now to double her workload, the pressure at times seemed intolerable to Marjolaine, though Mercier did eventually make good his promise of hiring more help and, eleven months later, four new chars had been added to the mansion's staff, all eager and ready to begin their daily menial chores. However, it wasn't long before it became obvious that a couple of the so-called domestics had been taken into service more for their expertise in the boudoir than their domestic capabilities.

To make matters worse, the recent barrage of galas in the great house were almost more than she could bear. The majority of these opulent balls were a result of the peaceful alliance with their former enemy, the Mohawk Nation. The natives would arrive at the receptions in full regalia and, though by nature rigid and formal, their natural versatility and intelligence allowed them to swiftly adopt French mannerisms such as kissing the hand of a lady on first meeting – a sight not to be missed by the Governor's guests.

Things had gone well for a while once she'd trained the new chars in their specific duties. She'd had more time to herself, was well rested, and for the first time since she could remember, was beginning to enjoy her life. Then, as luck would have it, two of the girls, upon realizing their duties were to include satisfying Mercier's lust at any given time, stormed out of the mansion in a huff.

How Mercier managed to maintain his stalwart reputation among the other high-ranking officials was something she could only guess at. She prayed daily that the posters she'd pinned to the walls at the local shops, appealing for domestics, would soon be answered.

The resounding tone of the large brass doorknocker woke her with a start. Sitting up, she caught a glance of Claudette scurrying down the hall toward the front entrance.

"Who might that be?" she wondered. Rarely did anyone approach the Governor's front portal without invitation and, if they did, it was of the utmost urgency.

The mouth-watering fragrance of freshly baked apple pies wafted from the kitchen, whetting her appetite and reminding her she hadn't yet had breakfast. Retrieving her cleaning supplies she walked into the hall, nearly tripping Claudette with the birch broom she'd tucked under her arm.

"Who was at the door Claudette?" she asked. "Another peddler?"

"No, it is a girl applying for the domestic's job. Seems like someone finally read your notice. I sent her around to the back so you could interview her. She seems quite strong and able, though her French leaves a lot to be desired."

"Merci Claudette. I'll be there in a few moments."

Marjolaine, like everyone else, thought the world of Claudette. An assiduous woman with a round dimpled face and heart of gold, she'd survived three Mohawk raids in which she'd witnessed the slaying of her family, including her husband of forty-five years. Rather than quashing her will to live, the horrors she'd survived had woven around her a natural integument against all pain and she'd managed to retain a joie-de-vivre of sorts. Animated and jovial, her profound sense of humour, thought by many to be a survival strategy, was unparalleled. She was a marvelous cook, particularly when called upon to organize sumptuous buffets for the visiting Mohawk guests.

Admittedly she and the other chars, bored out of their minds at times with their dreary existence, looked forward to the festivities involving the Indians, particularly when the men brought their women along. These charismatic women with their dusky complexions were the highlight of conversation among the domestics for days following their visits. They were particularly struck by the absence of coquetry among the Indian women, a feminine wile employed by their French sisters, as natural to them as breathing. As for Marjolaine, she looked forward to the end of the day when she could return to the small cabin she shared with Henri, her husband of fourteen years. Situated on the outskirts of the Governor's estate, the cabin was a haven for them, a welcome diversion from the hectic life inside the mansion proper.

Their wedding had been a hasty affair, occurring while the Governor was en route to France. Knowing full well Mercier had designs on Marjolaine, Henri took it upon himself to ensure the ceremony took place as soon as possible following their employer's departure. Ruby and Eli had stood up for them at the ceremony, and though Ruby's mood had been festive, Eli's constant whining and morbid referrals to Mercier's wrath upon his return very nearly ruined the day. As it turned out, Mercier was indeed livid and he would have dismissed Henri on the spot but the thought of Marjolaine leaving his employ prevented him from doing so. In the meantime he'd continue to satisfy his lust with the domestics in his employ who were less then virtuous as well as the various high-society wives who sought momentary diversion.

✠

Eve made her way to the back of the mansion according to Claudette's instructions, pausing every now and again to drink in the magnificent surroundings. The rich architecture of the mansion, offset by sumptuous gardens boasting stone benches and exquisitely sculpted bronze statues left her breathless. The heavenly scent of lilacs permeated the atmosphere. Never in her wildest dreams had she imagined anything so splendid. Growing up as she did amongst the natives, there'd been nothing to compare to this, though Claude had, on occasion, attempted to convey to her the lifestyle of the wealthy French class, but she thought he was merely spinning yarns to entertain her.

The mere sight of such beautiful surroundings excited her, stirring in her a promise or rather a delusion of the grandeur that might one day involve her personally. Possessed of an unnatural love for material things, she had for the past three months, with little else to occupy her time, caroused the local shops, fawning over the latest fashions imported from France, a pastime she never tired of.

Her separation from Lucien, a sordid affair in which he'd found her in the arms of the local blacksmith, allowed her plenty of time for her fashion excursions. She, of course, had blamed Lucien for her indiscretions, his extended trips to the native camps in search of furs leaving her lonely and desolate. As for Lucien, he'd been forced to confront what he'd suspected for some time now. Eve was a capricious, fickle trollop, an opportunist, incapable of being faithful to any man. In the future he'd limit himself to his native wives secured safely at the various villages where he traded for furs, leaving Eve, once and for all. Since they'd arrived in Ville Marie eight months previous she'd given him no indication of wanting to be intimate or loving, always ready with an excuse, however lame. But despite it all, he'd remained faithful to her, justifying her behaviour on the grounds that her new surroundings were strange and she needed time to adjust.

On her own now and forced to seek employment, Eve would leave their tiny shack every morning and head for the village proper where she'd spend untold hours strolling the wooden walkways lined with small shops where she'd enquire as to whether or not she could be of help. She never tired of the sights and sounds: soldiers in white uniforms gartered to the knees; ladies in hooped-skirts with powdered hair and lace bonnets; transients hovering close to the shops with hats extended in hopes of a meager donation; working classes with their hair in little pigtails and short skirts and the clip-clop of horse drawn wagons, their shafts groaning and squeaking.

She was rather surprised at the number of settled natives residing in Ville Marie and though they were rarely seen in town, she felt a twinge of homesickness for the village of her captors upon encountering these natives on occasion, a sensation she marked up to being overtired and slightly anxious. Entering a shop one afternoon, the door was held open for her by a young native girl who smiled up at her. Eve glared angrily at the youngster before turning her head in dismissive contempt, refusing to enter until the baffled child, uttering an obscure apology, rambled quickly away.

Touring the shops, she'd longingly covet the abundance of garments, foods and knick-knacks. And so it was she happened upon Marjolaine's poster while browsing through the local milliners. Claude's insistence regarding her French lessons was coming in handy at last.

131

Claudette was waiting for her as she approached the back door.

"Come in and make yourself comfortable. Mistress Marjolaine will join us in a moment," she chirped, attempting to keep the mood light for fear of conveying to Eve, the dire need for another pair of helping hands. "Would you care for a nice piece of fresh apple pie and a cup of tea?"

"Oh yes!" Eve replied, perhaps a little to quickly as she had been numb from hunger for a few days now. The very thought of sinking her teeth into the source of the heavenly aroma pervading the kitchen was almost more than she could bear.

"Is Marjolaine here, Claudette?"

Claudette turned toward the door where the obviously agitated Mercier stood. Clad in his saffron taffeta morning robe and clutching a fistful of papers, his eyes lit on Eve who was in the process of removing her moccasins. Quickly stepping back into the hall lest the young woman see him in such disarray, he motioned to Claudette to follow him.

"Send Marjolaine to my office immediately. I need help with these blasted invitations to next month's gala." Then, as if an afterthought, he continued, "Who is the young woman Claudette, is she a friend of yours?"

"No Sir," she replied while swiping a fly from the apple pie she was about to slice. "Her name is Eve, Sir. She is applying for the job as domestic. Marjolaine will be here in a moment to interview her."

The wheels in Mercier's head spun wildly. The girl was a not only deliciously young but she was a real looker. Extremely rough around the edges and obviously a stranger to Ville Marie, her coarse, almost untamed demeanor suggested an interesting challenge regrettably absent in his present mistress.

"She's hired, and don't forget to send Marjolaine to my office immediately!" Returning to his private office he happened upon Marjolaine in the hall.

"Follow me," he ordered. "We have work to do. And don't worry about the new girl – she's hired. Come quickly!" he squealed, shoving her away from the kitchen door.

"Just let me leave my cleaning supplies here," she said curtly before dropping everything at the entrance of the kitchen door, catching but the slightest glimpse of the new char who stood at the far end of the room. A sudden anxiety swept over her, a vague terror and sense of apprehension she couldn't understand. She turned and followed Mercier to his office.

CHAPTER TWENTY-TWO

A warm rain fell steadily as Blood Sky wormed her way through the horde of villagers: the urgency for solitude and spiritual regeneration guiding her toward the forest. Her intrinsic spirituality required consistent nourishment and only through short periods of solitude, silence and prayer was she able to reconnect with her inner self and her Creator. She had been preoccupied with dreams of Wind Hawk, counting the days until he returned to make her his wife. Also, the events of the last few days had taken its toll on her as well as the other villagers who were initiating the ancient celebration of the *Feast of the Dead*, a grim ritual that is guaranteed to leave in its wake, an overall mood of sadness and melancholy.

Executed every ten to twelve years, the sacred rite involved the retrieving of corpses from their temporary resting places of scaffolds and graves, whereupon they were placed in a common burial pit. Those individuals from neighboring villages who wished their dead to be buried, as well those who wished to honor the ceremony, were invited to attend. Although she'd been too young to recall with clarity the last such ceremony, she still remembered the hideous cries and wailing of the people as they tearfully carried out the obligatory task in respect to members of their families who'd crossed the great River of Tears.

"Blood Sky, can we come with you?"

Startled, she looked down into the eager face of Little Wolf, his small hand clinging to that of his younger sister, Walks With It, who was struggling madly to break his grip. A sudden pang of sadness ripped through Blood Sky's heart for she knew it was just a matter of time before they'd be scraping away the flesh still clinging tenaciously to the bones of their parents, a distasteful but necessary part of the age-old custom.

Not wanting the children to see the sadness in her eyes, she reached out and tousled their hair.

"I must be alone for awhile, but when I return I will have a special gift just for you!"

"*Aaaii, atatawi, atatawi* – A present just for us?" Little Wolf cried out, freeing his sister's tiny hand before fleeing back toward camp to share his good fortune with the other youngsters, his chubby little ward following on his heels. Their enthusiasm dissolved her tears.

Moments later she stood at the base of her beloved tree. Having been struck by a thunderous clap of lightning years ago, the tree had survived, a healer in its own right. Extending her arms, she warmly embraced the giant cedar, kneading her cheek gently against its craggy bark. Within seconds the familiar waves of tranquility caressed her rigid spine, soothing and releasing all tension from her body. Loosening her hold slowly, she arranged herself on the ground, and pressing her back against the charred and most powerful area of the sacred tree, contemplated the disappearance of Corn Child. Her instinct told her that all was well with her adoptive sister; that her sudden departure from the village had in fact been a carefully executed plan. She also knew intuitively that they'd meet again, though when and under what circumstances remained a mystery to her.

A gentle breeze from the river swirled about her, it's relaxing quality urging her eyes to close for a brief moment of silent prayer, a prayer for strength.

With a fresh lightness in her step, she made her way back to the village where the ceremony was under way. Her mother was somber, almost gloomy, for the time had come to bid a final farewell to her departed husband, Black Whirlwind. Even the familiar chatter of the women, busying themselves preparing food for the great feast that would follow the common burial, failed to lift her spirits. The men had long since began the task of retrieving bodies of the departed from their temporary resting places to be transported back to the village. The people had donned their best outfits in preparation of the sacred ceremony; their garments colorfully decorated with porcupine quills and shell beads, a few of them depicting pictures of small animals, actualized by dipping a thin stick into a mixture of fish oil to which was added ochre. Earrings fashioned from animal teeth, bone and feather complimented the women's necklaces that had been hammered and cut from European coins. A few of the younger women had woven flowered wreaths into their hair.

Mimicking the beat of a fading heart, the slow pounding of a water drum alerted everyone to the ceremonial circle. Placing a trembling hand on her mother's arm, Blood Sky whispered, "It is time. We must see to father."

Walking from their cooking fire they joined the other women somberly heading toward the area where their deceased relatives were neatly laid out in rows. Once there, the drums ceased, a sign that the great Sachem White Thunder would soon vacate the small crude hut in the distance.

Having entered the tiny dwelling two days previous to sing the proper songs and prepare himself spiritually for the solemn ceremony at hand, White Thunder gently replaced the sacred eagle feather he'd worn for two days back inside the deerskin bag. An extremely respected individual and one of the few men privy to the necessary rituals required to appease the eagle's spirit, White Thunder had fasted while singing the necessary songs for days. Laying a fresh round bowl of corn and venison in front of the deerskin bag, he uttered a final prayer, and with his typical staggard gait, vacated the hut to begin the initial duty of unwrapping the hundreds of corpses awaiting him.

Briefly addressing the people, he approached the first corpse and proceeded to deftly peel away the aged layers of skin. Sporadic cries rippling from the crowd accompanied his task as, one by one, each family came forward to reclaim their own. Thus began the terrible responsibility of scraping and removing all remaining flesh from the bones of their loved ones. Muffled sobs graduated quickly to eerie shrill screams, the hideous noise blanketing the chanting of medicine men and frightening the children.

The overall mayhem took Blood Sky back to her sixth summer, the summer she'd first been exposed to the somber custom of burying the dead. She recalled how the unearthly wails had threatened to shatter her tender heart until furtively, she'd found refuge behind a great gnarled tree, and huddling beneath it, loudly voiced her fears to the Creator. Having slipped away from the others to relieve herself in the bushes, Cloud Woman had overheard the tiny girl's pleas. Adjusting her skirt, she'd approached the child who sat hunched against the tree, her small hands clasped tightly over her ears to block out the plaintiff cries. Squatting beside her, the heavy woman gently freed one ear by clasping the tiny hand in her big warm fist.

"*Wa'kerennhane,*" she said. "I got used to it; you will too. When I was a little girl, I too was frightened and distraught in the midst of such gloom, but I've since learned it is necessary to the balance of our souls. Just as good balances evil, and age balances wisdom, so must death balance life. Pleasant experiences are necessary to balance out the unpleasant; for only when our souls are in balance will our lives be tranquil."

The explanation had made sense to Blood Sky despite her tender age. She'd hugged Cloud Woman for helping her understand and the two of them returned to camp hand in hand. In the years to follow, Cloud Woman would become her closest friend and confidant. It was she who would teach Blood Sky the importance of learning from all animals: patience from the spider, curiosity from the mouse and from the panther she'd learned to jump. More importantly, she explained to the young girl that silence is the voice of the Creator or provider.

"Remember little one," she'd said, "In silence we receive our most important messages for in silence we hear with our hearts and not our ears."

Piled neatly in front of her, the moistened bones of Black Whirlwind glistened from the steady stream of tears flowing from Dancing Leaf's eyes. His death had left her with an aching gap in her soul and Blood Sky longed to comfort her, but knowing the necessity of mourning, held back. She'd been taught that grieving was designed to cleanse the soul of accumulated grief that might otherwise simmer, resulting in emotional sickness.

Reaching down to retrieve a large bone, Dancing Leaf paused, withdrawing her hand as if physically incapable of touching the remains of the man she'd loved more than life itself. Once more she reached forward and once more her empty hand returned to her lap. A fresh flood of tears escaped from her eyes. The haunting melody of a cedar flute drifted from deep within the forest.

Focusing her attention once more on Little Wolf whom she'd been assisting, Blood Sky observed his small hands neatly placing the bones of his parents in a large fur bundle while his sister, lulled to sleep by the repetitious chanting in the background, lay curled up

beside him, her corn husk doll clutched tightly to her breast. A cloud
of turkey buzzards loomed above the brilliant orange maples, the
rhythm of their wings in tune with the shamans' rattles.

The last to finish, Little Raven rooted among the fast dwindling
heap of furs, searching for a pelt small enough to wrap the miniature
bones of the still born infant she'd lost two moons before. Clutching
her small bundle, she joined the trail of people hiking toward an
immense area that had been cleared within the forest. Ahead of her,
borne on stretchers by family members, were the corpses of those
who'd just recently crossed the River of Tears.

As they entered the burial area, a light rain began to fall on the sad
procession, causing the numerous fires encircling the area to hiss and
spit. A group of children sat cross-legged around a high scramble of
sticks, peeling the bark to prevent the fires from smoking. Scattered
on the ground beside them were baskets containing the sacred
tobacco; boxes of pipes; nested baskets; piles of blankets and furs;
round hand and water drums, and other paraphernalia required for the
ceremony.

Inside the circle of fires yawned a freshly dug pit about thirty feet
wide by ten feet deep, surrounded by a scaffold upon which were
situated a number of cross-poles. By means of ladders, all bundles
were soon hung from the cross-poles under the direction of White
Thunder who stood upon the scaffold, strings of wampum beads
dangling from his topknot. One had only to view the number of
bundles of bones to realize the severity of the *O'seronni's* strange
diseases. Never in the memory of the *Onqwanonhsioni* had so many
died from unnatural causes. The wind spirit moaned through the trees.
A young mother berated her child for spitting into the fire, an act
rarely, if ever, seen among The People.

The great booming voice of White Thunder commanded their
attention. All eyes lifted toward the top of the scaffold. He began his
discourse wherein he extolled the virtues of the departed. He called
upon their friends and relatives to recall and even imitate them in
some way. Meanwhile, deep inside the pit, a group of men busied
themselves lining the earth with beaver skins and robes, offerings for
the dead – then they lay upon it a bed of tomahawks, beads,
necklaces, bracelets of wampum, and other things given by relations
and friends. All corpses that remained whole were handed down to

the twelve braves who were responsible for neatly arranging them prior to covering them with furs and layers of tree bark, earth and large pieces of wood.

By the time the funeral games started the sun was waning, causing thick veins of diffused light to creep slowly over the participants, bathing them in a strange reddish hue. Everyone participated in the games – the winners receiving prizes given in honor of the dead. Tired and restless, scores of youngsters slept on their mother's laps. It was nearly dark before the multitude repaired to the village for the night, the final stages of the ceremony to be completed in the morning.

The sun was still sleeping the next day as, amid discordant shouts, all remaining bones were thrown into the pit. Arranging them with long poles, the men had summoned the villagers to hurl assorted logs, earth and stones inside as a finale to the ceremony proper. They then returned to the village in anticipation of the feast.

Spirals of smoke from the cooking fires snaked their way skyward. Great platters of venison, moose, caribou, beaver, squirrel, rabbit, hare on a spit, partridge, wild turkey, bustard, geese, pigeon, snipe, salmon, eel, haddock, and sturgeon had been laid out for the famished crowd. The children, delighted to see such a variety of food, put behind them the glum events of the morning and ran to fill their plates. Everyone indulged in the banquet before the dancing began.

CHAPTER TWENTY-THREE

Marjolaine wasn't the least bit surprised when Mercier suggested to her that Violet, one of the chars with which he'd been dallying of late, vacate her room next to his quarters thereby making room for Eve. She stifled a giggle at his failed attempt to imitate someone who actually cared for Eve's welfare when he mumbled somewhat sheepishly, "The new girl might feel safer if she knows there's a man closer to her during the night."

'Oh yes', Marjolaine thought. 'She'll feel really safe. I wonder how she'd feel if she knew there was a secret passage from Mercier's apartment into the bedroom where he's installing her?' She found it even more ludicrous that Mercier thought he was pulling the wool over her eyes.

Upon being told she was to immediately vacate the magnificent suite in favour of the squalid closet sized bedroom with a hidden entrance off the main lobby, Violet, a competent housekeeper, albeit slow-witted, burst into tears. Lacking the common sense to know Mercier had used her, she was confused and hurt beyond description. Marjolaine knew only too well the futility of attempting to intercede on Violet's behalf; the best she could do was try comforting the wistful girl before packing her few belongings in a portmanteau, making sure to leave behind, according to Mercier's instructions, all the gowns and finery she'd acquired since being in his employ.

Ushering her from the luxurious quarters, Marjolaine felt helpless as Violet wailed inconsolably, retching between sobs. A naïve girl completely devoid of malice, Violet had truly believed the Governor had loved her; after all, hadn't he told her that time and time again as he'd entered her bed?

Precariously leading Violet to the fake door leading to the minuscule room that was musty and dark as a tomb, Marjolaine hesitated before entering, visions of the room's horrific disarray and filth giving her pause. Stepping into the room, she placed a small candle in the ancient holder on the wall, nearly jumping out of her skin at the startling crash of thunder followed by a flash of lightning that illuminated a horrendous spider clinging to its web just inches from her face. Void of all furnishings save a tiny dresser; its missing leg causing it to lean haphazardly to one side; and a naked mattress strewn in the corner, the room was bare. With no beneficence of latrine, Violet's eyes rested on an aged, badly stained chamber pot that was occupied by a large half rotted rat.

Overcome with sympathy for the jilted girl Marjolaine, attempting to make her voice as cheerful as possible said, *"Fretta de do pas ma petite, vous viendrez et rester avec moi er Henri jusqu' a nous nettoyons et joli cet endroit vers le haut* – Don't worry my pet, you will come home with Henri and me until we can clean and pretty this place up. Come now and have a cup of tea and some of Claudette's fresh baked cookies and rest awhile. The day has been very emotional for you but things will soon look up."

Too overcome with sorrow to speak, Violet reached out, her wistful eyes damp with tears, and clinging to Marjolaine, turned her attention toward the filthy window and lowered her head.

Thinking it best to leave her alone for awhile, Marjolaine returned to the kitchen to find Claudette arranging hydrangeas in a vase while Eve, attempting to demonstrate her expertise in the kitchen, busied herself paring vegetables for dinner. Again, Marjolaine experienced the alien sensation, the wild thumping of her heart. Passing it off as being overtired, she bid Eve follow her to her new lodgings, but not before Claudette enquired as to why Marjolaine was looking paler than usual. Before Marjolaine could respond, a pitiful wail emanated from the room where Violet had been set up. The agonizing tone was chilling.

Turning on her heel, Claudette dropped the flowers before scurrying off to comfort Violet while Eve, paying little attention to the girl's obvious misery, deduced that Violet was very much loved. Not remotely sympathetic under any circumstances she was impervious to the women's concern, labeling them as sentimental fools. Removing her apron she approached Marjolaine who sat at the table, her hands covering her face in sorrow and frustration.

"Bien, allez-vous me montrer la suite ou pas — Well, are you going to show me the suite or not?" she inquired in a most insolent tone of voice.

✠

Overcome by the posh ambiance of the suite, Eve was exalted. The spacious rooms were meticulously furnished. The bed; an enormous canopied four-poster, adorned with carved angels and bedecked with rose satin coverings; had been placed royally upon an exquisite oak dais and was the focal point of the oversized room. Having thus far been exposed only to the bare essentials in life, Eve thought she must be dreaming. Gasping audibly she carelessly tossed her threadbare valise onto the lush carpet and slowly walked toward the superb piece of furniture with outstretched arms.

"Is this really where I am to sleep?" she asked in amazement.

As if on cue, Mercier strode into the room, walking brusquely past Marjolaine, and with a move of considerable cunning, wrapped his arm around Eve's shoulders in a most familiar manner, his long delicate fingers resting just inches from her bosom.

"Is the room to your liking my dear?" he whispered, grinning perversely.

"Oh yes, it is so beautiful I shall never want to leave it!" she uttered in the most innocent manner she could conjure while thinking to herself, 'and I'm sure you'll see to it that I don't.'

With the cunning of a predator, Eve knew exactly what the Governor was after and she would see to it that he got it. Though she found him slightly abhorrent and far too feminine, she was delighted at the turn of events, her mind racing with possibilities. Her instincts also cautioned against being too easy as he gave the impression of one who lived to manipulate defenseless young women. Feigning a shy smile, she looked at him with reverence before turning her eyes to the floor, hoping to give the impression she was too timid to prolong eye contact.

"Now you get settled in your new surroundings my dear, tomorrow is time enough to begin your household duties."

Glancing at Marjolaine he said, in a most churlish manner, "Marjolaine will bring you a fresh pot of tea."

Marjolaine was livid, and it wasn't until she left the room that she realized she'd driven her nails through the flesh of her hands in frustration. She couldn't wait to get to the kitchen, to escape the negativity that besieged her while in the presence of Eve, a powerful sense of maliciousness or obscure memory she was unable to clarify. Nearing the bottom of the stairs, her ears were assaulted by the sepulchral howling emanating from Violet's room but there was something else amiss. The cries were not Violet's, they were Claudette's. Running toward the source of the wailing, she abruptly halted at the door of the grimy area.

Kneeling on the floor, hands clasped as in prayer, Claudette was sobbing her heart out, the lifeless body of Violet hanging from a rafter directly above her.

Unfettered by the news, apart from the morbid satisfaction he felt knowing the girl truly loved him, Mercier ordered Henri to immediately transport the girl's body to her parent's cottage on the outskirts of Ville Marie, while in the same breath reminding Marjolaine that Eve was still awaiting her tea.

Moments later, with shaking legs, Marjolaine carried Eve's tray upstairs to her suite, stopping for short periods to lean against the banister and catch her breath. Knocking at the door to no avail she let herself in and placed the tray on the night table. Turning to leave, her nostrils were assaulted by the heavy scent of bath oil permeating the room. The splashing of water told her Eve was bathing.

"Marjolaine, is that you?" Eve called from the cabinet de toilet.

Tempted to ignore her and just slip out the door, she thought better of it. After all, she'd just have to come back. Of that she was sure.

"Yes, it's me, Marjolaine," She shouted back. "Your tea is here."

"I don't want tea I want some towels and I can't reach the wardrobe from the tub. Fetch them for me will you?"

Passive by nature, and slow to anger, Marjolaine slammed her fist on the table, very nearly upsetting the tea. There was a dead girl downstairs; the Governor's Wednesday night soiree was this evening and she hadn't even started to prepare. Now this impertinent little trollop had the temerity to expect her to comply to her every whim! Taking a deep breath she made the sign of the cross before entering the cabinet de toilette. A billow of steam rising from the gigantic four-clawed tub faintly obscured her vision through the French doors, but she could make out the figure of Eve climbing from the tub, muttering something about the lazy char in the other room who couldn't even fetch her towels.

"That's it!" said Marjolaine aloud turning to leave, then, as an afterthought she decided to berate Eve for her haughty behaviour. Spinning around to open the French doors, her mouth open in preparation of telling Eve where she could go, Marjolaine was struck dumb.

The last thing she saw before fainting was the mark behind the girl's naked thigh, a birthmark in the shape of a serpent.

✠

Henri's mood was as dismal as the day – an unnerving bleakness hung over him. The snorting of the horses alerted him to the cottage in the distance.

Built of wood with a timber frame and filled with horizontal, squared logs the cottage sported a steep thatched roof constructed to shed snow. His eyes were drawn toward the smoke escaping from the chimney and whirling upward toward the pewter sky. He pictured in his mind the cozy domestic scene inside the whitewashed walls.

A young buck, his antlers still in velvet, leapt across the road, causing him to pull on the reins in order to slow the horses' pace. He needed time to cogitate on what he could possibly say to the parents of the dead girl who lay shroud in a blanket at the back of the carriage. He began to pray for them, unable to stop the flow of tears escaping from his eyes.

Henri was a man of deep faith and spirituality, believing that everything happens according to God's plan. With that he was comfortable, but he was also aware that everyone didn't share his degree of faith and for this he was sorry. Climbing from the wagon he dried his eyes and headed toward the house. The large, rather eloquent brass knocker looked sadly out of place on a door so badly in need of repair. About to knock, the door opened, startling him and leaving him momentarily speechless.

"*Bonjour*, how may I help you?"

The agreeable aroma of freshly cooked meat and cabbage spilled into the hallway behind the short, thin woman with gray hair standing in the doorway. It was apparent to him that this was Violet's mother. Possessed of the same obtuse look and vacuity of eyes she stared up at him like a child. Before he had a chance to offer an explanation, a large boned man, wiping the grease from his chin and sucking his teeth, appeared behind her, his lips set in a thin disapproving line. With a conciliatory smile, Henri blurted out a stumbled apology for having disturbed their dinner. The couple nodded their heads, waiting for an explanation as to why he was standing on their doorstep. Feeling the sweat break out on his forehead, he blurted out in a gravelly voice, "I…uh…I'm from the Governor's mansion and I…uh…"

Before Henri could compose himself enough to pour out the dreadful details the woman began screaming.

"There's something wrong with Violet isn't there? Arthur, Arthur, something's happened to our Violet," she cried, clinging to her husband's shirt like a tiny child. Lowering his eyes for fear of them seeing the pain in them, Henri thought it best not to be vague at this point.

"I'm afraid she's dead Madame. I'm so sorry."

And indeed he was. Mute from shock, the woman's mouth opened but no sound came out.

"The Governor sends his regrets to you both regarding this most unfortunate accident and" – he hesitated; trying to recall what Mercier had told him to say next.

"How did it happen?" the man asked, his thin lips trembling.

"She fell Sir, lost her footing on the stairs."

The woman gasped, and without releasing her breath, gasped again. It was as though she was unable to breath, as if the horror of her only child's death brought to a halt, her will to live. Pulling her to him, her husband embraced her, caressing her back, his lips brushing the top of her head. Worming herself out of his arms she glanced through the open door toward the waiting carriage where, unbeknownst to her, lay the body of her beloved Violet. Like pools of despair, her eyes welled with tears as she faltered toward the back of the house. In silence, Henri escorted Violet's father across the expansive lawn, glittering with hoarfrost. As they reached the carriage, the sound of pitiful screams from the bowels of the cottage reached their ears.

"Elle mort, Ella mort - -she's dead, she's dead!"

In empathy, Henri's eyes began to sting. The mournful cooing of a turtledove drifted toward him.

✠

It was dark when Henri arrived back at the cabin; the absence of the familiar candlelight glowing from the window telling him that Marjolaine was still busy at the mansion. An ominous stillness flooded the room as he crossed the threshold causing him to shudder. The floorboards complained under his tread as he searched the room for the source of a tiny animal-like sound coming from the far end of the cabin. Assuming it was just another renegade mole, he made his way to the source of the noise to find Marjolaine whimpering in the dark.

She lay on her back, her fingers laced, staring at the ceiling, her cries soft and mournful.

"Marjolaine, Marjolaine, wake up, your having a bad dream," he cried, but her lack of response told him something was very, very wrong. Lighting a candle from the smoldering fireplace, he placed it on the mantle in an effort to shed some light on the area housing the bed. Gently shaking her shoulder he whispered, "Marjolaine, it's me Henri, what's wrong…what's happened?"

She started to scream, the fear in her eyes terrified him and he could see she was hysterical, her mumbling words indecipherable.

Lifting her tenderly into his arms, he attempted to soothe her disquiet with his tender voice. It grieved him to see her like this and he rocked her as one would a child in an effort to mollify her. He began to hum her favourite tune and gradually felt her taut body relaxing. She gazed up at him, the confusion in her eyes slowly vanishing.

Still in his embrace, she related the afternoon's incident to him; her voice, lacking inflection, was delicate and hushed. He knew of her experience following the delivery of the Langevin infant as she'd recounted the story to him on more than one occasion leading him to believe she had been traumatized by the episode.

"It was such a bad feeling," she'd often said to him. "It was like the infant carried with it some form of evil – I felt strange even touching her. I can't explain it but there was something wrong with her and I felt it."

She'd let it go at that and then, several months later she'd recount the story to him again.

"But my darling" he said, holding her closer, "there must be more than one person in this world with a snake shaped birthmark behind their thigh. Besides, the Langevin infant died in the raid along with her mother, at least that's what you told me."

"But the feeling I had while in the company of Eve even before I saw the birthmark – and Eve told Claudette she'd been kidnapped by the Mohawk so it makes sense—it must be her, it must!"

Henri had to agree. He held her all night and prayed she'd rise above this. He loved her so very, very much.

CHAPTER TWENTY-FOUR

The day was blustery. Stooping to her labour, Blood Sky emptied the basket of corn into a large, well-worn vat containing boiling water to which ashes had been added. A few of the other women broke into laughter provoked by a humorous story involving one of their offspring, when the eager yelps and whoops of children split the air.

"*Rononha rontorathonhne* – the ones who went hunting have now returned!" Craning her neck, her eyes narrowed against the sun, Blood Sky was able to make out the figures of the men walking toward them in the distance, a few of them weighed down by the game slung over their shoulders, the others lugging great sacks of meat with which to share with the village.

Then she saw him. His gait was unmistakable. Chewing her lip thoughtfully, she debated as to whether she should join the other women who leapt up to run and greet their husbands and sons. She decided against it. She dreaded the idea that he'd think she took for granted that they were now a couple, even though their last encounter confirmed their special bond, at least to her way of thinking. Never having been involved with a man before she was unsure of what it is she must do, or say, or how she should act.

As if in answer to her indecision, his voice cried out: "Blood Sky, Blood Sky," and she saw him rushing in her direction; his hands now relieved of their burden, extended toward her. Sweeping her up from where she sat, his strong arms embraced her as if he'd never let go and she knew that's where she belonged.

They were married in the season of *Tsothohrha* – the time of much cold. The wedding feast was spectacular and Blood Sky, chastely enveloped in her beaded wedding dress, danced along with the guests until dusk.

Following the ceremony Wind Hawk led her to the tiny cabin reserved for young couples that married during the winter and thus were unable to spend their *nikarihwehsha* – First Time Alone in the forest, as was the custom. Many times Blood Sky had heard the other women discuss details of their *nikarihwehsa*'s as new brides, and she'd always wondered what her experience would entail. She was quite nervous yet eager to consummate their love.

Once inside the cabin she was aware of Wind Hawk studying her. With a knowing smile he gradually moved closer, hypnotizing her with soft murmurs of assurance. With a sense of urgency he lifted her up, and gently laying her upon the lush warm fur that lay beside the fire, began to remove her clothes. Her senses swimming, she was overcome by a desire, the likes of which she'd never known. When he touched her bare flesh for the first time, his hands caressing her shoulders, breasts and stomach with agonizing slowness, she thought she'd faint. Unable to reciprocate, she lay there moaning, delighting in the sensation of Wind Hawk's gentle touch. His hands moved lower, to her woman parts causing her to involuntarily part her legs, and when he entered her it was as though she'd been born for just this moment. Their lovemaking was passionate and try as he might to savor the moment, Wind Hawk's need for her was too great. When it was over she cried tears of joy. She came to him again during the night.

The morning found them wrapped in each other's arms – a sense of love was tangible in the air.

"Why can't I tell anyone about us Herbert?" Eve whined as Mercier climbed from the bed. Tiring of his evasions and dense enough to believe she was now Mercier's one and only, she couldn't understand why he forbade her to mention their relationship to anyone. All her begging, pleading and cajoling fell on deaf ears and he constantly skirted the issue by changing the subject. He had however, unambiguously enlightened a handful of his oldest cronies as to his situation with Eve after tiring of their assiduous inquiries guaranteed to be accompanied by knowing winks. Swearing them to secrecy and stressing how mortified he'd be if anyone caught wind of the fact that the Governor of New France was dallying with a mere char, the subject had then been closed save for the unrelenting crude jokes and innuendos during those occasions when he and his friends had tippled more than their fair share of champagne.

Conniving to trap Mercier as quickly as possible, Eve abolished her daily routine of ingesting herbs to prevent pregnancy in hopes of conceiving Mercier's child, a ruse she knew would unite them for life; however, in a weak moment brought on by too many glasses of claret, he'd divulged to her his inability to father a child. Due to a genetic disorder, his infertility was, to him, a great blow to his manhood, no doubt the psychological root from which sprang his indiscriminate womanizing.

Mercier was aware of the fact that Eve's housekeeping skills were incompetent to the point of being non-existent other than the sporadic bouts of dusting whenever the mood struck. Possessed of numerous foibles, she was churlish and rough around the edges with little command of the French language. As well, the slut was insolent and conceited, lacking the slightest knowledge of social graces or niceties to speak of. He found himself constantly dismissing her if anyone of consequence was present for fear she'd behave too familiar with him whilst in the company of the visitor – a social faux pas guaranteed to leave him shorn of reputation.

Even on those rare occasions when she was wont to whisper specious endearments to him, it was to her own end, for she never tired of wanting something – be it money, clothes or jewelry. Mercier refused to fulfill these requests on the grounds that the closets in her suite were crammed with clothes and accessories, supposedly left there by Deidre, his unfortunate cousin who'd met an early demise. Truth be known, Deidre never existed, the wealth of chattel having been left behind by his former whores. When he denied her requests with a firm "No," she'd smugly repeat the word, imitating his intonation before lapsing into a mood of petulance like a small child denied a new toy.

She was a mass of contradiction, one day attiring herself according to her station and showing up the following day dressed in the most garish costumes, ignoring the other domestic's suggestions that her dress was out of place. Mercier overlooked her inappropriate dress as trifle, justifying her vulgar taste on the grounds that, compared to her, his former lovers had been mediocre at best.

He'd even gone so far as to disregard the recent concerns of Marjolaine and Claudette when they'd reported a number of rare *object de art* mysteriously missing from their respective display

150

shelves in the great hall simply because he knew where they were. He hadn't taken too much notice at first when a few of the treasures turned up on her dresser, but lately her quarters were literally filled to capacity with a confused cluster of exceptional pieces she'd pilfered from the main quarters. He prayed it was a temporary aberration.

On more than one occasion he'd been obligated to seriously ponder her uselessness outside of the boudoir, but validated her presence as a necessity since she provided a much needed therapy of sorts, a physical relief if you will, after his busy days in office. The thought never occurred to him that she was partially responsible for his exhausted state.

He'd been obligated in the past to fire chars who lacked the sense to keep their intimacy in the boudoir; flaunting it, albeit in a cloaked manner, whenever possible; thinking it would gain them an element of respect among the more influential visitors to the mansion. However none of them had been so deliciously depraved between the sheets as Eve, her sexual appetite matching, if not greater than his, a vixen much to his liking. As well she was defiant, ill tempered and habitually succumbing to rage with a vehemence unlike anything he'd experienced in the past – traits that for some inexplicable and bizarre reason, intensified his passion, so much so that on more than one occasion he'd found himself purposefully provoking a row. She'd even had the effrontery to lecture him on his frailties from time to time. Expecting a retaliation, she'd been baffled by his amorous response unaware that her verbal abuse was his ideal form of foreplay.

There were times however when he wished her pliancy of disposition equaled the pliancy of her body whilst in the throes of passion. He couldn't help but compare her with Violet so profound were the disparities. Inarticulate as she'd been, Violet had always received him into her bed with open arms; submissive, yielding and truly incapable of the disparagement he'd endured since succumbing to Eve's bizarre spell.

A utilitarian, Violet had busied her day cleaning, dusting, baking and tending to the mansion's excessive greenery, whereas Eve, in her instability, chose to indolently while away the days in desultory seclusion, thinking of bizarre ways to alleviate her boredom. It never occurred to her to lend a helping hand to the other overworked chambermaids. Not including the main floor, the mansions twenty-one bedrooms were in dire need of weekly dusting, hence Marjolaine and Claudette were left to their own devices, hiring on occasion an extra char to come in for a day or two. And unlike Violet who was loathe to ask for anything except when absolutely necessary, and even then did so with confused supplication, Eve was consistent with her interminable requests, displaying a most childish petulance when her demands failed to be immediately met.

Add to this his recent, however reluctant, sanction regarding her attendance at the upcoming gala, a situation destined to be fraught with inappropriate behaviour on her part and loss of status on his. It was at times like this he was obliged to question his critical faculties believing he must have been mad to have agreed to her presence; but as usual her argumentive nature had weakened his resolve.

The altercation between them had happened last week in his study. With an abstracted gaze he'd been staring out the window. The day had been nasty; small chips of hail relentlessly peppered the leaded windows, the monotonous tinkling grated on his already frayed nerves. For one thing, Intendant LaValle had been well over an hour late for his 7:00 a.m. appointment, confirming Mercier's suspicions that tardiness was indeed an upper-class trait, the true meaning of 'punctuality' escaping the sagacity of those who were titled.

Killing time, he turned his attention from the window to peruse a document in as perfunctory a manner as possible when Eve burst into the room, her face white with rage. The windows shuddered as she slammed the mammoth arch shaped door before treading resolutely toward him, and striking her fist on the ornately carved desk, proceeded to berate the stunned Mercier.

"Etes-vous hors de votre mind! Isn't il assez que je suis votre esclave de sexe sans avoir l'attente de ro sur vos amis comme un char commun – Are you out of your mind Herbert? Isn't it enough that I'm your sex slave and now you want me to wait on your friends like a common maid! Eli just delivered my uniform, including a ridiculous looking apron, to my room! The uniform he says I will be wearing to serve the guests at the gala. I'll have you know I will be attending the party dressed in a beautiful gown like the other ladies, not as a servant in a uniform. You will not defile me like this!" she screamed in her fatuous manner, her slippered feet stomping the floor as if to

emphasize her point. "I intend to be feted in the dining room with the visitors, and will not be confined to kitchen duties like a common slave. Do you understand?"

Nettled by her audacity and complete lack of subtlety, he glared at her as if to usurp her momentary power over him. The idea of allowing an ill-behaved uneducated slut such as herself to attend his yearly gala was hardly prudent and ludicrous at best. Though determined to keep their affair inviolate from the upper crust, he felt himself weakening, mesmerized as usual by her delicious temper and was at once hesitant to alienate her; all the while fighting the urge to throw her to the floor, and burying his face in her panther coloured hair, satisfy his lust while she was still in a foul mood.

She was incorrigible, affecting him like an insidious disease from which there was no cure and he loved it. He fought the compulsion to facetiously remind her that she had, after all, been hired as a char even though she hadn't so much as washed a dish since setting foot in the mansion; not to mention her ignorance of even the slightest minutia of social etiquette; but hesitated as he knew only too well her low tolerance for taking offence. He affected to find an excuse powerful enough to nullify her but finally acquiesced, pandering to her whim under the condition she'd introduce herself as the daughter of an old childhood friend of the Mercier family and under no circumstances whatsoever was she to mention her relationship with him, all the while damning her for the siren like power she held over him, the insatiable sexual longing that consumed him day and night. She promptly agreed to the rules and Mercier, with imperfect faith in her ability to follow through, closed his eyes and inhaled deeply.

Sensing his mood was one of desire, and placated now that she'd gained permission to attend the ball as a guest, she decided to throw him a crumb. Fully aware of his predilection for teasing, she languorously hoisted her gown to her waist and with a brazen leer, revealed the nakedness of her lower extremities before making her way toward him, her steps sly and fluid like some predatory animal. With eyes glued to her exposed femaleness, he pushed his chair back, and with fumbling hands and feeble smile, hastily prepared himself for her. Slowly, very slowly, she mounted him, her masochistic tendencies delighting at his shaking hands and pleading eyes that squeezed shut in pleasure as she leisurely and dispassionately undulated her hips while covering his face with kisses.

It was this dichotomy of her nature, this *esprit de contradiction,* that so captivated him and she knew it. Within seconds he was satiated and laying his head on the back of the chair with eyes closed, was barely aware of her weight lifting from his lap.

A few moments later Eli, bearing a tray of hot biscuits and tea, tapped lightly on the door. Upon entering, the sight of Mercier in repose prompted him to tread lightly so as not to awaken his master. It wasn't until he rounded the desk that he noticed the pants of the ordinarily meticulous Governor, lay crumpled around his ankles, the simulacra of semen on his upper leg removing all doubts from Eli's mind as to why Mercier's slumber was accompanied by a gratified smile. Quietly placing the tray on the desk, he turned and scurried from the room, his shoulder coming in contact with Intendent LaValle who was about to enter despite the fact he was more than two hours late for his appointment. Hastily closing the door Eli attempted to alter the expression on his face to one of professional demeanor.

"If you please Sir, the Governor is indisposed at the moment. Would you be so kind as to wait in the foyer?"

CHAPTER TWENTY-FIVE

Indeed Mercier's galas were a site to behold – albeit a distant echo of the larger and vastly more splendid court of Versailles. Display to Mercier was everything and he maintained as much protocol and ostentation he could devise by adhering to the sacrosanct barrier of classes, ensuring that the majority of his guests were strictly of the upper echelon to be entertained with a luxury totally detached from the lives of mere colonists who believed that sumptuous and magnificent meals, dances or galas were dangerous and licentious recreations.

Aside from being attended by the most noteworthy individuals in New France, Mercier's finest hours were those in which the various tribal delegates were invited, as he could flaunt his wealth and high living standards in front of what he thought were the most disadvantaged people on earth. As for the natives, they felt anything but envy as material things meant little to them, and they were more than ready to leave at the galas finale.

As well, the majority of his native guests pitied Mercier. Masters of body language, they could see he was shallow, attempting to live vicariously through his position and possessions and that the only one impressed was Mercier himself. As the celebrated Governor of New France, Mercier was often miffed by the passive faces of the natives who rarely altered their expressions, unlike the French who invariably displayed animated enthusiasm while in his presence.

The late afternoon was crisp and silent, the leaves brittle beneath her feet. A resonant hush of frosty air and a fresh scattering of light rain had transformed the ground into a pristine and sparkling carpet. The waning sunlight lowered to meld silently into the river as a hawk glided majestically above her. The winsome howl of a coyote echoed from somewhere deep within the woods, his cry somehow conjuring up hazy memories of her contented childhood. From the direction of the village Blood Sky could hear young voices excitedly yelling,

"*Yakohsatens, yakosatens* – The horses are coming!"

Thinking it just another game the children were playing, she continued on her way until a sound, much like the muted beat of a drum, obligated her to turn her head. Two men on horses were approaching her, waving their arms, signaling her to wait.

Sidling up behind her, the men dismounted. A fat white man with a round face lengthened somewhat by a scraggly beard glanced at her with dull gray eyes under thatches of bushy brows. Turning his attention from her, he began to root around in his saddlebag for something while the other stranger, an extremely mute-faced Indian: tall and spare to the point of being cadaverous, waited beside him, his grave eyes lowered. Drawing something from his bag the fat man waddled toward her in a rather tyrannical fashion, his puffy cheeks red and blustery from the cold. The Indian followed two paces behind. Turning to address his native companion in a most superior manner, the brevity of his attitude was sadly disparaged by his squeaky little voice. Blood Sky couldn't help but smile. She realized the native was his interpreter when he turned to her and said, "We were looking for Chief Black Whirlwind, said the Indian. Are you his daughter?

"Yes, I am Blood Sky, but my father has gone to the River of Tears."

"We know. They told us back at the camp" he retorted as he handed her an elaborate envelope before continuing, "I am Tall Pine and this is Monsieur Gamalain. In light of your father's death, Governor Mercier requests your presence at his annual Christmas gala at his mansion. Transportation will be provided there and back and your safety guaranteed."

"*Ka'nonwer tsi niwa* – Where is it?" she asked.

"In the land of our French brothers, a place called Ville Marie."

"*Kat-keh* — When is it?"

Explaining the agenda to her, he specified what day her transportation would arrive to escort her to Ville Marie.

There were so many questions she wanted to ask but her head was spinning. This was all so foreign to her and she'd never been far from her village let alone a place like Ville Marie. Before she had time to think, the fat man bowed and with a dismissive shrug turned and walked away, the Indian in tow. Mounting their snorting horses they turned and rode out of sight.

Although taken aback, Blood Sky felt honored. She knew her father would want her to represent him at the gala and she felt it her duty to help sustain, as best she could, the contemporary unity of the French and Mohawk.

"What will Wind Hawk say about this?" she pondered. Would he concur with her decision to attend the gala? There had been no mention of him during the brief conversation with the emissary; perhaps he'd assumed she was still unmarried. Her decision to consult Cloud Woman for assistance in determining the proper protocol was short lived when she saw Wind Hawk walking toward her waving.

"Wa'katitahko – I was looking for you," he said breathlessly.

Handing him the invitation she explained what had taken her so long. He looked at the envelope quizzedly.

"Yah tewakateryentare naho'ten tsiten – I don't understand. An invitation to the Governor's mansion in Ville Marie?" He frowned, noticing immediately the disillusionment in her eyes telling him how she longed to attend the gala. His love for Blood Sky was such that he'd do anything to make her happy and here was his chance.

"Kathseronn," he said with a smile. "I'm getting dressed up at last."

Elated she turned toward the village, eager to share the news with everyone, when he reached out and grabbed her skirt, stopping her in her tracks. Baffled, she turned to look at him.

"Yah ki' nonwa teskahtentyonh, he said with a gleam in his eye, "I am not going home right now."

"What do you mean?"

"I'll show you what I mean," he said furtively before tossing her onto a bed of soft leaves. Her laughter was cut short as he lowered himself on top of her and pressing his lips to hers made glorious and fervent love to his woman.

CHAPTER TWENTY-SIX

With a gust of enthusiasm Eve swung open the door to her rooms. The once immaculate suite had been desecrated beyond belief. Lacking even the slightest sense of order, her clothes and personal effects lay strewn on the bed, chairs, tables and floor. Obliged to maneuver around a pile of unwashed linen she'd been neglecting to do, she casually kicked it aside, making her way toward the elaborate cupboards by the window and with passionate avarice swung open the closet doors wherein hung an agglomeration of elegant gowns.

One by one she donned the exquisite outfits before prancing like a debutante in front of the triple full-length mirror. Delighted to find they were a good fit, and obviously purchased for an exorbitant fee, she was distressed to find each and every one of the dresses sported a prudent neckline though the current fashion dictated plunging necklines designed to expose as much bosom as possible. How could she have known that Violet, endowed with a more than ample bosom, had been paralyzingly self-conscious, never daring to publicly expose more skin than absolutely necessary?

Agitated, Eve tossed the gowns to the floor when it suddenly occurred to her how she might wear a high neckline to her advantage. By dressing modestly she'd thwart any suspicions Mercier might harbor in terms of her seeking out other men, thereby retaining her ascendancy over him. As well, she knew enough about the male animal to know it is what a woman covers rather than what she exposes that piques a man's interest.

Loyalty, being far from her strong suit, combined with her natural promiscuity, impelled her to lie awake at night conjuring up images of the handsome, well-heeled men she'd meet at the gala, before surrendering to sleep, images of dancing in their arms carrying over into her dreams. Loathe to lose what meager status she'd gained in the eyes of those contemporaries of Mercier, who surmised she was his mistress, she'd vowed to behave appropriately at the gala – at least when the Governor was in the immediate vicinity.

Of late, her relationship with Mercier was tenuous at best. Truth was, she cared not a whit for him and was quickly tiring of professing herself concerned with his conversational inanities and sexual demands. Repugnant to her, his incessantly groping hands and demonic sexual energy repulsed her, and only through her flagrant imagination was she able to endure their interminable sexual bouts. And when he finally succumbed to sleep, his stertorous breathing nearly drove her crazy, the gasping and snoring preventing her from sleeping, an irritation that found temporary relief by the morbid fantasy of smothering him with her pillow. As well, he was becoming increasingly critical toward her, and try as she might to humour him, more often than not she found herself giving way to sudden flare-ups of temper for which she'd later chastise herself. Knowing full well she ran the risk of being replaced at any given moment by a fresh domestic whose hidden charms Mercier wished to explore, she'd vow time and time again to curb her temper lest she be dismissed before meeting the man who could offer her a noble life; a union she reasoned that could only transpire under circumstances of her present affluent lifestyle.

A knock on her door was followed by Claudette's voice, pleading in its tone.

"Eve, can you please help us in the kitchen, we're not nearly prepared and the ball is tomorrow night. We need your help desperately!"

"We need your help desperately," Eve whispered to herself, mocking Claudette's frantic state.

"Quel casse-te – what a headache I have Claudette, just go away. I'm not feeling well and have to rest awhile. Maybe I'll come down later if I'm feeling a bit better." With that she crawled under the down-filled comforter and closing her eyes, fantasized once again about the men she'd meet the following evening.

Gold and crimson leaves drifted lazily onto the cobblestone avenue leading toward the mansion where a myriad of flaming torches shone brightly around the majestic sweep of the grounds. Upon entering the massive iron gates leading to the manor proper, the guests were welcomed by the site of hundreds of candles, like great jagged teeth, dangling precariously from the overhang of the elaborately decorated verandah. An assemblage of officers brandishing torches lit the way for the handsome carriages and high stepping horses making their way toward the mansions atrium, the jangling of bells heralding their impending arrival. The passengers, reclining on upholstered seats, were greeted by orchestral strains drifting from the magnificent gothic windows.

Welcomed by the concierge, the guests entered through the enormous carved doors leading toward the vast lobby where the Governor greeted them with elaborate formality. He held sway in the center of the room flanked on either side by a dozen or more officers with coloured uniforms and velvet waistcoats, their tailed periwigs topped by tricorn hats embroidered with gold; their swords buckled by their sides.

Mercier looked august. Aping the fashion of the French court he sported a rouen linen shirt decorated with batiste, his waistcoat buttons set with small rubies complimented his flame coloured silk stockings and matching cravat. The redolence of his strong cologne permeated the immediate area.

As usual, the first to arrive was Madame Le Jeune, a puerile, no-nonsense, aged dowager with rheumy eyes and mottled creped skin. Leading an extremely austere life since the death of her husband, Etienne, some thirty years previous, the mundanity of their marriage was a mere rehearsal for her widowed years. The Governor's annual gala was the sole concession she allowed herself for fear of being drawn into the intoxication of idleness and frivolity. Never appearing in public without her beloved toy poodle Fifi, a sinister looking animal encased securely in her arms, she walked toward Mercier who warily eyed the dog. He detested Fifi as the tenacious little fellow was wont to snap his teeth at all who dared venture near his mistress.

Mindful of the fact that Madame Le Jeune's disdain for ceremony would impel her to disregard both he and the servant offering to escort her to the ballroom, he ignored the slight in protocol and extended his bejeweled hand to the next guest, a Madame Shari Louis, a woman whose extreme wealth was handed to her via her marriage to her recently deceased husband, Seigneur Garnet Louis – soldier, landlord and patron of the local church which he personally built.

Having spent most of her married life in near seclusion due to her late husband's selfish preoccupation with his own life, she was known to be an extremely shy woman, stifled even further by his jealous nature. As Mercier clasped her hand it was blatantly obvious to him that the widow Louis had no intentions of leading a life of resigned boredom now that Garnet was out of the picture.

Modest of dress in the past, her current impropriety shocked even Mercier. Her neckline was cut perilously low, one of her nipples half exposed, causing more than one wide-eyed gentleman in the foyer to be rapped in mock reproach with his wife's fan. Affecting not to notice, Mercier reluctantly wrenched his gaze from her bosom and with a studied lugubriousness of tone, expressed his condolences before hastily welcoming the next guest lest he become overheated.

Piqued by her abrupt dismissal, Shari reluctantly clasped the extended arm of a stalwart looking servant who escorted her through the lofty doorway into the ballroom before enthroning her on a gold velvet lounge in close proximity to an insipid looking aged officer with weathered skin, mutton chop whiskers and minus one eye; his ancient uniform bearing dozens of decorous medals he'd acquired during his glory days in the service. Scanning the room for a more opportunistic seating arrangement, she spotted a group of young blades in boisterous conversation across the room. Her eyes widened when she recognized Daniel Lytle as one of the group.

Subtly intrigued by Daniel since their brief but unforgettable encounter at his father's wake some three years previous; the elder Lytle having been an acquaintance of her late husband; she'd thought of him more often than she cared to admit even to herself. His father's estate; albeit a derisory sum due to his poor business sense; had devolved to Daniel and word had it he was fast squandering what little he had on his numerous women. Shaking open her fan to better conceal her expression of delight whilst studying him, snippets of the beastly allegations against him, gleaned from the rumor mills, unwittingly pervaded her thoughts.

A roguish fellow of questionable reputation, Lytle's every move smacked of sexual overtones. Feckless in most other areas of his life, his rapacious sexual appetite was legend, leaving no doubt in anyone's mind he was possessed of the sinner's lust for debauchery as well, according to the ladies, as being pre-eminently endowed physically, a most dangerous combination indeed. In short, he was the embodiment of a true lecher having ruptured the trust of numerous women.

Being of the same ilk as Mercier, they were sometime friends and confidantes, their private sorties taking place here at the mansion lest anyone of consequence witness their convergence, for certainly if anyone saw the Governor of New France fraternizing with the immoral and much maligned Lytle, the grist mills of gossip would run for weeks. Mercier never failed to obtain vicarious pleasure from hearing, albeit second hand, Lytle's numerous sexual exploits, however twisted, and never failed to be awestruck by the rogue's most recent sexual conquests of which there were many.

Accused several years ago of the crime of 'rape and seduction', a misdemeanor punishable by death or sentence to the galleys, it had been Mercier who'd tactfully pulled the vital political strings with which to free Lytle.

A deviant of sorts, Lytle was known to have lay waste many an unsuspecting maiden, prompting more than one young lady's father to warn his daughter of the corroding influence surrounding the ignominious scoundrel who lacked even the slightest trace of scruple. Subject to a great deal of well-deserved derision, he was known to have sired as many as six illegitimate children without benefit of marriage. The infants, like all captured English children, were given to the Iroquois at Kahnawake, St. Regis and the Lake of Two Mountains west of Fort Montreal to raise. Their mothers, considered now to be females of bad character were compelled to heavy labour by the crown as deportation to France was not considered sufficient punishment for women with loose morals, commonly referred to as *putains* or whores.

Certainly with Lytle's sexual prowess, and had he been twenty-two years younger, he would have benefited from the newly established *King's Gift,* a monetary reward to encourage early marriage for males before age twenty and females before age sixteen. All couples producing ten children received three hundred livres and to those lucky parents of twelve, an amount of four hundred was awarded. The procreation rate of New France however, was too slow for the King's liking and a new law stipulated that men must marry before the age of twenty and girls before the age of sixteen or their fathers would have to appear in court every six months until the unwed child had found a mate. Many of the girls were married at the tender ages of ten to sixteen; a situation that helped increased the population somewhat. Still not satisfied with the birth rate, Mercier, along with Intendant LaValle and a handful of obtuse electorates, toyed with the idea that marriage between Frenchmen and native women was a sure fire way to increase the population, but rumor had it that native women nursed their children too long and as a result didn't procreate fast enough, a statement prompting one young man, obviously jealous of Lytle's numerous conquests, to exlaim,

"Perhaps the savage maidens haven't had the pleasure of bedding Lytle. He turns out offspring as swiftly as rabbits."

Failing to come up with any semblance of solution and wishing to end the meeting in order to do some serious drinking, the men had voted unanimously on a law forbidding any resident of Ville Marie to sit on benches in front of their houses after nine in the evening. Intendant LaValle reasoned the new decree would indeed encourage the people to procreate.

As Shari considered Lytle from across the room, he disengaged himself from the group to leisurely ambulate about the area as if searching for something or someone. Indeed, like the true sexual predator he was, he was seeking out the ideal spot wherein he could cultivate a most dashing and seductive stance guaranteed to catch the eye of every female who entered the room. Indeed it would be difficult to miss him, donned as he was in his trademark scarlet sateen pantaloons and high shone boots. Exuding an abundance of *savoir-faire,* the rascal had gained entry to the gala this evening strictly as an escort to Madame Solange La Pointe, an ostentatious and raconteurial character who'd had her day dallying with Mercier. Hence the Governor was obligated to allow Lytle entry lest Solange retaliate by making public the specifics of their affair, information that would do little to salvage his already shaken reputation. Mercier refused however, to acknowledge Lytle's presence by blatantly ignoring him, his latest fiasco still fresh in Mercier's mind. Having been accused, and rightfully so, of impregnating Anne Lauger, wife of Gilles Lauger, Lytle had been fined 20 livres and the unfortunate adulteress was expelled fromVille Marie for three years.

Halting about three feet from where Shari was seated, Lytle appeared to have found the preferred spot from where he could subtly eye his prey. Removing a cheroot from a thin silver case, he lit it, and drawing heavily, sensuously pursed his lips, allowing the smoke to spiral upward so as not to offend anyone. Shari decided to remain where she was despite the officer's annoying one-sided extraneous conversation. In an attempt to dissuade the voluble oaf from his oppressive chatting, she met his eyes with icy contempt before adjusting herself in such a way that his constant inconclusive snippets of useless trivialities were directed toward her back, an indignity prompting him to vacate his seat in order to seek an audience more receptive to his monotonous pontifications.

With secondary regret Shari realized she was now conspicuous in her isolation but was loathe to surrender her seat to another woman who might catch the infamous Lytle's eye. Turning her head once more in his direction their gaze met, and with a loose grin he scrutinized her in a most intrusive manner, no doubt undressing her with his eyes. In simulation of searching for another seat, she scanned the room for a few seconds before meeting his glance again. Never short of confidence, he sauntered toward her with exemplary demeanor and suavely bowed before her.

"*Enchante Madame,* I bow to your wishes my lady," he said half in jest. "Would you care to dance?"

Summoning up her best coquettish manner, Shari declined; not because she didn't wish to dance with him but her body was trembling so much she feared she'd be unable to stand.

"May I then beg to join you?" he whispered in a most obsequious tone, the gleam in his eye directed toward her half exposed nipple. He was seated before she had a chance to concur and following a short exchange of social niceties – including his regrets on the untimely demise of her husband – she began to relax. His well-rehearsed compliments, though extremely flattering, were taken with a grain of salt given his reputation, though she had to admit there was a certain authenticity in his manner. Eventually she deferred to his charms, a smile tugging at her lips. Moments later they were whirling about the dance floor, then, just as suddenly, were nowhere to be seen.

In the months to follow, Madame La Jeune would, with great pleasure, relate how she'd felt in need of stretching her legs, and vacating her chair at the far end of the ballroom, had meandered into the solarium for a bit of exercise. According to La Jeune, one of the giant hibiscus trees began shaking as if overtaken by some powerful spirit. Startled by the plant's reverberations and ecstatic moans, she jumped back, inadvertently dropping her claret glass. Gritting her teeth in preparation of the shattering sound as it smashed onto the stone floor, she glanced down to see the glass still intact having safely landed on what appeared to be a pair of men's scarlet pantaloons leading her to believe Lytle and Madame La Pointe were dallying behind the verdant plant. Returning to the ballroom, her face crimson with embarrassment, she was stunned to see Madame La Pointe standing at the doorway, her eyes scanning the room for, what Madame Le Jeune knew, was her mislaid escort.

The last to arrive were the Mayor and his wife. Striding toward Mercier in his insouciant manner, the floorboards complaining under his tread, Mayor Vidal Lacroix was an extremely tall man of more than considerable girth with extremely protuberant eyes and impassive stare, his face sunken where his teeth were missing.

Extending his hand he greeted Mercier, the raucous timbre of his voice echoing throughout the foyer. Miserable and contrite at the best of times, his few attempts at bon-homie failed miserably, though when it proved necessary to his standing in the community he could be affable enough. His wife, a bland, phlegmatic woman whose haggard appearance; a result of her profound fecundity resulting in the birth of fifteen offspring; found these gatherings tedious, spending the majority of the evening imploring her husband to beg their leave so she could return home to her precious brood.

Soon the ballroom was filled to capacity, the champagne and conversation flowing harmoniously. The time had arrived for the pretentious Mercier to make his grand entrance. In the midst of exchanging boisterous salutations, the guests, upon hearing the announcement of his appearance, collectively stood at attention out of respect for the Governor, though in many cases it was a feigned respect. Madame Le Jeune remained seated, vegetating, as was her way.

Mercier, lacking even the slightest measure of charisma or propriety, summoned up his best peremptory impression before sweeping into the ballroom, but the lack of enthusiasm on the part of his audience; save a few who clapped half-heartedly as he entered, was a grim reminder that he could have saved himself the trouble. Opening his mouth in preparation of a rather portentous speech designed to inflate his ego, the audience, ignoring his stance, drew back into their respective insularities leaving him standing there talking to himself, a sight prompting his oldest friend and confidante, Antoine Dubois to laughingly remark to the peeved Governor,

"When will you learn my dear Mercier that brevity is a salutary virtue? Let's have a drink."

Nodding abstractly, Mercier was about to follow on the heels of DuBois when he caught sight of Eve making her entrance. The orchestra once again struck up, filling the room with a delightful melody inciting many a wife to drag her recalcitrant husband to the dance floor. It was obvious to Mercier that Eve was in her glory, her mood buoyant as she flit about the great room in her gold damask gown cut modestly high and complimented by the dangling ruby earrings that Mercier had loaned her for the auspicious occasion – treasures that had once adorned the ears of his grandmother. Delicate wisps of hair escaped saucily from her elaborate coiffure intertwined with gold and scarlet ribbons. Unlike the other ladies of the court who'd mastered the skill of lifting their gowns high enough to prevent them from tripping, yet low enough to avoid displaying their ankles, Mercier shuddered as Eve carelessly hoisted her skirt in such a manner as to allow all and sundry to scrutinize not only her ankles, but her calves and knees as well.

Eyeing her with a mixture of curiosity and mistrust, Mercier's closest friends and confidantes were baffled as to why the Governor would tolerate the presence of his mistress during such a prestigious occasion. Despite her fine clothes and sexually mesmeric presence, it was obvious the girl was nothing but an ill-bred and feral harlot, her command of the French language like that of an illiterate child. Various suppositions among the elitists perpetrated numerous queries regarding the girl's background; queries that met with redundancies and passed off by Mercier in his habitual arbitrary manner, all the while cursing himself for his prurient self-indulgence that led to Eve's presence at the ball.

Snubbed by the majority of females whose finely tuned intuition saw her for what she was, Eve adroitly honed in to areas of the room occupied by the most handsome and hopefully, most successful men of more than ordinary influence, and with practiced vivaciousness, struck up animated conversations peppered with subtle nuances and unmasked references to sex. Lacking a proper sense of delicacy, she derived great pleasure from the shocked yet fascinated responses of the men to her winning smile. Her temerity was such that she cared little if the gentleman in question was married or single – an error prompting more than one of her victims to hastily excuse himself before disappearing into the mass of guests, his irate spouse on his heels.

About to scan the room for the perfect, still evasive potential mate, she became aware of a gradual hush as one by one the guests craned their necks toward the entrance of the ballroom. From where she stood she was able to make out the figure of a native woman speaking to one of the interpreters.

'The token guests of the evening have arrived I suppose,' she thought.

About to turn her attention back to the eligible males in the room, she caught another glimpse of the Indian woman, her long black hair tightly fastened at the nape of her neck with a colourfully beaded clasp. With heightened interest she observed the woman walking with a slight limp behind one of the interpreters who was headed toward Mercier and DuBois standing at the far side of the room sipping champagne and making small talk with a few of the guests. Unable to tear her eyes away, she watched as Mercier, with feigned delight, bent down to kiss the woman's hand; the hand of her despised adoptive sister, Blood Sky.

With an audible gasp, she spotted Wind Hawk enter the room with his easy stride and savage eloquence, obviously unfettered by the pomp and splendor. The melodic strains of music hung in the air as the guests gesticulated and gaped in a most discourteous manner, the majority of them whispering to one another. Any guests who had previous notions regarding the savage nature of the Mohawk, were taken aback by Wind Hawk's imposing and refined presence; his certain reserve and guardedness so inconsistent with his untamed good looks and salubrious visage. Many a fugitive titter escaped from the amused audience as they viewed the incongruous spectacle of Mercier, resplendent in tails and sporting more lace it seemed than everyone else in the room combined, bowing chivalrously to the buckskin clad Indian towering above him. Within minutes a gathering of awestruck females, endeavoring to be introduced to the handsome native, circled round him batting their eyelashes and coyly fluttering their fans.

Though overwhelmed with exhilaration at the sight of Wind Hawk whom she never in her wildest dreams thought she'd ever see again, she couldn't comprehend why Mercier hadn't informed her that members of the very tribe who'd abducted her as an infant were to be guests of honor at tonight's gala. Truth be known, Mercier simply couldn't marshal the courage to tell her beforehand given her history of unpredictable reactions.

Upon their arrival in Ville Marie the previous evening, Wind Hawk and Blood Sky had been escorted to the home of Monsieur Victor Collacier and his charming wife Lynda, who'd cordially welcomed them with open arms and a meal fit for a King. When asked if they'd care to bathe before retiring, an obligatory query dictated by French hospitality, Madame Collacier was taken aback when they accepted. As for the French colonists, they rarely bathed believing it caused colic, headaches and vertigo and they were under the false impression that savages rarely bathed at all when in truth they did so every day.

Bathing in a tub was an incredible indulgence for Blood Sky, never having experienced the sensation of immersing herself in warm, soapy water. So soothing was the experience she found herself nodding off, a novel experience guaranteed never to repeat itself in the icy waters of the St. Lawrence.

A modest woman possessed of a smoother grain than most; a gift no doubt bestowed upon her by divine providence; Madame Collacier struck an instant rapport with everyone who came in contact with her. Unlike the majority of wealthy resident wives in Ville Marie who chose to lead frivolous existences by devoting their time exclusively to pleasure via whirls of social distractions and spending excessive amounts of money on parties that displayed more pageantry than the Court of France, Madame Collacier chose to donate her time and money to the Ville Marie orphanage; an institution made possible solely by she and her husband's philanthropic generosity. Possessing a magnificent joie-de-vivre, Madame Lynda was constantly surrounded by people, her sparkling laughter guaranteed to light up any room. She'd been only too pleased to ride with her native guests to the party, doing her utmost to make them feel comfortable in their strange surroundings. Her husband Victor, a quiet, unpretentious soul, chose to remain at home, snuggled warmly beside the hearth.

Encircled now by a party of half-drunk, boorish guests vying for answers to their queries, Wind Hawk and Blood Sky joined their interpreters for a brief respite on an exquisitely plush velvet sofa reserved for guests of prominence. A lean, swarthy-skinned officer in full regalia stood close by, thwarting as best he could, the incessant stream of curiosity seekers. Placing her head into the yielding cushions, Blood Sky's gaze was drawn to the cathedral ceiling of the great room. Overwhelmed by the mammoth chandeliers, she likened them to delicately carved chunks of ice hanging precariously from the high rafters. Boasting ten in all, the magnificent crystal fixtures were adorned with hundreds of glowing candles, their dancing light reflecting ten-fold in the gigantic gilt mirrors situated strategically throughout the ballroom. The strains of a delightful minuet, followed by the patter of footsteps heading toward the dance floor interrupted her reverie. Her eyes lit upon the dancers, their movements fluid and most delicate as they sashayed across the parquet floor. It all seemed so absurd to her, for if the men not been wearing trousers she'd have had a difficult time differentiating them from the women as their elaborately curled hair and bodies were encased in a myriad of multi-hued velvet and lace, the majority of them sporting bows on their glossy black shoes.

Fighting the impulse to giggle by biting the inside of her cheek and diverting her eyes once again toward the ceiling she was aware of Wind Hawk's muffled laughter.

"*Oh niwathahsteren'tsheroten* – What kind of pants are they?" he asked the interpreter whose own laughter prevented him from answering.

Bustling through the mass of guests, waiters bearing trays and a multitude of hooped skirts and swishing crinolines, Eve maneuvered her way toward the couple who were by now inundated once again by a swarm of inquisitive guests vying for the attention of the Mohawk interpreters at their side. Biding her time until Blood Sky's head was turned, she rudely pushed herself to the front of the line, and standing directly in front of Wind Hawk, who was deep in conversation, reached down and clutched his arm.

"Kenahkwatshenryes," she whispered in her most seductive voice. "I'm looking for a partner to dance with."

He turned toward her, facing her in his usual phlegmatic manner, the interpreter with whom he'd been conversing making no attempt to disguise his miffed expression at her untimely and rude interruption. It wasn't until their eyes met that he recognized in them the familiar blaze of craftiness, unaltered by her heavy powder and elaborate makeup. His jaw dropped. He turned urgently toward Blood Sky, alerting her to the fact that Eve was present, and together they awkwardly offered their greetings. They enlightened Eve on the latest news from home including their recent marriage. The announcement left Eve speechless, her fists involuntarily clenched shut as her nails dug painfully into her skin. Then, with practiced solicitude, she congratulated the couple, shifting her gaze for fear they'd detect the look of jealousy in her eyes.

Reluctant to continue conversing with them lest her voice tremble she turned toward the dance floor, feigning interest in the antics of the acrobats Mercier had hired for the night, their haphazard leaps and bounds mimicking the beating of her heart. In an attempt to betray her deep core hatred of Blood Sky she altered her expression to one of exuberance and turned to once again face the couple only to find Wind Hawk and his interpreter engaged in conversation with an elderly couple leaving her to face Blood Sky who remained sitting on the lounge. Her features, Eve noted with envy, were even more beautiful than she remembered. Thinking it best to stifle – for the time being at least – her usual venomous barbs, she chose instead to shamefully ingratiate herself, a ploy in which to deter any suspicions Blood Sky might harbour in terms of her lingering attraction toward Wind Hawk. In a most affable manner she sat down beside her before proceeding to confess her adventures with Lucien, embellishing her story by concocting a yarn wherein she'd met the Governor through her former employers – a wealthy couple with close ties to Mercier's family. Daring to go one step further she proudly announced her upcoming engagement to the Governor, stressing the importance of telling no one as yet since Mercier wished to make the announcement himself. She went on to describe in great detail, the numerous females in Ville Marie who'd be sadly disappointed, as they had fervently desired to secure the Governor's hand in marriage.

"*Wa'khena'tonhahse,*" she said with a proud sneer, "I showed them didn't I?"

Blood Sky, totally without guile, smiled.

"*Wake'nikonhrahseronn* — I am pleased for you Corn Child," she whispered in keeping with Eve's instructions to be secretive lest there be an interpreter close by.

True to her spiritual nature Blood Sky truly was pleased for her and felt perhaps the prayers she and Cloud Woman had offered to the Creator on her behalf were being answered.

As for Eve, her contempt and hatred for Blood Sky was magnified ten-fold for not only had she married Wind Hawk, the man of her dreams, she was present tonight as guest of honor at the Governor's mansion while she, the woman he slept with, was obligated to keep their relationship a secret! She cursed the Mohawk bitch and was more then ever resolutely determined to wound her as best she could.

Searching the immediate area for Wind Hawk, she spotted him, still engaged in conversation not three feet from where she sat. Surrounded by a crowd of curious spectators he looked uncomfortable, vulnerable somehow, like a caged animal pleading for freedom. She watched as one of the female guests reached up to sensually rub his chest on the pretext of admiring the texture of his buckskin shirt; while another less attractive woman, held his hand tightly, refusing to let go as she rambled to him in a language he couldn't understand. She watched as he gently pulled his hand free to feign waving to someone before nonchalantly clasping his hands behind his back.

Eli, looking splendid in his finest uniform, entered the room bearing an immense silver tray filled to capacity with champagne filled goblets. On his heels Claudette, pushed a large mahogany cart laden with exotic teas, coffees, cream and sugar for the benefit of the small number of abstainers in the crowd. With a disparaging look, Eve scrutinized Claudette's freshly starched uniform, complete with lace apron and ridiculous looking cap and couldn't help but compare the outfit with the exquisite gown she wore.

The idea came to her in a flash; a delicious plan in which to erase that damned smile from Blood Sky's face. Excusing herself, she vacated her seat next to Blood Sky, and lifting her skirts, bustled toward Claudette.

"Just half a cup of the strongest you have Claudette - no cream or sugar."

With a forced smile Claudette poured the steaming liquid into an exquisite antique mug. No sooner had the mug been half-filled than Eve roughly grabbed it from her, spilling a few drops of the boiling fluid onto Claudette's hand causing her to gasp. Ignoring the incident, Eve disappeared into the crowd without so much as a *"merci"*, and headed toward the great dining room.

The great room was empty, save for a couple of hired maids bustling about the mammoth table now half filled with the evening's fare. Quickly making her way toward the liquor cabinet, she searched the bottles until she found the silver carafe in which the café liqueur was stored. An unpopular spirit; it's taste being almost identical to extremely strong coffee; she filled the mug to the brim before slamming the cabinet door shut and making her way back to where Wind Hawk was chatting via the interpreter to the same woman who, bereft now of his hand, desperately clutched his arm. She observed him wrestling his arm free before following the interpreter to the cabinette de toilette. As they weaved through the crowd, the interpreter, an elderly native man with a blank incurious stare, was unimpeded by the intrusive guests attempting to strike up conversation with Wind Hawk, waving them away in a manner unheard of in the native community.

Biding her time until Wind Hawk disappeared into the toilette she swiftly made her way across the room, gripping the mug with both hands lest she be jostled by one of the exuberant guests. Twice she nearly tripped on her skirt but managed to make it to the entrance of the cabinette de toilette without spilling a drop. Emerging from the latrine a few moments later, Wind Hawk hesitated, obviously waiting for his interpreter. Sidling up next to him, she smiled.

"Here," she said, passing the cup to him. "The Governor sent this over for you. It's his own personal blend of coffee and rarely, if ever, does he share it."

"*Wakenya'tathenhs* – I am thirsty," he said, receiving the cup from her hands. *"Yah nonwenton tetiwakatkahthonhh* – What kind of drink is this? I have never tasted it before," he said, sniffing the contents.

"It is a drink made from crushed beans called coffee," she retorted. "It comes from the other side of the world and is much sought after. Drink up, you will enjoy it." He paused, staring at the contents suspiciously before enquiring if there was any alcohol in it.

"Of course not," she said, smiling ingratiatingly at him as if he were a child. "The Governor knows better than to serve alcohol to an Indian. Come on now. *Enwakena'khwen'onh* – I will be angry if you don't drink it."

Taking a small sip, he licked his lips, finding the taste rather pungent though far from unpleasant. *"Yawekon* – it is good tasting," he said with a grin before emptying the contents of the cup.

"There is plenty where that came from and after all, the Governor did tell me to make sure you received anything you asked for."

Before he could answer, the interpreter emerged from the toilette, a pained expression on his face, his fingers rubbing his elbow as if to soothe it.

"Katenentshawi'takahrewahtha" – I banged my elbow on the door. I must see if there is any ice about. I won't be long."

Excusing herself on the pretext of recognizing an old acquaintance she hadn't seen in years, Eve disappeared back into the throng of guests with full intentions of refreshing Wind Hawk's drink. As luck would have it, she encountered Eli awkwardly balancing his mammoth tray, laden now with assorted liqueurs. Filling a large crystal goblet with more than an ample amount of café liqueur, Eve looked up to spot Mercier standing a few feet from her, his eyes focused on her every move like a hawk ready to move in for the kill. Pretending to sip from the goblet, she smiled innocently before blowing a kiss in his direction – an action she knew would cause him to turn his attention elsewhere lest someone sense their familiarity.

Scurrying back to where Wind Hawk stood she collided with Claudette whose arms were filled with loaves of bread, a few of which toppled to the floor. Acting completely out of character, Eve bent over to retrieve the loaves before mentioning to Claudette the Governor's request that Blood Sky be given a complete tour of the mansion; a ruse on her part in which to separate her from her husband for a while. Uncomplaining as usual, Claudette merely said she'd have one of the other chars attend to it, as she was far too busy at the moment.

Still hemmed in by curiosity-seekers, speaking to her via the interpreter, Blood Sky was curious as to the whereabouts of her husband, her obvious lack of concentration on the guest's queries prompting the interpreter to whisper to her with a smile,

"*Akta tsi kanhokaronte ithrate* – Don't worry, he's standing over there beside the doorway."

She glanced over and saw him discussing something with his interpreter, unaware that Eve was slowly headed in his direction with yet another drink of alcohol for him, biding her time until she witnessed Blood Sky being greeted by Edith, a part-time maid endowed with an eye-catching widow's peak. With a great deal of enthusiasm, Edith took hold of Blood Sky's arm to escort her from the room to begin their tour of the great mansion.

Hustling back to Wind Hawk who stood recumbent against the wall and obviously doing his utmost to understand the questions thrown at him by a beastly looking woman with a pallid complexion, whose attempts at sign language were atrocious to the point of being comedic, Eve was unable to suppress her amusement at the spectacle. She hesitated for a moment in an attempt to control the laughter she felt bubbling up within her. That being done, she then approached her to inform her that the Governor had requested a few moments respite for the guest of honor whereupon the woman stomped angrily away talking to herself. Waiting for the woman to dissolve into the crowd, Eve nonchalantly handed the goblet to Wind Hawk.

"*Khnekiraha* – Drink up," she said with a smile, "It will do you good and it tastes much better cold."

"*Niankowa* – Thank you," he retorted before proceeding to empty the contents in one large gulp before turning his attention to the dancers – his body swaying to and fro in time with the music. Unbeknownst to the great warrior, the potent effect of the alcohol's spirit was very much alive in his unsuspecting soul. The expression in his eyes was softer, more convivial and yielding; his laughter flowed easier and there was an obvious and most pronounced camaraderie overlapping his usual reticence. Consciously unaware of his altered demeanor and sense of euphoria, Wind Hawk found himself having a good time; his laughter flowed and he was deluged with a sense of power. As well, his sensations had reached a pinnacle of acuteness he'd never known; the sights, sounds and sensual scents of parfum imbued in him a fresh lust for life and pleasure.

Good-naturedly slapping the back of the puzzled interpreter on his arrival from the kitchen where he'd secured an ice pack for his swollen elbow, Wind Hawk jokingly asked him if he'd care to have a dance.

"Kenonnyyaweyenhon," he said with a grin. "I am a good dancer!"

Although not a self-appointed arbiter of abstinence, the interpreter could have sworn Wind Hawk had been imbibing. Clinging to his impaired elbow he glanced toward Eve with an interrogating look. Feigning ignorance she simply smiled and asked sympathetically about his elbow before excusing herself to fetch some more liquid refreshment for her target of seduction, her beloved and most unsuspecting Wind Hawk.

CHAPTER TWENTY-SIX

Dinner was announced much to the delight of the famished guests who moved en masse into the great oak paneled dining hall where a sumptuous buffet had been laid out. Groaning with a profusion of delicacies set upon superb lace coverings and exquisitely embroidered napery, the overall appearance of the table was nothing short of regal. A large marble column displaying a bust of Mercier commanded one corner of the room, but the guest's eyes were automatically drawn to the far wall.

Lavishly banked on either side by oversized potted plants, an exquisitely carved fountain, boasting a life-sized statue of a nude male evocative of Michelangelo's David, held precedence. To the amusement of the guests, it soon became apparent that the liquid flowing from the statue's penis was not water, but champagne. Within minutes a swarm of good-natured individuals were lined up beside the fountain, crystal goblets in hand, all vying for an opportunity to refresh their drinks from such a novel source.

As she entered the room on the arm of her husband, Madame Jodi; a rather eccentric woman whose scandalously low-cut neckline was tempered somewhat by the gardenia wedged between her ample cleavage; broke from his arm, and staggering toward the fountain, ran to the front of the line to situate her lips around the statue's nether region with the intention of imbibing without use of goblet. All eyes watched as copious streams of champagne poured from the corners of her mouth; an obscene spectacle prompting gales of laughter from even the most jaded guests. Everyone that is, except her husband, a prudent man of deferential temperament who stared at her with implied reproach before disappearing from the room in mortification, the rude gesticulations of the crowd accompanying him as he lowered his head in shame.

Relishing the attention almost as much as the champagne, Madame Jodi held her ground just as Monsieur Guy La Flamme, private tutor to the offspring of the wealthy, entered the room. An erudite man with ascetic features, the overtly religious La Flamme was steeped in knowledge and lived an abstemious and prosaic life, far removed from the depravity of his employers. Turning his attention to the ruckus in the corner, his small, squinty eyes widened dramatically at the incredulous sight of Madame Jodi, a regular member of his parish, performing what appeared to be, an obscene yet highly successful act of fellatio on the auspicious statue. The pleasurable reaction of the guests to Madame Jodi's sexual satire, coupled with the numerous provocative gestures of the men in the room, confirmed his long held belief that good taste was not a prerequisite for class. Lacking even the flimsiest thread of moral resiliency, he clenched his fists and in an earsplitting timbre, voiced his passionate condemnation to the occupants of the dining hall.

"*Ainsi c'est la voie que nous enseignons les heathens au sujet Christ! Le Gouverneur devrait avoir honte de se!* – So this is the way we teach the heathens about Christ? The Governor ought to be ashamed of himself!"

Startled from their joviality, the guests looked toward La Flamme, two or three of them obviously abashed in the realization that Ville Marie indeed had been founded with the sole design of bringing the gospel to the natives, and as tonight's guests of honor were Mohawk, they had to admit the sexual overtones of the evening had been an egregious error on their part. As for the other revelers, they were having too much fun to be interrupted by La Flamme's untimely history lesson and continued their vulgar revelry without batting a lash.

Infuriated beyond belief, La Flamme, piously and with tremendous indignation, spun around in his eagerness to escape this corrupt milieu and swiftly heading toward the door, wedged his right foot in a brass cuspidor sitting inauspiciously on the floor. Unable to dislodge his shoe from the cuspidor and embarrassed to the point of wanting to die, he hastened into the ballroom, the calamitous din of the cuspidor drawing everyone's attention to the disconcerted scholar whose face was beet red with chagrin. Unable to regain his aplomb he decided that vacating the gala would be the better side of discretion, and so it was he vacated the premises without so much as a "*Bonsoir*". According to the gossip-mongers, he'd later cancelled all tutoring appointments for the next three weeks.

Throughout La Flamme's tantrum, Madame Jodi's lips remained glued to the statue's penis, infuriating the other women who were awaiting their opportunity to take a few swigs from the same source.

Eyeing the lewd scene with indifference, Monsieur Pierre Le Blanc, a surly character bereft of any semblance of humour, concentrated instead on the lush buffet before him. With severe observation he scrutinized the diverse delicacies, his eyes glazed and mouth watering.

Heavily jowled with silver hair, he was possessed of a vociferous appetite, apparent by his gargantuan bulk. Akin to a starving vulture he whiled away the remainder of the evening hovering over the table, wolfing down great amounts of canapés and cursing his luck as one of the guests, a chirpy little fellow with an extremely large head and short bowed legs, reached out with thin little hands knotted with blue veins, to snatch the heftiest cut of pheasant from under his nose.

Alerted to the dinner bell, the face of Wind Hawk's interpreter had lit up. Grabbing Wind Hawk's arm he'd started toward the dining room but the pensive Mohawk was dreamily considering the enormous cathedral ceiling decoratively painted with scenic splendor and refused to budge from where he stood. Once more the interpreter tugged at his sleeve but to no avail as Wind Hawk's gaze was now fixated on the glorious spectrum of colours radiating from the chandeliers looming above. The slightly miffed interpreter turned on his heel and rushed toward the buffet, ignoring Eve whose eyes were still peeled to the door for any signs of Blood Sky's return.

Alone now with the man of her dreams, she placed her hand on his arm. *"Teyohsahe'tahnekonnyatha* – would you care for more coffee?"

Nodding his assent, she insisted he accompany her this time, if for no other reason than to view more of the mansion's grandeur.

Mercier, frenzied with the numerous plaudits being piled upon him from one of the guests; a toothless old crone with a clubbed foot who had him cornered, failed to notice Eve and Wind Hawk slip from the room.

Unsteady now on his feet, the handsome Mohawk was fast losing interest in anything but a soft bed and a nap. On the pretense of allowing him to view more of the mansion's grandeur, Eve led him to the empty lobby where she swiftly undid the hidden latch on the concealed door, before ushering him inside – all the while searching the area for any lurking witnesses to her dastardly scheme.

Insensible with drink and totally unaware of his atrocious surroundings, Wind Hawk stumbled over an old basket lying in the middle of the room. His speech was so slurred Eve barely understood when he asked where they were.

"Ttsi yotahshetahkwen – in the bedroom," she whispered. "Would you like to lie down for awhile?"

"Hen'en – Yes," he said while thinking to himself, 'Before I fall down.'

Guiding him to the old cot, he fell onto the putrefied mattress with a heavy sigh, his eyes drawn to the tiny gothic window beside him. Fascinated by how the moonlight cast traces of dappled light upon the bed, he failed to notice Eve swiftly removing her clothing at the far end of the room.

She was on him before he knew what was happening; caressing, searching, her body engulfing his in a manner he'd never experienced. As a rule Wind Hawk's integrity would have been impenetrable by such a union, but in his deluded intoxicated state all sense of moral values had been temporarily numbed, subjugated instead by the basest of human passions that raged throughout his soul. Incapable of recognizing the temporary suffocation of his profound spirituality, and despite his weariness, Eve's sexual expertise aroused in him an enormous desire and aggressiveness he'd never known. Though his features were obscured in the darkness, the truncated words of passion he cried out, though unintelligible to Eve, elated her, nourishing her desire until she thought she would faint from happiness.

Upon awakening he was unable to recall whether he'd passed out or just fell into a deep sleep, but snippets of his deplorable and unfaithful actions immediately began flashing unmercifully from his inner recesses; a realization that tore deep into his heart. Then, like in a dream, the face of his beloved Blood Sky took precedence over his derelict and much wounded mind, and he was at once strongly compelled to find her and hold her tightly in his arms, allowing her goodness to eradicate the deep shame within his tarnished soul.

Within minutes, his spasmodic wretched sobs echoed mournfully within the confines of the filthy room.

Fighting the urge to remain clasped in his warm strong arms and drifting into a deep sleep beside him, Eve had reluctantly left his side to shake the dirt and spiders from the gown she'd hastily thrown to the floor, all the while endeavoring to compose herself before returning to the ballroom lest her absence become obvious. A smile crossed her lips as she smugly congratulated herself for having succeeded in seducing Wind Hawk despite the risks involved and for carrying out her plan with such élan.

Her entrance to the ballroom coincided with that of Blood Sky and Edith having just completed their tour of the mansion. Blood Sky, settling into the first available vacant chair, yawned wearily while half-heartedly scanning the room for her husband whilst attempting to show some semblance of interest in her neighbour's pithy attempts at sign language. Taking advantage of the situation, Eve dashed toward her and with passionless solicitude enquired as to whether she'd care to retire for the evening, the pitch of her voice piercing the air in an attempt to compete with the raucous sound of the orchestra. Declining the invitation on the grounds she must wait for Wind Hawk, Blood Sky sank back in the chair with a heavy sigh thinking to herself, '*Kariwehs tsi rohtentyonh* – He's been gone a long time.'

Scanning the massive room for one of the interpreters who'd likely know his whereabouts, she noticed the crowd had thinned considerably whilst she'd been touring the mansion. Thinking perhaps the interpreters had left for the evening, she fought to keep her eyes open until her husband returned to her.

Accompanying a party of guests to the lobby, Mercier's eyes locked with Eve's who had settled next to Blood Sky. With a sly wink she pursed her lips as if to throw him a secret kiss. Not only was it uncharacteristic of her to flirt with him but also there was a definite languor in her eyes, signs that immediately gave Mercier pause. He knew immediately the wink was fraudulent, but why? Reflecting a moment his gaze zeroed in on her facial expression, perplexed as to why she bore a palpable look of happiness such as he'd never witnessed, but as he was preoccupied with seeing his guests to the door, he pushed her odd behavior to the back of his mind for the time being.

As the small party crossed the threshold into the lobby they stopped in their tracks, curious as to why an assemblage of men had gathered in the corner, their wives huddled together at the opposite end of the room, their faces bearing looks of befuddlement. Dashing toward the group of men whose inaudible whispers piqued his interest further, Mercier noticed their eyes appeared to be glued to the floor.

"Ce qui va sur ici, chacun à l'écart! What's going on here, everyone out of the way"!

The crowd reluctantly dispersed as Mercier glanced to the floor. His mouth opened in shock.

"Mon Dieu, le sauvage est ivre! Quelqu'un cherchent son épouse immédiatemen! My God, the savage is drunk, someone fetch his wife immediately!"

Slouched on the marble floor with half-closed eyes, chanting eerily to himself, Wind Hawk was oblivious to the fact that a myriad of eyes were focused on him. His chanting continued as he tried unsuccessfully to obliterate the degrading image of Eve's throes of passion from his mind.

A rancorous hatred directed toward Wind Hawk for sullying his gala in such a degenerate manner caused Mercier to lose his composure. Cursing, he paced furiously back and forth across the vast lobby from which numerous alcoves and secret entrances had been strategically placed when he noticed the doorway to Violet's old room was slightly ajar. Upon further inspection he saw the bed was in disarray, his eyes drawn to a sparkling object lay strewn upon the lone filthy pillow. Stepping into the room he gingerly retrieved the object, recognizing it immediately as one of the ruby earrings Eve had so proudly worn tonight. Mercier clutched the earring tightly in his shaking hand, an uncontrollable rage kindling inside him.

"You deceptive bitch!" he screamed, finding little relief in the fact she wasn't as deceptive as she thought she was.

Through half-closed eyes, Blood Sky spotted the interpreter dashing at full speed toward her.

Tewakhsterihenh, karo nonkati – Hurry over this way!" he cried out, grasping her wrist in an attempt to pull her from the chair before literally dragging her into the lobby. Her husband lay comatose against the wall; Mercier, red-faced and obviously livid, kicking at him in an attempt to revive him.

"Tekta's, tekta's," she cried. "Stop, stop!" Running toward Wind Hawk she knelt by his side only to be assaulted by the odorous stench of alcohol permeating from his pores. She was speechless. This couldn't be her beloved husband; he'd never let alcohol cross his lips. This she knew as well as she knew herself, just as she knew intuitively that Corn Child was responsible for her husband's condition.

Wrapping her arms around his broad shoulders, she held him close to her breast, murmuring lovingly to him, assuring him all would be well and reminding him that everything happens for a reason; a truism they both believed strongly.

His eyes slowly opened, their vague remoteness foreign to Blood Sky, almost unrecognizable. *"Wa'khnekira,"* he sobbed, "I drank."

With compassion she hugged him even closer to her breast, asking no questions, allowing him to talk at his own will.

"Tsi tetkanonnyahkwa wa'tyakayaterane' kiken' tsyakothonwisen – I met this woman at the dance," he whispered to her in a choking voice, tears of shame escaping from his eyes. Wind Hawk, inept at lying didn't even attempt to distort the truth as he poured the story out, however, Blood Sky's natural astuteness told her the circumstances long before he did. An expression of compassion stole across her face for she knew how devious Corn Child could be, especially when it came to something she wanted, and she had lusted after Wind Hawk since they were children. There was no pain of betrayal in her heart, for she knew her husband was staunchly loyal and hadn't purposefully betrayed her; indeed it had been her so-called twin sister, her adversary since childhood.

Angry beyond words, Mercier thought it best to retire to his suite, the ruby earring burning in the palm of his hand. Once inside his rooms, he headed directly toward his private bar, stumbling in his rush to retrieve yet another much needed drink. Fumbling with the cork he realized the earring was still clenched in his fist. Slowly opening his hand, he glared at the sullied piece of jewelry, an act that sparked a recurrence of his initial anger and strengthened his resolve to punish Eve for her infidelity. Transferring his rage to the earring he flung it across the room before filling his brandy snifter to the brim and sinking into the cushions of his favorite chair to plan his strategy. He drank all night, oblivious to the initial rays of sunlight washing over his inebriated body. Seconds before he blacked out, a sardonic smile crossed his lips, the solution to Eve's punishment realized.

Eve on the other hand, fell into a deep and victorious sleep, the trace of a faint smile on her treacherous lips.

CHAPTER TWENTY-SEVEN

The invasive chimes of a Grandfather clock woke him with a start. Glancing about the unfamiliar surroundings his eyes were drawn to Blood Sky who lay sleeping beside him. Realizing he was back at the Collacier's home, he couldn't for the life of him recall how he had gotten there. His head pounded and waves of nausea swept over him causing his stomach to lurch. Shakily rising from the bed, he hastened to the cabinette de toilette where he wretched. Beads of sweat dripped from his brow, the throbbing in his head swiftly graduating to excruciating pain. Rinsing his mouth and face he strolled toward the bed to silently kneel on the carpeted floor to study the face of Blood Sky who still slept. Placing his hand on her forehead to gently caress her warm skin he leaned forward and kissed her forehead, his tears of repentance sprinkling onto her brow. Footsteps resounding on the stairs reminded him of their planned departure later that day. With narrowed eyes he searched the well-appointed room for articles to be packed for their long journey home when he spotted their baggage, neatly packed and ready to go, thanks to Blood Sky's inability to sleep the night before. It was all he could do to awaken her to prepare for what promised to be a long and tiring day.

True to her nature, Madame Lynda Collacier served them a delicious and hearty breakfast. Incessantly good-natured, her very presence helped alleviate the dreadful memories of last night's events. No sooner had they finished eating than one of Mercier's officers appeared at the door to inform Madame Collacier he'd come to fetch the Mohawk couple to meet with the escorts who would assist them on their journey back to the village.

"Napoleon, get out of there!" scolded Marjolaine as she reached into the small valise in an attempt to retrieve the curious feline by his tail. Glancing over her shoulder she was more than a little relieved to find she hadn't awoken Eve. She began placing the meager contents into the valise, all the while shaking her head in a failed attempt to eradicate the echo of Mercier's screeching voice playing over and over in her head.

"Marjolaine, you are to immediately pack only what Eve arrived here with. Do you understand? Nothing, and I mean absolutely nothing else leaves her suite," he'd bellowed following his untimely intrusion into the pantry where she'd been planning next week's menus. *"I have already instructed Claudette to inform Eve that she must vacate the premises before noon, and under no circumstances will I be available to see or speak with her. Is that understood?"*

Dumbfounded, Marjolaine nodded her assent, stepping back as Mercier moved closer to her, the timbre of his voice raised another three octaves.

"Arrangements have been made to send her back to that savage Mohawk village where she belongs. I'm sure she'll be delighted to find she'll be traveling with Blood Sky and her drunken husband Wind Hawk."

Literally spitting out Wind Hawk's name, droplets of saliva flew from the corners of his mouth as he stamped his foot. Again Marjolaine nodded, praying he would vacate the pantry as her head was splitting, aggravated as well by the thought of a confrontation with Eve. Moments later, accompanied by Napolean, she'd crept silently into Eve's suite to retrieve her old valise before replacing the few puny articles Eve had brought with her to the mansion.

A light tap on the door signaled Claudette's arrival and Marjolaine scooped up the valise, and with Napoleon in tow promptly left. Less than a minute later the sound of loud voices and a great smashing of something against the floor told her Eve had been informed of her immediate banishment. Nervous as a cat, she nearly jumped out of her skin when the doorbell rang, heralding the arrival of two large officers who'd been appointed by Mercier to escort Eve from the mansion. Directing them to Eve's suite, Marjolaine returned to the kitchen for a much-needed cup of hot chamomile tea.

Moments later, hands tied securely around her back, a small threadbare valise dragging on the ground behind her, a sobbing Eve was led to the waiting carriage by the officers who refused to answer any of her questions, leaving her in the dark as to her destination, a destination that became painfully clear upon arriving at the docks.

Literally wrenched from the carriage by one of the soldiers, her mouth dropped at the sight of Wind Hawk and Blood Sky stepping into the vessel that would take them back to their village. She was aghast to think Mercier was sending her back to camp with Wind Hawk and Blood Sky as traveling companions. Though inordinately stubborn, she knew there was no chance of her escaping the situation. Seething inside, she clenched her fists, gritted her teeth and, true to her erratic behavior, spat directly into the eye of the attending officer who'd grasped her arm to lead her to the boat. Obviously agitated, the officer wiped the spittle from his eye before pitching her roughly into the craft, her weight falling directly onto a startled Wind Hawk. Repulsed by the physical contact, Wind Hawk in turn heaved her to the floor where she lay sobbing, the fluid movement beneath her body alerting her to the fact she was indeed on her way back to the Mohawk village, leaving behind forever, her life of indolence and dreams of an affluent future.

Shocked by this unexpected turn of events, Blood Sky and Wind Hawk exchanged concerned glances before turning their attention once more to Corn Child whose shaking hands covered her tear sodden face. Wind Hawk, mortified at the idea of being in the canoe with both women, averted his attention to the native guides Mercier had hired to escort the small group back to their village, initiating a most superfluous conversation in an effort to distract his mind from the awkward situation in which he found himself.

Blood Sky turned her attention to Corn Child who lay in a heap on the floor of the canoe. The compassion reflected in her eyes belied the short-lived twinge of jealousy she'd felt upon hearing Wind Hawk's sporadic confession last night.

Corn Child felt a hand lovingly caressing her back as if to soothe away her fears. Confused as to her surroundings, the cry of an eagle soaring above brought her back to reality and her tears welled up once more.

"I want to go back! Please make them take me back! I beg of you!"

Though Blood Sky knew it was useless to try and placate her, she merely whispered, *"Sotsi teyoteryen'thara ne' eh yahonne* – It is too dangerous for you to go back there! Return to the village with us, it's where you belong."

Too ashamed to make eye contact, Corn Child averted her face to conceal her guilt, the reality of the situation churning in her gut. Reaching down Blood Sky grasped her hand, squeezing it reassuringly as though she were an infant. The compassionate act triggered in Corn Child, for some inexplicable reason, a compulsion to confess her appalling deeds of the previous evening; a noble thought, so uncharacteristic of her thus far, yet there seemed to be an immediacy, an inner desire to absolve herself of past wrongs against Blood Sky. It was as though her adoptive sister's innate goodness had engulfed her, embraced her somehow, altering her psyche in such a way as to fill her with the spirituality she'd lacked since birth. Gently releasing her hand from Blood Sky's grip, she took a deep breath, the dipping and dribbling of the paddles soothing her trepidation. Lowering her head, she said softly,

"There is something you must know; something that happened last night between Wind Hawk and myself."

"I know everything Corn Child. My husband told all despite being very sick from the alcohol you gave him. *Tenhske tsi nihronkwe'tiyo* – he is truly a good man, it was the bad spirit alcohol in his body, *ne'e karihonni eh nahatyere* – that is the reason he did it. It is over now. Today is a new beginning, let us not speak of it ever again."

Overcome with gratitude for the undeserved acceptance, it was she this time who reached out for Blood Sky's slim, dusky hands, grasping them tightly as a drowning man might cling to a life-line, for indeed Blood Sky's goodness had offered her a new life, a fresh beginning, a chance to make up for the damage and hurt she'd so carelessly inflicted on others. Suddenly anxious to get back to the village, she jokingly inquired as to whether Coyote had done Claude in yet with her voracious sexual appetite.

"Wahonnise thikenhne' – It's been a long time since I've seen him, it will be good to see him again." Swatting a fly from her forehead, she then turned her attention to the scenic view before her, drinking in the beauty of the distant trees and calm water as though viewing it for the first time.

Blood Sky, raising her face upward with closed eyes, gave thanks to the Creator for answering the prayers she and Cloud Woman had, for so many seasons, diligently offered on behalf of Corn Child. The oarsmen had begun chanting. Their voices, combined with the smooth gliding of the canoe lulling both women to sleep.

The following morning was chilly, the nip in the air bringing with it an unknown sense of peace for Corn Child, a glimmer of a better tomorrow and the promise of a new relationship with her adoptive sister. She couldn't understand what had altered her way of thinking so suddenly and unexpectedly. Reflecting momentarily on her life, she was able to see, for the first time, the tremendous amount of pain she'd brought to others in the past: the energy she'd wasted conniving, lying, arguing and stealing.

'Why this change of heart?' she asked herself again. Other than Claude, she was devoid of any friends in the village of her captors and it hadn't taken her long to alienate the other domestics in Ville Marie. As far as she could recall not one person had treated her with the kindness and understanding shown by Blood Sky, particularly in light of what she had done to both she and her husband Wind Hawk.

CHAPTER TWENTY-EIGHT

The familiar scent of dried apples and tobacco greeted them as they entered the longhouse. Corn Child, slightly anxious as to whether or not she'd be welcome, felt awkward at first as she stood in the background and observed the large extended family warmly greeting Blood Sky and Wind Hawk. Startled by the large hand gripping her shoulder, she turned to see the smiling face of Claude.

"Bienvenor – Welcome!" he cried, reaching out to embrace the girl he'd tutored in French since she could talk.

Immediately she felt better, able to converse with Claude, sharing with him bits and pieces of her life in Ville Marie, albeit altering the facts somewhat, telling him she'd returned home of her own accord. She knew Blood Sky or Wind Hawk would never discuss the details of her banishment from Ville Marie. As Blood Sky had stressed, *"Today is a new beginning, let us not speak of it ever again."* and Corn Child knew she was as good as her word.

Little by little the others gravitated toward her, extending their hands in greeting, their acceptance making her feel more comfortable. The scent of roasted beavertails and onion sauce whet her appetite as she approached Cloud Woman who sat hunched over the cooking fire. Offering to help prepare the food, she began sorting the baskets that lay on the ground.

One look in Eve's eyes told Cloud Woman her prayers and the continuous burning of sage on her behalf had finally worked their spell. With a toothless grin the older woman embraced her warmly, bading her rest until the meal was fully prepared, a suggestion she couldn't resist.

Climbing into her old bunk, Corn Child drew the warm furs around her tired body, the familiar sounds and smells of the longhouse filling her with a warm sense of belonging and an even greater sense of gratitude. With moist half-closed eyes she observed a group of women across the aisle, shaping pots and paddling designs on unfired vessels while the unique scent of Indian corn wafting from the cribs at the end of the lodge lulled her into a deep, dreamless sleep such as she'd never before experienced.

�֎

Blood Sky and Corn Child assisted Dancing Leaf in the preparation of crushed leaves of the wild geranium; a medicine guaranteed to alleviate the painful stomach ulcer Claude had developed. The winter had been unusually cold, allowing Blood Sky and Corn Child time to bond during the long dark days spent together in the longhouse, their friendship growing stronger as winter turned to spring. As well, the rapport between Corn Child and Wind Hawk had gradually elevated to the point of comfortable friendship.

But all was not as it appeared. Corn Child's monthly flow had ceased, and she suffered from sporadic bouts of nausea. She knew she was pregnant with Wind Hawk's child. How badly she wished to confide in Blood Sky for she was well aware that her adoptive sister's forgiving nature was unconditional, yet she couldn't bring herself to divulge her pregnancy until the time was right.

The opportunity arose a few weeks later as she and Blood Sky walked together toward the river to fetch water for the evening meal. The morning air smelled fresh, whirling about their faces before playfully raising their braided hair toward the sunlit sky. With a deep breath Corn Child halted and lowering her basket to the ground, gently grasped Blood Sky's arm.

"My sister," she whispered, staring at the grass, "There is something I must tell you but I don't know how – the words won't come." Placing her basket on the ground beside Corn Child's, Blood Sky embraced her, smoothing her wind blown hair.

"There is nothing you can tell me that could stop my love for you. Look me in the eyes and relieve whatever burden it is you carry. Together we will face it."

"I am with child," uttered Corn Child, staring toward the ground, her whisper so low Blood Sky thought she misunderstood, until realizing the expression on her adoptive sister's face was one of great seriousness. A cloud of disbelief swept over Blood Sky's eyes, her mouth dropped and then, much to Corn Child's delight, she began to giggle as though she were a small child. Unsure as to what that meant Corn Child whispered haltingly, "Why are you laughing, do you not hate me?"

"*Yah non-wa' o'nen, Wa-ke'-ni-kon-hrah-se-ro`n:-nih* – No, not anymore, in fact I am pleased about it."

"But my child belongs to Wind Hawk, your husband," she protested. "How can you be pleased for me? I don't understand. *Wak-hswe`n-honh* – I detest myself, surely you must hate me!"

"*Yah non-wa` o:-nen khe'kenha* – Not any longer sister, you have proven to be a good woman and most precious friend. What's in the past is in the past. Now I have something to tell you," she said, her eyes smiling. "I too am with child."

Overcome with emotion, Corn Child reached out and hugged her as tightly as she could. They cried together, their tears and hearts intermingling with joy, a joy that was to be short-lived.

CHAPTER TWENTY-NINE

'Where is she, she should have been back by now?' thought Blood Sky to herself. She was concerned about Corn Child who, like herself, had reached the final stage of pregnancy and could give birth any day now. Her unease stemmed from Corn Child's insistence on scaling the steep hill toward the river to wash clothes, a chore she'd refused to abdicate just because she was heavy with child. Anxious to make up for her past behavior, she'd toiled as much, if not more, than the other women in camp despite their obvious gratitude and foiled attempts to slow her down.

Completing the turtle rattle she'd been fashioning for her unborn child, Blood Sky held it up against the blazing sun to ensure there were no glitches in her craftsmanship that might prove harmful to the infant. Satisfied, she struggled to pull herself up from the ground, but her large stomach made it awkward to stand. Suddenly, a gush of water escaped from her, followed almost immediately by agonizing cramps that forced her back onto the wet blanket; her knees drawn up to help ease the pain. She'd estimated the infant's birth time would coincide with the next full moon but the severity of the contractions belied her calculations; coming as a complete, though not unwelcome surprise.

"Aieee, aieee, wakenekwen'tanon`nwaks – my stomach hurts!" she screamed, alerting a handful of women returning from the cornfield to her side. Among them was Little Current who'd taken over the role as official midwife following the death of Crippled Sparrow some ten years previous. Fleeing to her side, she knelt down and placed her hand on Blood Sky's stomach, timing the contractions.

"Onen thoha enyakoweyennenta'onh," she cried out to the other women. "She will be ready very soon, help me to assist her to the birthing hut."

"Corn Child, where is Corn Child?" Blood Sky cried out, a tone of urgency in her voice, an urgency stemming from the pact she and Corn Child had made to be present at the birth of each other's baby.

"Someone fetch Corn Child. Tell her Blood Sky's time is here!" cried Little Current while attempting to brush the annoying fly from her eye without losing her grip on Blood Sky who walked with faltering steps toward the birth hut situated behind the longhouse.

"I'll fetch her!' cried Singing Goose, breaking from the others to run at top speed toward the river.

Having made her way to the river's edge, Corn Child had cautiously stepped across the slippery rocks before placing the large basket of soiled clothes on the ground. Removing a badly soiled tunic, she awkwardly knelt down to place the article in the water when she was overcome by a severe cramp. The tunic she'd been about to wash slipped from her hands as she grasped her stomach, the seat of the pain. Gradually the pain subsided and thinking it best to return to the village as soon as possible lest she be in labour, she began to stand up, but her bulk, combined with the slickness of her moccasins from the water's residue, caused her to plunge head first onto the unforgiving rock, upsetting the laundry basket; it's contents swept away on the river's current.

Everything was black – the bittersweet taste of blood oozing from the gash on her temple trickled into her mouth. Unable to move, she lay there moaning, until finally, a warm sense of peace swept over her and she became vaguely aware of Blood Sky kneeling beside her – comforting her in her gentle way. She could feel herself floating; the sensation was indescribably beautiful, and then, nothing.

From the top of the hill, Singing Goose spotted her lying on the rock. At first glance it seemed she was merely resting; a natural conclusion since her time of delivery was almost upon her. Not wanting to startle her by yelling she hastened to the bottom of the hill when her eyes were drawn to the pieces of clothing floating in the river. A cold chill passed through her as a large turkey buzzard circled the stone where Corn Child lay.

Breathless from running down the hill, Singing Goose quickly knelt beside Corn Child's motionless body and pressed her ear against her chest. Unable to detect a heartbeat, she frantically grasped her wrist, searching for a pulse. A muted squeal caused her to let go the

193

limp wrist, her eyes probing the area for the source of the sound. Again she heard it, louder this time – the high squeaky timbre emanating from beneath Corn Child's skirt. With shaking hands she gingerly raised the deerskin sarong, nearly fainting at the sight of an infant female, the tiny writhing body still attached to her dead mother by the umbilical cord.

Lowering her head, she severed the rope-like appendage with her teeth.

✠

"Push, push!" coached Little Current, signaling one of the other women to wipe the perspiration from Blood Sky's face with a damp deerskin cloth, before turning her attention once more to the head of the infant, the slick black hair visible now at the birth entrance.

"Tewakhwihshenheyon – I'm tired," moaned Blood Sky, "It hurts so bad!"

"Wakyenta'teke' wakyenta's kanonhkwatsheriyo – Take this medicine, it will help ease the pain," whispered Little Current as she prepared to spoon a small quantity of crushed snake rattle into Blood Sky's mouth.

"Aieeeee," she screamed. The baby's coming!"

Tossing the medicine to one side, Little Current reached into the birth canal to grasp the slick head of the infant before assisting it into the light of life.

"Oh naho'ten o – What is it, what is it?" cried out Blood Sky, overcome with emotion at the first cries of her newborn.

"Iken yeksa'a yohskats Onekwenhsa Karonya – It is a female child Blood Sky. You have a beautiful daughter! Wind Hawk will be pleased!"

The infants had come forth into the world at precisely the same instant; their initial cry was simultaneous, their first breath drawn in unison – a unison that bordered on the uncanny.

A short time later, Singing Goose entered the birth hut carrying a small bundle in her arms. Spotting her from where she lay on a pallet suckling her newborn, Blood Sky's face lit up. "Did you find Corn Child?"

Too filled with emotion to speak, Singing Goose looked deeply into her eyes, her arms tightening ever so slightly around the infant she clasped to her breast. Unable to stop the flow of tears streaming down her face, she lowered her eyes in silent response to Blood Sky's query. A great sigh escaped from Blood Sky; a sigh of acceptance, for she knew her adoptive sister was dead.

Singing Goose, between sobs, briefly explained what had transpired before lowering the newborn into Blood Sky's outstretched arms. Kissing the top of her tiny head, the new mother placed her at her free breast, gently rocking as the miniature tongue sought, then found her nipple. Tears of sadness for Corn Child, blended with tears of thanks for the infants, trickled lightly upon their soft little faces.

To this day, the Grandmothers speak of the Sacred Rock by the river, where, on the evening of Blood Sky's death at age seventy-eight, a group of villagers witnessed the spirits of two young women contentedly nursing their infants. From that day forward, on those rare evenings when the sky is red as blood, the spirits appear upon the sacred rock. It is said that if you listen hard enough you can hear the new mothers crooning the 'Growing Song" to their babies.

About the Author

Author of "Intuition: Success Strategies" and "Sing the Brave Song" Judith Ennamorato's Mohawk heritage combined with an avid love of history was the inspiration for her first novel "Blood Sky". When she's not writing, Judith conducts writing workshops composed of fiction, non-fiction, research and brain structure, all of which involve her extensive study of left/right brain activity. on "Intuition and Fiction", sharing her own experiences in terms of allowing her inner, creative voice to be applied in her writing regardless of how ludicrous or irrelevant the idea may seem initially.

Printed in the United States
1092900004B